Frank turned away from the waterlogged car, leaving it and the body to the two technicians from the state crime lab and to a queasy looking Chris Fredericks and his camera. Jack's description hadn't done the body justice. Pale as a slug, it was so bloated it looked as if it would pop if someone stuck it with a pin. The right side of the short-sleeved shirt was covered with a dark stain, presumably blood. Not as grisly as the walking corpses in horror movies, maybe, but even more grotesque. And real.

As Jake had said, the hair—thick and long and gray—proved that it wasn't Lou Cameron.

But who was it?

★

MURDER
IN THE
BLOOD

Gene DeWeese

W🌐RLDWIDE.

TORONTO • NEW YORK • LONDON
AMSTERDAM • PARIS • SYDNEY • HAMBURG
STOCKHOLM • ATHENS • TOKYO • MILAN
MADRID • WARSAW • BUDAPEST • AUCKLAND

MURDER IN THE BLOOD

A Worldwide Mystery/December 2004

First published by Five Star.

ISBN 0-373-26513-1

Printed in U.S.A.

For Ed Gorman, not just because he's the editor,
but for all his kind words since
the YANDRO days and for some terrific books,
particularly the Sam McCain series.

PROLOGUE

THE MIDNIGHT AIR hung thick and sultry over the weed-choked remnants of Resurrection Cemetery.

For nearly an hour, the two men had taken unequal turns with the spade. Their only relief from the relentless August humidity was an occasional sluggish breeze from the surrounding woods, too feeble even to scatter the cloud of mosquitoes that whined around them in the hazy moonlight.

Now the shorter man, grinning with excitement despite blistered hands and aching muscles, struggled out of the two-foot-deep hole and leaned on the spade to catch his breath. His companion silently jerked the spade away, lowered himself into the hole, and took up the attack on the hard-packed clay. Clothes plastered to his body with muddy sweat, the shorter man went down on one knee to watch.

The chipped and eroded headstone they had searched out lay on the ground like a piece of gray granite roadkill, half devoured by the knee-high tangle of ironweed and milkweed and a dozen varieties of nettles and burdocks. Four hundred seasons of rain and sun and ice and wind had weathered the deeply carved lettering almost out of existence, but enough fragments of letters and numbers remained to tell them that this was the spot they had been looking for: the grave of Jeremiah Arthur Ingram, 1837–1883.

And people think history's dull! the resting man thought, unable to keep from laughing in a sudden burst of nervous exuberance. "This is crazy," he said, not for the first time, ''you know that? We're crazy—out here like a couple of grave robbers, for God's sake!''

The man in the hole grunted and jabbed the spade into the dirt.

''Hell, there are laws against digging up graves,'' the shorter man went on. ''Just because Resurrection's abandoned and there hasn't been an Ingram around here since the First World War—''

He broke off to flail at the ever-present mosquitoes. ''If we had the sense of a rat terrier, we would've waited until morning,'' he chattered on, still too euphoric to sound as if he meant it. ''More light. Fewer bugs.''

''Here,'' the man in the hole snapped, straightening as he thrust the handle of the spade toward the other. ''If you have so damned much energy and enthusiasm, dig!''

The shorter man hesitated only a moment, then grabbed the spade and lurched back into the pit as the other climbed out. Despite the heat, despite his blistered hands, he was relieved to be digging again. Anything was better than fidgeting at the side of the grave, babbling as compulsively as a nervous kid on his first date. Even in the heat, even with his gut muscles cramping, he felt a shiver go down his spine.

The last ten hours had been weird. Who'd have thought anything as wild as what he and the Englishman had stumbled across could have happened here, in a town where everybody knew everybody else? How in God's name had that kind of secret been kept for a hundred days, let alone a hundred years?

And how on earth had he let himself be talked into this ghoulish, spur-of-the-moment expedition into a backwoods corner of Granger County? They hadn't notified the proper authorities or asked permission or anything. What they should have done, of course, was—

The spade handle twisted painfully in his blistered hands as the blade jarred against something solid.

My God, he thought. *There's something here. It's real!*
Gulping, he let the spade fall and dropped to his knees.

"What?" demanded his companion.

"I've found something."

His shaking fingers scrabbled at the loosened soil. Barely
two feet down, this couldn't possibly be Ingram's coffin.
Something else did share the century-old grave!

The taller man seemed to have stopped breathing. At length
he said, "Let's have a look." A tense expectancy colored his
voice. An instant later, a yellowing flashlight beam spilled
into the hole.

"Probably just a rock," the kneeling man said, laughing
nervously as he continued to claw at the dirt.

His fingers touched what the spade had struck. He hadn't
thought his heart could pound any faster or harder, but it obviously could. A momentary dizziness made the jagged sides
of the hole sway around him as he cleared away the last of
the dirt and saw—

A rock.

A rock, still brown and slippery from the clay, four or five
inches across.

In an instant, his giddy excitement turned to stomach-
wrenching disappointment. What an idiot he'd been! How
could he have imagined that, after a century of heat and cold
and rain and decay, anything solid could remain?

"Well?" his companion asked from behind the flashlight.

"A rock. Just a goddamn rock."

"Are you certain? It's still half buried."

"See for yourself." Grabbing the spade, he jabbed it into
the dirt next to the rock and almost broke the handle levering
the rock and a chunk of soil loose. He flung the entire mass
into the weeds at the other's feet. "Now let's fill this back up
and get the hell out of here and hope nobody ever finds out
what idiots we've been!" Steadying himself with the spade
he lurched upright and climbed out.

Angrily, he began shoveling the dirt back into the hole.

"Let's not be too hasty," his companion said with a sudden bark of laughter.

He grimaced. "If you don't want to help—" he began, turning sharply toward the taller man.

He stopped, his mouth falling open.

His companion was looking not at the rock but at the underside of the clump of dirt that clung to it.

And at what protruded from the dirt.

There, in the yellowing beam of the flashlight, were what would have looked like nothing more than four blackened pebbles—if it hadn't been for the nearly intact human jaw in which the teeth still rested.

ONE

OCCASIONALLY FRANK DECKER'S sheer bulk—six-five and over two hundred fifty pounds—stood him in good stead, even if it did harbor more flab than he liked. Back in Whitford High more than fifteen years ago, he'd been the football team's leading scorer in both '66 and '67 despite mediocre speed, average coordination, and not all that much interest in sports. And now that he was sheriff of Farrell County—another job that had come looking for him rather than vice versa—belligerent drunks thought twice about defying him. And the county board hadn't yet gotten overly zealous in its attempts to force him to wear the gun the sheriff's manual required.

Most times, though, his size just made him self-conscious. And right now, as he stood looking at Harry Truitt's ruined garden, it only intensified his feelings of helplessness and frustration. Yesterday the old man's backyard had been filled with weed-free, geometrically perfect rows of dozens of varieties of flowers. Today it held only a mass of ripped-up roots, wilting blossoms and scattered dirt.

Standing beside Frank, Truitt grimaced, wiping away a mixture of angry tears and the sweat that the morning heat had already simmered out of his tightlipped, weather-creased face.

"Sorry, Frank. I know it's just a piddly bunch of flowers, but Wilma and I used to work on them together, and—"

The old man stopped abruptly, pulling in a deep breath as

he wheeled about and silently headed back along the concrete walkway toward the front of his green and white bungalow.

Most crimes had motives, Frank thought, following. Greed, anger, revenge, something that made sense! But this—sheer meanness, nothing more, which made it virtually impossible to get a handle on. Seven episodes in little more than a month, and he still didn't have a clue who was doing it. His easygoing, "reasonable" approach to being sheriff just wasn't hacking it. Sam Butterfield, his head-busting predecessor, had probably had the right idea all along. With his kick-their-butts-and-throw-them-in-a-cell approach, he might've caught the son of a bitch by now, or at least scared him into retirement. Maybe—

From behind the closed windows and drawn drapes of Truitt's house came the muffled jangle of a phone.

So. Just like all the others.

With a deep breath to cover his uneasy anger, he brushed past the old man. "I'll get that for you, Harry," he said.

Reaching the front porch, he was relieved to hear the old man say, "Sure, Frank, thanks." He pushed through the door into the dim, relatively cool interior, his heart pounding.

The phone hung on the kitchen wall, beyond a small living room crammed with furniture from the older, larger house where Harry and Wilma had lived until their kids had left home. Crowded or not, the room was spotless, everything down to the smallest knickknack arranged with military precision. Even the photos of Harry and Wilma and their daughters and grandchildren were arrayed on one wall like an organization chart.

He managed an emotionless monotone as he snatched up the receiver. "Yes?"

"Oh?" the familiar taunting voice said. "Answering the phone yourself these days, are you, Sheriff Decker, Sir? Is this a new county service? Part of the victim assistance program?"

A young-sounding voice. A teenager. Insolent. "Mr. Truitt is busy."

That brought a chuckle. "Taking it badly, is he?"

"Not particularly."

Frank could almost hear the shrug on the other end of the line. "But how about you, my friendly neighborhood sheriff?" the voice went on, filled with the same derisive sarcasm that had grated on Frank's ears on six other occasions over the past five weeks. "How are you taking it? Feeling like even more of a clueless jerk than last time?"

"I'll survive," he said, glancing over his shoulder to make sure Truitt was still outside. "Which is more than they'll be able to say for you when I get my hands on you," he went on distinctly and deliberately. "I'll really enjoy sticking it to a chicken-shit coward like you, someone so gutless he sneaks around in the dark to make his little messes and then hides out behind a telephone." He forced a snort of laughter. "I guess I should feel sorry for you, you pathetic loser, but I just can't manage it, not for someone so yellow he can't even face the people he dumps on, let alone me."

His lines delivered, Frank hung up. As he strode back through the house, he wondered if the phone would ring again. There had been no second calls any of the other times, but Frank hadn't been the one to hang up on those.

Nor had he issued a challenge until now. At first he'd reacted exactly the way the caller probably wanted—loudly and angrily. Later, he had tried to talk calmly and rationally, but the results had been the same—more gloating, more taunts about what a sorry excuse for a sheriff Frank was and how dumb he was not to be able to figure out what was going on.

By the time he reached the porch, it was clear that, whatever reaction his little speech had stirred up, it hadn't been a desire to call back and debate. Maybe, just maybe, he'd actually done some good this time. Maybe he'd made the son of a bitch angry enough to pick Frank himself as his next target. Or at least to make some dumb mistake, whoever he picked.

Truitt was sitting on the steps, absently kneading the reddish-brown fur of a floppy-eared mongrel the size of a large beagle. At the sound of the closing door, the dog eyed Frank briefly before retreating lazily into the shade of the bushes that flanked the steps.

"Wrong number," Frank said.

Dry-eyed now, Truitt looked more like his true age of seventy-five than the eighty or more he had seemed in the backyard. He shrugged as he stood up and stepped onto the porch, his body assuming the military erectness that, more than twenty years after his retirement as a full colonel, still seemed his natural state. That and his jaunty salute to each customer had become his trademarks during the fifteen years of his second career as manager of Sloane's Cones, the ice cream parlor down the street from the grade school.

"Figured it was," Truitt said with a hint of a grin. "Sounded like you really gave the bastard what for."

"You heard?"

"Enough. Still don't recognize the voice, huh?"

"You know about the calls?"

"Hell, Frank, everybody knows about the calls. Just because you wouldn't let Del put it in the paper doesn't mean it's a secret."

Frank sighed. "I guess not. No, I didn't recognize the voice. What about you? Any idea who it might be?"

"Not a clue." Truitt lowered himself into the old-fashioned porch swing suspended from a pair of hooks screwed into the ceiling. He sat as erectly as he stood. "You know, Frank," he went on, "I was in the army for thirty years. Lived all over the damned world, Wilma and me, and nothing like this ever happened to us. Oh, sure, things happened, but never like this, for no reason at all."

"Any neighborhood kids you've had trouble with?"

The old man shook his head. "I don't keep up with the

kids so well since we left Sloane's, and especially not since Wilma died. Not even that girl of yours. What's her name again? Betsy?''

"Close. Beth.''

Truitt grinned. ''I remember now. Elizabeth Joyce, right? She always went for the double fudge. How's she doing these days?''

"Just fine. She'll be a sophomore this fall.''

"Already? Hell, it seems like just a couple years ago she started school. She always stopped at the store on the way home, and she and Wilma would—'' He broke off, perhaps adding up the years and realizing just how long it had been since he and Wilma had retired from managing Sloane's.

"How's she like you bein' sheriff?'' Truitt resumed. ''I suppose with kids her age, it's not the most popular occupation in the world. Like bein' in the army, I'd guess.''

"No problems like that with Beth,'' Frank said. ''She likes the sheriff business just fine. Helped with my campaign, as a matter of fact. Put posters up all over town. Even tacked them up on the trees in front of her house—until her mother saw them. No, her biggest problem is, we can't get that custody judge to listen to sense and let her move in with me and her grandmother.''

"Judge Hastings? He the one? Didn't Del run an interview with him the other day? From what I remember, his judicial philosophy is that the husband is unworthy until proven perfect, and perfection doesn't exist in the Midwestern male.''

Frank grimaced. ''He's the one. As far as I can tell, Harve Pressman's the only father who's won a custody fight in front him in the last five years, and that was only because his ex's live-in boyfriend turned out to have two priors for child molesting.''

Truitt shook his head in sympathy. ''Endorsed Butterfield in the election, too, didn't he?''

"So did Beth's mother.''

"Irene, right?''

"Right. It's Irene Bailey now."

"Got married again, huh?" Truitt's eyebrows climbed. "Sure didn't waste any time."

Frank sighed. "The divorce was more than five years ago, Harry."

"That long?"

"Beth was nine, almost."

The old man sighed. "Years don't last as long as they used to."

"I've started noticing that myself," Frank sighed, "and I'm only thirty-five. But to get back to last night—"

The muffled crackle of a two-way radio coming to life cut Frank off.

"Your chariot's tryin' to tell you something, Frank," Truitt said with a nod toward the squad car drawn up to the curb.

"Be right back." Lumbering down the sloping lawn, Frank grimaced as he saw that a patch of sun had slipped between the elms and now glinted off the roof of the closed and locked car. In a town as small as Whitford you'd think it would be safe to leave a car, particularly a sheriff's squad car, with its windows rolled down, but since the vandalism had started, Frank had turned paranoid on the subject. The last thing he needed was "Negligent Sheriff's Car Trashed" running as a headline in the *Gazette*.

"Frank?" A scratchy version of his mother's voice was filtering through the dash-mounted speaker as he opened the door and slid into the bake-oven interior. "Frank, are you there?"

"Hi, Mom," he said, pulling the mike from its cradle under the dash. "So Phil let you steal the radio again."

Phil Biggs, a high school math teacher before he'd retired and become a deputy, theoretically took care of the phone and radio during the day shift, but he rarely turned down anyone's offer to relieve him. And Frank's mother, who'd reluctantly taken on the jail matron's job not long after his election, had been offering relief both to Phil and to Steve Waymore, the night deputy, more and more often lately. Some days she put in more hours than both men combined.

"Mr. Wetherston called," she said, ignoring his comment, "Mr. Nathaniel Wetherston. Personally. He wants to see you right away, at his office in the bank."

"What does he want?"

"He didn't say. He just said it's important."

"Unless somebody's holding up the bank, tell him I'll be along when I finish up here. Or, since you're taking care of the radio, you could send Phil over."

"I suggested that, but Mr. Wetherston didn't want—"

"Then he'll have to wait."

"Frank, this is Nathaniel Wetherston," his mother said, as if she couldn't believe he'd heard her the first time. "Don't you think you'd better get right on over?"

"He can wait his turn like everyone else. I'll get there when I've got time. If he doesn't like it, too damn bad."

Replacing the mike under the dash, he moved the car out of the patch of sun, rolled the windows down, and rejoined Truitt. As he climbed the porch steps, he twisted his arms behind himself to loosen the sweat-soaked back of his short-sleeved brown uniform shirt, plastered to his skin during his brief stay in the car.

"Someone else get trashed?" Truitt asked.

"Not unless it's old man Wetherston. He wants to see me. Didn't say what about."

Truitt snorted. "I can just guess. Wonder what sort of trouble that kid of his has gotten himself into this time."

"Allen?"

"I surely didn't mean Garrick!" Truitt chuckled. "Allen's been back in town at least a month, and that's twice as long as he ever behaved himself when he was growing up. You did know he was back, didn't you?"

Frank nodded. "I've seen his car. And heard the rumors."

"That he's reformed and old Nathaniel's welcomed the lost sheep back into the fold? Don't you believe it, Frank. That's one leopard that's never going to change its spots, any more than his old man's going to quit bailing him out and bitching about it.''

"You know something I don't, Harry?"

Truitt shook his head. "Just common sense. Hell, you should know the kid better than me. You went to school with him, didn't you?"

"He was a couple years behind me. Garrick was a year or two ahead."

"Now there's a whole different story—Garrick. Hard to believe the two of them are part of the same family, isn't it? If he wasn't so rich, I'd feel sorry for Garrick, that wife of his always off somewhere, and him trying to run Nathaniel's businesses practically single-handed ever since the old man decided to 'retire'."

"It could be worse," Frank said with a smile. "But, Harry, much as I like to gossip, how about getting back to last night? Your garden?"

Truitt's face sobered. "Not a hell of a lot to tell, Frank. Everything was fine at ten, when I let the mutt in, so it had to be sometime after that."

"You didn't hear anything when it happened?"

"You think I would've let the bastard get away if I'd heard him? No, I didn't hear anything. Had the air conditioner going full blast in the bedroom, so it's no wonder. Barely hear the TV with that thing running." He sighed grimly. "I just looked out this morning, and there it was, all ripped to hell. Guess I'm lucky he left the house alone."

"Probably knew better than to do anything that'd wake you up."

"Damn right!"

"But you don't have any idea who it might be?"

"Nary a one. No enemies I know of. No arguments, unless you count when the paperboy tried to collect twice last week. No mysterious phone calls or anonymous letters, none of the things you asked all the others about."

Frank smiled. "Guess that wraps it up, then. Except you should come down to the office and get something in writing."

"Sure, why not?" Truitt stood up from the swing. "Think I'll let it go till tomorrow, though, if that's okay with you."

"That'll be fine."

"I think I'll spend today in the garden."

"Harry—"

"Don't worry, Frank," Truitt said, grinning as he went briskly down the steps. "I'm not losing my marbles. I was going to work out there today anyway, and now— Well, if I just get my butt in gear, there's a lot I can probably salvage. Flowers are like people, Frank. Some of 'em are a hell of a lot tougher than they get credit for."

Returning to the squad as the old man marched toward his backyard, Frank eased his bulk behind the wheel, glad that he'd left the windows down. The ventilated seat cushion helped, too, but it also forced him to slouch to keep his dark brown crew cut from being crushed against the roof.

Starting the engine, he turned on the blower, aiming its feeble stream of air at his sweating face, then pulled quickly away from the curb, the wind through the open windows helping far more than the blower. If the county ever decided to spring for a new "fleet" of squad cars, at least one would have air conditioning, even if the extra money had to come out of his own pocket.

After a couple of blocks of relative comfort, his mind went back to Wetherston and his mother's call. Harry had probably been right. It almost had to be about Allen. After all, with the black sheep of the family back in town after—what? ten years?—what else would someone like Nathaniel Wetherston want to see the sheriff about?

Frank blew a disgusted sigh up his face. Nathaniel Wetherston was the ultimate big fish in Whitford's little pond and wasn't about to let anyone forget it. Grandfather Leander had founded the Farmer's and Merchant's Bank in the eighteen-eighties, and his pigeon-spotted statue adorned a wooded glade in the city park. Even his original office, nearly a century old, was carefully preserved and kept on display in the Farrell County Historical Society museum.

And now grandson Nathaniel was the bank's president and chief stockholder, as well as the outright owner of a substantial fraction of everything else worth owning in the county, including several huge tracts of farmland that hadn't been worked since the U.S. Agriculture Department had decided to pay people not to grow crops.

And for the last ten years, since his wife had died and he had turned the day-to-day management of most of his businesses over to his elder son Garrick, Wetherston had been on the County Board of Commissioners, which held the purse strings of just about everything in county government, including the sheriff's department. Nathaniel wasn't chairman of the Board, but whoever was chairman—Dwayne Schalmeyer, currently—always listened to Wetherston. Carefully, as did almost everyone else in and around Whitford.

And with good reason. Even before he'd been elected to the Board, Wetherston had been a one-man civic improvement committee, donating to and raising money for endless local charities. He'd sponsored studies to find ways to improve the local school system and to lure new business into the community. He'd started a scholarship fund. He'd even managed to get Carlton Lake, the county's only tourist attraction, cleaned up.

And then there were the political fundraisers he hosted, one after the other.

Even so, few people—certainly not Frank—believed that an unselfish love of Farrell County humanity prompted Wetherston's endless civic activities. All were too purposely public for that. Nathaniel himself was obviously ill at ease whenever he had to deal with the recipients of his attentions, even the politicians. He made the appearances, shook the necessary hands, said the required words, and withdrew as quickly as tact would allow. As far as Frank could tell, Wetherston was "looking after his family's town," and not particularly enjoying it.

And now that Allen was back—

Frank stiffened abruptly, tightening his grip on the wheel. Fifty yards ahead, a car had pulled out of a driveway onto the wrong side of the street and seemed to be aiming itself directly at the squad car.

TWO

HITTING BRAKES and horn, Frank wrenched the wheel toward the curb.

A moment later, the other car—a subcompact almost small enough to fit in the squad car's trunk—veered wildly toward the opposite side of the street and clipped the far curb before rocking to a stop.

Frank let up on the horn and pulled up next to the car. The neatly bearded and very apprehensive looking driver was, of course, one of the flock of visitors from Whitford's "sister city" in England. They'd been in town since last Thursday, but some of them still occasionally had trouble remembering which side of the road to drive on.

Frank eyed him sternly for a moment, then sighed. "Just be careful, okay?" he said through the open window, and waved him on.

The man nodded gratefully. In the rearview mirror, Frank watched him drive with exaggerated caution down the street and look both ways at least twice before turning right onto Cleveland. Probably heading for the city park a half mile to the south, where Mayor Hardesty doubtless had more activities lined up to keep the visitors entertained. Frank hoped it wasn't practice for the softball game Hardesty had scheduled for tonight. If the mayor had any sense—not something Frank would guarantee—he'd postpone any outdoor physical exertion until that cold front the weather forecasters had been promising since Saturday actually came through.

Pulling out onto Main, barren of trees since the widening

a dozen years before, Frank found himself assaulted by the acrid exhaust fumes of the nine-fifty Greyhound from Springfield. He dropped back into clearer air, letting his thoughts settle again on the Wetherstons. Particularly Allen.

The old resentment twisted at his gut. Or was it jealousy, even now?

He had been jealous often enough in school, watching Allen Wetherston—a gold-plated son of a bitch if there ever was one—rolling in money and getting away with everything short of murder, while Frank himself had to watch every cent and struggle with a part-time job to make it through two years at Davis Tech. Wetherston Senior's scholarship committee had turned him down: two-year schools weren't considered "acceptable," a memory that still rankled.

But there was no point in getting worked up before he knew for sure what Wetherston wanted. Now that he thought about it, Wetherston might be wearing his community service hat today. He might even want to talk about the reward he'd hinted he might offer to help catch Whitford's busy new vandal. One of the early victims had been a loan officer at the bank, and that was when Wetherston had first mentioned the idea. But talk was as far as it had gone. Three more messes, four counting Harry's flower garden, had been made since Wetherston's last hint. Maybe he had decided to go ahead with the reward.

And if he hasn't, Frank thought with a grim smile, maybe I'll sneak out to the park tonight and spray paint an opinion or two on old bronze Leander. That would get the reward offer made official quick enough.

Parking in the sizzling asphalt lot, Frank glanced at the time and temperature display on the bank's marquee. Nearing ninety already. A block and a half to the west, on the parched courthouse lawn across the street from the jail, another digital display showed the same temperature but also the "discomfort index," the summer version of wind chill. It hadn't dropped much below a hundred, even at night, since the current mass of swampy air had moved in.

Sweating heavily, Frank pushed through the massive plate glass doors into the air-conditioned bank lobby. The tellers smiled as he passed their cages, and most of the bank officers looked up from their desks and nodded or spoke briefly.

The door to Wetherston's mahogany-paneled inner sanctum at the rear of the bank stood open. Wetherston, thin-faced and white-haired and wearing a wrinkle-free pale gray three-piece suit, got up and came around his desk to meet Frank at the door. He looked impatient, a familiar enough expression, but Frank thought he sensed an edge of nervousness as well.

Wetherston gripped Frank's massive hand in his own wiry but powerful one for a too-deliberate second. Yes, definitely nervous.

"Sheriff Decker," he said, urging Frank inside and closing the door behind him, "I don't have a great deal of time. Senator Downs is due in at noon, and I still have things to do before our lunch at the Inn."

Naughty boy, you didn't come running when I called, he might as well have said. Frank suppressed a scowl. "You said you had something important to talk about?"

"Most assuredly," Wetherston said, motioning Frank into the plush chair facing the massive desk and then lowering himself into his own soft leather swivel chair. "And delicate, Sheriff, most delicate. I assume I can trust in your discretion."

Damn, Frank thought. *It's not the reward, just Allen.*

"Of course," he said. "Incidentally, I just came from Harry Truitt's place. The same s.o.b. that trashed your loan officer's car hit Harry last night. Ripped his flower garden to shreds. That makes seven."

Wetherston blinked at this sudden change in direction of the conversation, opened his mouth with an annoyed-sounding breath, then seemed to think better of the reaction. "You still don't have any idea who's responsible, then?"

"Not yet. To tell the truth, I was hoping you'd thought some more about that reward you said you might offer."

After a moment, Wetherston dredged up his standard faint smile. "No, I hadn't, but I can see that I've delayed too long. I'll have an announcement drafted for the next edition of the *Gazette*. Perhaps we can make your job a little easier."

"Thank you, Mr. Wetherston."

"And you said Harry Truitt was the victim this time? Didn't he manage Sloane's until a few years ago?" When Frank nodded, Wetherston went on briskly. "Tell him to stop by the Garden Shop. Tell him he can have whatever he needs to repair the damage, free of charge."

The Garden Shop was in the shopping mall on Wetherston-owned land out on the bypass. Sloane's Cones, Frank remembered now, was one of the businesses the Wetherston conglomerate had absorbed back in the fifties.

"But right now, Sheriff," Wetherston went on, "there is another matter I wish to discuss."

Of course. Offering the reward was simply good public relations, but the offer to help Truitt had been aimed at Frank alone. Softening him up. The matter Wetherston wanted handled with "discretion" *must* have to do with Allen.

"As I was saying," Wetherston went on, "this is a most delicate matter, and your discretion, I trust, can be taken for granted."

"It depends on your definition of discretion," Frank told him. As in cover-up, maybe? "I'll do what I can."

Wetherston frowned. "I merely meant that I would like this matter handled as quietly as possible. I would appreciate it if you do not charge about like the proverbial bull in a china shop. That is all."

"I can't promise anything until I know the facts, Mr. Wetherston. You know that. I can only repeat, I'll do what I can."

"My dear Sheriff Decker," Wetherston began, but stopped abruptly, his frown deepening. Then he sighed. "Oh, very well. But I warn you, if this gets out of hand, I will hold you personally responsible. I hope that is fully understood.''

And if I want any help getting re-elected, I can go whistle, Frank thought, but he said only, ''Of course. Now maybe you should tell me what the problem is.''

''You are aware that I am chief stockholder of Allied Insurance?''

''I know that your family controls it, yes.''

''You may also be aware that Louis Cameron has sold insurance for Allied, on a part-time basis, for several years. You are, I believe, acquainted with Mr. Cameron.''

''I was in his history classes in high school, yes, a long time ago.'' Frank didn't add that Cameron, just out of college then, had been his favorite teacher, a man who really came alive in the classroom. He was the only one who had ever managed to make history interesting, not only to Frank but to many others, including Frank's daughter Beth. Outside the classroom, though, he was colorless, not really the sort to make a good insurance salesman. Or so Frank had always thought, but Cameron had apparently been fairly successful at it.

But what the hell did Cameron have to do with Allen Wetherston?

''Cameron is still a teacher, as I am sure you are aware,'' Wetherston said, leaning forward in mock confidentiality. ''He also has a wife and two children, both still in school.''

''I'm afraid I don't understand what you're getting at,'' Frank said.

''I know, I know. I am merely filling in the background, in the hope that it will help you to understand why this matter must be handled with the utmost discretion in order to avoid injury to the innocent parties involved. You see, we recently discovered that Mr. Cameron has, for a number of years, been systematically embezzling from Allied.''

''Lou Cameron? Embezzling? That—that's crazy! I don't believe it!''

Wetherston shrugged his narrow shoulders and leaned back in his chair. He seemed calmed rather than offended by Frank's startled disbelief. "I, too, found it nearly impossible to credit," he said. "I have known Louis Cameron at least as long as you have, and I trusted him. But rest assured, there is no room for doubt. He admitted what he had done in the note he left behind."

"Note? What note?" Frank stared at the old man. "Where is Cameron, anyway?"

"I have no idea, Sheriff. Now please, I understand your feelings, and to some extent I share them. But it will be best if you allow me to explain without interruption. As I was saying, Cameron's thievery was discovered only a few days ago, and only by sheerest accident. Like you, I found it hard to believe, so I proceeded cautiously. I checked the evidence personally, and rechecked it, not once but a half dozen times. I continued to hope it was all a mistake. Then Cameron apparently realized his activities had been discovered."

Wetherston paused, shrugging again, this time in seeming resignation. "Last night he decided to run. His wife found a note this morning, a note apparently written on one of the typewriters at the Allied office."

"Let me see it."

"All it said was that he was sorry. And that if he stayed, the situation would only grow more difficult, now that the truth was going to come out. Since mine was the only name mentioned in the note, Mrs. Cameron called me this morning when she found it. She woke me out of a sound sleep at four a.m., in fact."

"I said, let me see that note!" Frank said impatiently.

"I'm sorry, but that is impossible."

"Like hell it is!"

Wetherston shook his head. "No, Sheriff, it is impossible. The note has been burned."

"Burned? How the hell—"

"Mrs. Cameron and I both thought it best, once I explained

matters to her. Please, Sheriff, do me the courtesy of allowing me to finish.''

''Destroying evidence, under any circumstances—''

''You still don't understand, Sheriff.''

''Then make me understand, Mr. Wetherston,'' Frank said through gritted teeth. ''Make me understand!''

''The crux of the matter is this,'' the old man replied, seemingly unperturbed. ''As far as I am concerned—and therefore as far as you and the law are concerned—there has been no crime. The note therefore was not evidence. I am not going to pursue a complaint against Mr. Cameron. I intend to write the loss off. I will charge it to—to experience, let us say. As I'm sure you are aware, Sheriff, I can afford it. And I want as little publicity about this as possible. None at all would please me best. Publicity would not be fair to Mrs. Cameron or to the children, for one thing. They had nothing to do with the crime except to unwittingly spend some part of the money. They are victims in this affair as much as I myself am a victim. Do you understand now?''

''No, I don't, damn it. If you're trying to keep the crime a secret, then why the hell are you telling me about it?''

''Primarily because I need your cooperation. Mr. Cameron is gone, God knows where. Even though Mrs. Cameron herself has agreed not to ask for a missing persons investigation, others surely will. Others who do not know—and do not need to know—the circumstances surrounding his leaving. Officials at the school, for example. His co-workers at Allied. His friends. They will want to know what has happened to him. They will want an investigation, I am sure. As of course will his children.''

''They haven't been told?''

''Only the daughter. She was with her mother during part of our conversation this morning. The son is visiting his uncle—Mrs. Cameron's brother—out of state.''

''Then the three of you are the only ones who know?''

Wetherston nodded. "And you, of course. And the manager of Allied. And my son Garrick."

"But you don't want Cameron caught and arrested? You don't want to even try to recover the money you say he took?"

Wetherston shook his head. "No, I do not, for the reasons I have stated. In fact, just the opposite. I have already offered Mrs. Cameron employment, in whatever capacity she might wish, within reason. And I plan to provide whatever is necessary to see the children through college. It hardly seems fair that they be deprived of an education because of their father's ill-advised actions. It was, after all, none of their doing."

"Jennie Cameron agreed to all of this?"

"Not in so many words, at least not yet. As you might expect, she is badly shaken. Perhaps in shock. I have arranged for my own physician to help her through these first few days. I can only say that she has not opposed any of my suggestions as yet. And she did agree that burning the note was for the best."

"For the best! You steamroller her into something as harebrained as— Look, Wetherston, didn't it occur to you that the note might have been a forgery? A forgery that we will damn well never be able to prove now that you've burned it?"

Instead of looking angry, Wetherston smiled faintly and shook his head. "In the first place," he said with exaggerated patience, "the note was merely confirmation of what I already knew. In the second place, the note was not written but typed."

"But the signature—"

"There was no signature. There was no way of proving who did or did not write it. The most anyone could have proven was that it was indeed written on a typewriter used at our office, which was immediately evident in any case."

"No signature? Christ, man, didn't that seem just the slightest bit suspicious to you?"

Again Wetherston shrugged. "As a matter of fact, it did.

But Mrs. Cameron assured me that it was quite in keeping with her husband's previous behavior. He rarely signed things, not even the personal letters he wrote. He always typed his name at the bottom, she said. He didn't even like to sign Christmas cards. A personal idiosyncrasy, apparently. She would usually sign both of their names.''

''What about fingerprints?''

Wetherston shook his head brusquely. ''I am afraid the possibility did not occur to me. Criminal investigation is not my forte. But it is too late. The note is gone. And in any case, no complaint will be made, therefore the note cannot concern you.''

Frank scowled silently for a moment. ''All right,'' he said finally, ''looks like you've got me. But I still won't believe Lou Cameron could have done what you say.''

''Speak with his wife, then, Sheriff. Speak with his wife.''

''I will. But if you change your mind and decide to press charges after all, you'll be sorry you burned that note.''

''I will not change my mind, Sheriff. You can take my word on it.''

''I suppose I'll have to,'' Frank said. ''But what I won't take your word for is this burst of generosity. According to you, Cameron has been stealing from you for years. Why are you so willing to write off however many thousands of dollars he allegedly took? Why are you willing, even eager, to help his family in his absence? I'm sorry, Mr. Wetherston. You may support your share of charities and then some, but you've never struck me as the fairy godmother type.''

Wetherston's eyes met Frank's for several seconds. Finally the old man pulled in a breath and let it out in a sigh as he leaned back, gripping the arms of his huge leather swivel chair.

''Very well, Sheriff,'' he said, ''if you need the whole truth before you will cooperate, I suppose you must have it. The truth is—and I tell you this in strictest confidence—I do not want it known that Cameron was able to take the amount of money he took. The method he used was extremely simple. Any employee in Cameron's position could duplicate it. All anyone needs is the idea and the time.''

''You're saying you're afraid that if your other loyal employees got wind of what you say Cameron did, they'd be tempted to do the same?''

''No one is above either temptation or suspicion. Cameron himself is ample proof of that, I would think.''

''But—''

''There is nothing more to discuss, Sheriff. I would gain nothing by trying to have Mr. Cameron arrested, other than the remote chance of recovering whatever money he has not already spent. On the other hand, if his methods came to light, I could lose a great deal more.''

''What about the college expenses for Cameron's children?''

''Think of it as part of my scholarship program. And as insurance. It should greatly reduce the chance that Cameron's wife will ever be inclined to reveal the truth, for whatever reason.''

Wetherston, glancing at his watch, stood up and moved briskly to the door. ''I take it I can trust in your discretion, Sheriff?'' As Frank stood up, frowning, Wetherston held out his hand, as if in a peace offering.

Frank ignored the hand. ''I won't tell anyone that Lou Cameron is an embezzler, if that's what you mean. As far as I'm concerned, he's not.''

Wetherston let his hand drop. ''I don't suppose I could ask for more than that,'' he said, opening the door.

The hell you couldn't, but you know it wouldn't do you one damn bit of good, Frank thought, but all he said as he strode through the door was, ''I'll be in touch.''

THREE

ERUPTING FROM the cool oasis of the bank, Frank stalked across the parking lot and heaved himself into the blistering squad car. He cranked the window down, bulled his way into traffic and headed west, past the jail on the right, the castle-like courthouse and its Civil War cannons on the left.

Burning the damned note, for God's sake!

But it shouldn't have surprised him.

None of it should have surprised him, least of all the high-handed way the old tyrant was trying to sweep the whole affair under the wall-to-wall carpet of Wetherston money and influence. Whitford was Wetherston's town, and Wetherston undoubtedly thought of Frank as "his" sheriff.

A block past the jail, the squad's tires squealed as Frank cut north onto Jefferson. Angrily anxious to reach the Cameron house and get Jennie Cameron's version of what had happened to Lou, he almost gave in to the temptation to use the siren.

As he drove, however, he realized that it was more than simple anger that he felt. Behind the anger lurked an ugly and unwelcome fear. Much as he tried to resist it, much as he admired Lou Cameron, there was a slim chance that Wetherston was telling the truth. Stranger things had happened.

The late Reverend Einar Lindstrom had proven that, with a vengeance.

Lindstrom had died Frank's junior year in high school, but his memory was evoked every time anyone did anything spectacularly out of character. "Pulling a Lindstrom," it was called.

From his first day in Whitford, Lindstrom had been the picture of contentment and impeccable morality. His wife, as pretty as he was handsome, was totally devoted to him. His children, if not quite as perfect as Lindstrom himself, were the envy of every parent in Farrell County. Lindstrom himself was never too busy to give counsel to members of his congregation or to take over the running of yet another charitable function that others couldn't or wouldn't find the time for. In his fifteen years at the Third Street Church, he was never once heard to utter an angry word, let alone a profane one, never once seen to take a drink or smoke a cigarette.

Then, on his fortieth birthday, Lindstrom quietly left the party his congregation had thrown for him in the church basement, went next door to the rectory, locked himself in the bathroom, ran a tub of warm water, placed his neatly folded trousers on top of the laundry hamper by the door and his shirt and underwear inside it, lowered himself into the water and slit his wrists. If a motive was ever found, it was never made public.

Grimacing at the memory, Frank turned left off Jefferson onto the roller coaster hills of Second Street. "Cameron's no Lindstrom," he muttered harshly. The fact that one too-good-to-be-true Bible thumper had indeed turned out to be too good to be true didn't mean that everyone with a facade of virtue had some dark secret devouring him from the inside out.

Lou Cameron an embezzler? Ridiculous!

Parking at the curb in front of the Cameron house, Frank pulled in a deep breath to loosen the knot in his stomach. The front door of the modest two-story frame house was open, and as Frank stepped onto the small front porch, the faint buzz of an electric fan drifted through the screen door. If Lou Cameron had embezzled as much as Wetherston had hinted at, you'd think he'd at least have bought an air conditioner.

Hurried footsteps responded the moment he pressed the

bell, and Sheila, the Camerons' sixteen-year-old daughter, appeared at the far end of a narrow hallway that ran the length of the house. As she saw Frank's bulky form filling the door, the frown on her plain, freckled face deepened.

"I suppose you're here to search the place or arrest Mom or something equally gross!" she said, coming to the screen door but not offering to open it.

"Nothing like that," he said, sympathizing with the girl despite her hostile tone. "Can I come in for a minute?"

"Could I stop you? I suppose you've got a warrant or whatever."

"No warrant, and I don't want to arrest anyone," he said patiently. "I just want to talk to your mother. If it makes you feel any better, I don't think your father stole that money any more than you do."

The girl snorted. "Now I've heard everything! King Wetherston says my father's a crook, and the loyal Sheriff of Nothingham doesn't believe him?"

He sighed. "And you're all set to be Robin Hood, is that it?"

"Somebody has to be," she snapped. "Now what do you want?"

"I told you. I want to talk to your mother."

"Sheila? Who is it?" A woman's tired voice came from the far end of the narrow hall. Before Sheila could reply, Jennie Cameron appeared. She was neatly dressed in light blouse and slacks, but her hair, short and curly with a touch of gray, was tangled, her face haggard. "Who is it, Sheila?" she repeated.

"Just the local Gestapo, Mom. Didn't I tell you they'd be around?"

Mrs. Cameron's angular face remained blank a beat longer than it should have before an off-center smile of recognition appeared.

"Come in, Frank, come in." Then a glance at Sheila, and a frown, not quite in slow motion but as if a conscious effort were required for each action. "Sheila, what are you saying? This is Sheriff Decker."

"I *know* who it is, Mother!" The girl stepped back from the door.

In the kitchen, Jennie seated him at the table, across from the fan oscillating noisily on the counter. Sheila grudgingly got him some iced tea from the refrigerator, then leaned against the doorframe, arms folded belligerently across her chest.

"Just tell me what happened, Jennie," Frank said, feeling awkward, even after all these years, calling the wife of his former teacher anything but "Mrs. Cameron." "Wetherston said Lou left a note, but it was burned?"

She nodded, and continued nodding a beat too long. "That's right," she said. "He assured me it would be better that way."

"If you ask me," Sheila snorted, "the only one it's better for is King Wetherston."

"Sheila, please."

"That's all right, Jennie," Frank said quickly. "As a matter of fact, I think Sheila's right." He went on to explain about Wetherston's fears that, if the embezzlement became common knowledge, someone else would try the same thing.

"Serve him right," Sheila snapped.

"Sheila," her mother protested, "don't talk like that. Mr. Wetherston is being very generous. He—"

"Sure he is. He comes around in the middle of the night and has his doctor dope you up and tries to make us believe that Daddy's stolen his precious money and then he burns that lousy note so nobody'll ever find out that he probably wrote the stupid thing himself and then—"

"Sheila," Frank broke in, turning in his chair to face the girl. "Just hold on a minute. Yelling at me isn't going to help. It's just going to slow things down. The sooner I find out what really happened, the sooner I can figure out why Wetherston is lying."

He paused, looking into Sheila's still-angry eyes. "Truce?"

Finally the girl lowered her eyes and nodded, though her stance was still stiff with defiance. "Okay."

"Now, for a start," Frank went on, turning back to Jennie Cameron, "what's this about Wetherston's doctor doping you up?"

"Nothing of the kind," she said defensively. "Mr. Wetherston just had Dr. Edwards come over and give me something to steady my nerves, that's all. And Mr. Wetherston is paying for it."

"Big deal!" Sheila said with a sneer. "He can afford it. If he really wanted to help, he'd hire a bunch of private detectives to look for Daddy, not go around telling stupid lies about him."

"Don't worry," Frank said, trying to sound more confident than he felt. "I'll look for him. All right?"

The girl nodded, still stiffly defiant as she sat down at the table next to her mother and dabbed at her eyes with a wadded-up Kleenex.

"Now," Frank said, "for a start, tell me about the note. What exactly did it say? And where did you find it?"

Jennie Cameron, who had been watching her daughter anxiously, blinked as she turned toward Frank. "I—I can't recall the precise words," she said finally, a new look of distress tugging at her angular features.

"Did it say when he took the money? Or how much? Was there any hint about where he planned to go?"

Jennie shook her head. "Nothing like that. All it said was..." Her voice trailed off, her brow wrinkling as she tried to remember.

"It was only a few lines," she went on. "Something like, 'I'm sorry to bring this shame on you, but Mr. Wetherston has found out what I've been doing. I hate to leave you, but it will be better this way.' Something like that. I—I can't remember it very well, I'm afraid."

Frank's heavy eyebrows rose. "He didn't say specifically what he'd done? What Wetherston had found out about?"

"No, but Mr. Wetherston said—"

"Sheriff Decker," Sheila broke in, her voice firm again, "I didn't see the note—if I had, King Wetherston would never have gotten away with burning it. But Daddy couldn't have written it! He wouldn't've stolen anything in the first place, and even if he did, he never would've run out on us like that, not in the middle of the night and not without explaining things to us, not in a million years." Her voice broke. "So it doesn't matter what King Wetherston said."

"I know that, Sheila," he said quietly. "But I'm a little confused here, so just let me get straightened out, okay? Let's go back to the note, Jennie. You're telling me there was nothing specific in it, right?"

Jennie nodded.

"Nothing about stealing any money?"

"No, nothing."

"And there was no signature? Just his name typed at the bottom?"

Again she nodded. "But that's just Lou. He hardly ever signs anything unless he absolutely has to."

"How did you find the note? Where did he leave it?"

"It was dropped through the mail slot in the front door," Jennie said, "around three or three-thirty this morning."

"You didn't actually see who left it? Or hear anyone?"

"I suppose I did hear the slot cover clank, but I didn't know it at the time. I was sleeping—dozing, really—in there in the living room. When Lou didn't come back from the museum, and I couldn't find him anywhere, I was too worried to go to bed, so I—"

"The Historical Society Museum, you mean?"

She nodded. "He's been there a lot lately, what with all this fuss about the English visitors. He was there until they closed Sunday afternoon, and he went back, after supper. He said there was something he had to do. He was going to meet us at the party later.''

The party, at the country club out by Carlton Lake, had been another of Mayor Hardesty's events staged for the English. Frank had stopped by briefly himself, chatting with Hardesty and Laura Young, the gung ho president of the Historical Society.

''And he never showed up at the party?''

Jennie shook her head. ''I called the museum. And the house. But he wasn't either place. Then I drove up to the museum, but it was all locked up, just the night lights on. And he still wasn't at home. I even went back to the party. I thought we might've missed each other on the road, but he hadn't been at the party at all. I talked to Laura, but she had no idea where he was. She'd been expecting him all evening, but she hadn't seen him since the museum that afternoon.''

Jennie's voice had been rising as she spoke. Last night's anxiety was resurfacing despite whatever Edwards had given her. Frank put one hand over both of hers where they lay on the table, fingers intertwining nervously.

''I went back to the museum a half dozen times,'' she went on. ''I kept hoping he—he'd stepped out for a minute or something. Finally, I just came home and waited. When I hadn't heard anything by midnight, I called your office.''

''And they told her not to worry,'' Sheila put in harshly. '''Call back in the morning if he still hasn't turned up!''' she mimicked.

That sounded like Steve, all right, Frank thought. The night shift deputy wasn't always as diplomatic as he could be, particularly when it came to missing spouses. One of Steve's uncles tended to disappear every few months, only to turn up the next morning, sleeping it off in his car somewhere. Steve seemed to think everyone behaved that way.

''I'm sorry,'' Frank said, ''but Steve couldn't've done anything you weren't doing already.''

''I know,'' Jennie said, calm again. ''I'm not blaming him

for anything.'' Sheila's sideways glare granted no such absolution.

"Did he say why he was going back to the museum? You said there was something he had to do. Did he say what?''

Jennie shook her head. "It wasn't like him, but he didn't.''

"What about Sunday afternoon? Was he doing anything special at the museum then?''

"The same as always, I imagine. On weekends, he and the others from the Society show visitors around and answer questions. The other things—the indexing and the genealogical research and all that—all get done during the week, when there aren't so many people coming through.''

Frank nodded. It was the indexing of the Society's hundred-and-ten-year run of the Whitford *Gazette* that had led to the visit by the English in the first place. Last fall, when Laura Young and the Historical Society had started microfilming the Gazette, Lou Cameron and a small group of history buffs had tackled the indexing, filling out index cards by the thousands.

In one of the August 1883 issues Cameron had found an article that warranted more than just a three-by-five card. It told how a group of travelers from an English town, also named Whitford, had come visiting for a day. They had been on a three-month "tour of the colonies,'' the article said, and when someone had pointed out the existence of an American Whitford only a few miles off their planned route, they had decided on the spur of the moment to have a look.

Cameron had shown the article to Del Richardson, the current editor of the *Gazette*. Richardson had been almost as fascinated as Cameron, and he put the original article on the front page, along with a story about how Cameron had found it. Naturally, Mayor Hardesty saw the story. On a whim he contacted the mayor of the English Whitford. One thing led to another, and within days a three-week visit in honor of the centennial of the original visit had been arranged, with the visiting English set to stay in the homes of local host families.

A lot of interest in the Historical Society resulted. People wanted to see the microfilmed newspapers, and if there was one thing Lou Cameron enjoyed almost as much as digging through the papers themselves, it was answering questions about what he found in them.

"Nothing different about this Sunday?" Frank asked.

Jennie Cameron shook her head, but after a second Sheila said uncertainly, "Daddy was kind of excited about something."

"Did he say what?"

"No, and when I asked him what was up, he just said it was because the English were here and all that stuff. But he had an envelope with him, one of those big brown ones, when he came home for supper. I saw him looking at some papers in it."

"You didn't ask him what the papers were?"

The girl shook her head. "I guess I figured they were something he was working on for the museum. Stuff that happened a hundred years ago isn't really my bag," she said, sounding a little defensive.

"But he seemed excited? Not worried?"

"Definitely not worried. He wasn't grinning exactly, but you know how it is when you're trying real hard not to?"

Frank nodded. "That's the way your father was acting? Not upset, but like he was looking forward to something?"

"That's right." Sheila's belligerence revived. "Don't you believe me?"

"I didn't say I didn't believe you. I just want to—"

"You think I'm making it up!" she flared. "Because if he'd been stealing that money and he knew King Wetherston had found out, he would've been acting worried or something, not excited."

"Sheila, please," her mother cut in. The girl clamped her mouth shut and lowered her eyes to glare at the table top. "I'm sorry, Frank, but you can understand that we're both on edge."

"Of course. I'm sorry I have to keep asking questions. Now

these papers that Lou brought home yesterday afternoon—did you see them, Jennie?''

''I—I think so. But Lou is always bringing something home to work on, from school or from the office.''

''Did he take the envelope with him when he went back to the museum?''

''I don't know. I suppose so.''

''Do you mind if I look around? Look through his clothes and things? What did he take with him, by the way?''

Before her mother could collect her thoughts on this new subject, Sheila snorted loudly. ''Nothing!'' the girl said. ''He didn't take one thing except the car. His clothes are still here, and his suitcases and his books and his spare keys and everything!'' She paused, her jaw trembling again, her eyes angrily meeting Frank's. ''He didn't take one single, lousy thing except what he was wearing. Which certainly ought to tell you *something*.''

FOUR

BACK IN THE oven-like squad car, heading for the civic center, Frank was just approaching the abandoned railroad tracks that angled across Harrison south of the town's water tower when the radio crackled to life.

"Beth called," his mother said curtly. "She wants to talk to you."

A twinge of guilt pricked at him. Since the election, he hadn't seen nearly as much of his daughter as he should have. "Did she say what she wanted?"

"Just that she'd like to talk to you and that you could call her at the Hyland place. She's babysitting there. In case you didn't know. And she sounded upset, if you want my opinion. She said it wasn't anything really important, but I didn't believe her for a second."

"All right, Mom," he sighed. "What's the address? I'll stop and see her right now."

A note of satisfaction in her voice, his mother gave him the address. Then she added, "What did Mr. Wetherston want?"

"Some craziness about Lou Cameron," he said. "I'll tell you all about it later. When half the county isn't listening to us on their scanners."

Replacing the mike under the dash, Frank made a left on Seventh, past Farrell County Consolidated High School, where Beth would be a sophomore in less than a month.

His mother, like his own conscience, had been urging him for months to "do something" about his relationship with the girl. He had to admit he'd done little but make excuses, hoping that things would go back to the way they had been during the first years after the divorce, when he had seen more of Beth than Irene had, custody award or no custody award. He'd lived in a three-room flat over the electronics repair shop he and Jerry Peterson ran, and hardly an evening went by that Beth hadn't at least stuck her head in the door. Often they would end up going to a movie or driving to the amusement park in Creighton, where he could barely squeeze into the bumper cars that, for most of one summer, had been one of her major passions.

Then he'd been elected sheriff—and moved into the five-room living quarters attached to the jail. Beth loved it, but Irene threw a fit whenever the girl so much as mentioned wanting to visit.

Why? God only knew. The most he was ever able to get out of his ex-wife was an icy, "If you can't understand why I don't want my daughter hanging around a jail, then there isn't any way on His green earth I can explain it to you!"

Even when his mother, Beth's grandmother, for God's sake, had taken on the matron's job and moved in with him, it hadn't cut any ice with Irene. Her mental picture of a jail— her mental picture of damn near everything, he used to think—had been formed and frozen long ago, and she wasn't about to let an ex-husband or former mother-in-law confuse her with facts. If it wasn't in a "good" neighborhood, surrounded by a well-kept lawn and freshly painted snow-white picket fence, Irene wanted nothing to do with it.

Irene had remarried not long after the election and the situation had gone from bad to worse. Frank hadn't talked to her new husband, Gordon Bailey, since the wedding, but he knew the man as well as he wanted to. A salesman at Krueger Ford, he fit the jovial, backslapping stereotype of a used car salesman almost too well to be believed. His son David, two years older than Beth, was already following in his father's footsteps.

Grimacing mentally, Frank pulled to the curb in front of a small, one-story house with cream-colored siding half hidden by waist-high evergreen shrubs. His daughter's bicycle was chained to a lamp post next to the sidewalk. The doors and windows of the house were all shut tight, and the backside of a massive air conditioner hummed and dripped in a side window.

Locking the car, he crossed the steeply sloping lawn to the front door. From inside he could dimly hear TV talk show voices over the vibrating hum of the air conditioner.

The moment he rang the bell, the voices were silenced. A second later, the door swung open.

"Daddy!" Beth, red-haired and pretty like her mother but already four or five inches taller than Irene's five-three, threw open the screen door. A broad grin lighted her face, and Frank found an answering grin spreading across his own.

"Hi, Pint Size," he said, using the nickname they had fallen into a couple of years before, when it became obvious that, though she had gotten her looks from her mother, she'd be getting her height from her father. "Your grandmother said you called, so here I am."

"She said you were out working. I didn't think—"

"She got me on the radio. And she said something was bothering you, so I figured I better find out what it was. Besides, we haven't been seeing enough of each other lately."

Her smile broadened for a moment, but changed to an exaggerated pout. "You know how Mom is."

"I know. But she worries about you," he forced himself to say. "That's all. Now are you going to leave me melting out here, or invite me into the air conditioning and tell me what the trouble is?"

Her green eyes became serious. "Sure, come on in," she said, turning and stepping inside. A baby eight or nine months old lay asleep in a crib across the room, a pacifier in its mouth. For a long moment, Beth stood with her back to her father,

looking at the baby. "I don't suppose you've had any luck
with that judge yet," she said finally.

"Afraid not. And now that your mother's married again—"

"What is that old man's problem?" she burst out, turning
away from the crib and sprawling onto the couch. "It's crazy!
I mean, you're the sheriff, and that jerk she married is just
a—a used car hotshot."

"Don't be too hard on him," Frank said without a lot of
conviction. "He can't be all that bad or your mother wouldn't
have married him."

She snorted. "You don't have to live with him. Or with
that creepy kid of his."

He suppressed a smile. The boy was fifteen, about a year
and a half older than Beth. The few times Frank had seen
him, he'd seemed like a nice enough kid. "And just how is
David 'creepy'?"

"For one thing, he's always barging into my room like he
owned the place. He doesn't even knock or anything, just
barges right in."

Abruptly, Frank's mood darkened, a mixture of apprehension and anger stabbing at his stomach. He'd heard all too
often over the years what stepbrothers and stepfathers—even
brothers and fathers—sometimes did to children. And since
he'd become sheriff, he'd been called in on a couple of local
cases and seen the ugly problem first hand.

"Has he tried to do anything to you?" he asked sharply,
his hand going out to touch her shoulder.

"It's nothing like that, Daddy. Or at least I don't think it
is. He's just trying to bug me. He had the room for ten years
before Mom and I moved in, and he just keeps forgetting
there's a new tenant. He says." She shook her head angrily.
"I've had that room for three months, and he's not that dumb.
He may be creepy, but he's not dumb."

"What about locking the door?"

"There's no lock! And when I tell Mom about it, she just

takes his side. I started propping a chair under the knob, but yesterday Mom tried to get in, and—''

She broke off with another shake of her head. ''All she says is, I'm 'overreacting.' She takes that creep's side all the time, no matter what. And would you believe, she's decided I don't need to go to college after all?''

''What? But that's all settled. I've been giving her money to put into your college fund.''

''Maybe so, but I heard her talking to Gordon last night— Mr. Creep Bailey wants me to call him 'Gordon,' did you know that? Anyway, I heard them talking last night,'' she rushed on, the words now pouring out, ''and he was telling her how he needed the money she has in that special account, and how I'd never even know it was gone!''

''You're sure about this?''

''I told you, I heard them talking.''

''But why should he—''

''I don't know! I didn't hear that part, but a couple weeks ago he started driving this brand new Cougar. He—''

''Don't worry, I believe you,'' he said, wondering how low a man would have to sink to steal from his stepdaughter's college fund. But surely Irene would never go along with it. Would she?

''Look, Pint Size,'' he said, standing up from the couch, ''I'll talk to your mother. I'll get things straightened out. And don't worry about college. I don't know what's going on, but one way or another, there's going to be enough money when the time comes. If you want extras, like pizzas or lipstick, you'll probably have to get a part time job like I did, but there'll be enough for the necessities. Okay?''

She was silent for several seconds, her face still half turned toward the sleeping baby. Then she nodded and stood up herself. ''Okay.'' After another silence, she looked up at him, her green eyes solemn. ''Thanks, Daddy.''

FRANK'S FIRST IMPULSE, to drive out to Krueger Ford and confront Bailey, lasted less than a block.

First, he'd better get Irene's version. If the boy, David, was barging into Beth's room the way she said, and her mother was turning a blind eye to it, he didn't want to waste any time. He hoped to God Beth was right, that all the boy wanted to do was bug her, but no way was he going to take chances with her safety. After he talked to Irene and maybe Bailey, he'd see Beth again, and then—

Then, unless he felt a lot differently than he did now, he'd tell Beth that, if she thought she was in even the slightest danger from her stepbrother, she should simply come to the living quarters in the jail. Under the circumstances, he was certain his lawyer could get an emergency order, if not from Hastings, then from some other judge.

But Irene wasn't home. While curious eyes watched from a neighboring split-level, he tore a sheet from the notebook he carried in his shirt pocket and scribbled a message, telling her to call as soon as she got in.

As he left, his stomach rumbled faintly, reminding him it was well past lunch time and he hadn't had so much as a snack since the Instant Breakfast he'd gulped on the way out to answer Harry Truitt's call.

TOSSING HIS chili dog wrapper and a half dozen napkins into the parking lot trash barrel, Frank hurried up the worn concrete steps to the main door of the Whitford Civic Center. The Historical Society office and museum took up one entire wing of the two-story brick building which had, until a decade earlier, housed Whitford High School. The massive door with its metal push bar was unchanged from when Frank, as a student, had barged through it at least a thousand times. Inside, it was all but unrecognizable. The classrooms were now meeting rooms or recreation rooms, filled with card and pool tables instead of desks and blackboards. The long, echoing hallways had long ago been painted a cheerful yellow instead of the institutional greenish gray he remembered. And the room where Lou Cameron had been his teacher—

Forcing Lou's image out of his mind, Frank hurried down the half flight of stairs and pushed through the swinging doors that marked the entrance to what had been the machine shop annex but was now the Farrell County Historical Society museum.

A sharp scent of age overlaid the breeze that trickled down from the air conditioning vents just below the ten-foot-high ceiling. The room itself was filled with a hodgepodge of display cases, whatever the Society had been able to get their hands on. Along one wall stood a pair of waist-high glass display counters given to them by Whittenberger's Hardware when the store had gone out of business five years ago. Now they were filled with Victorian knickknacks instead of electric drills and saber saws. Next to those, a huge, glass-fronted bookcase held photos and clocks and dishes and statues and ancient typewriters and whatever else would fit on the shelves, even a book or two. Through an open archway on the right he could see a buggy, a hay rake, a butter churn, and a rugged wooden bench with dozens of odd-looking tools carefully laid out and tagged. Beyond a matching archway on the left was an ancient, canopied bed covered with a faded patchwork quilt and surrounded by bureaus and chairs and a treadle-operated sewing machine, even a spinning wheel.

A dozen yards along the north wall, Laura Young was standing up from her battered but well-polished roll top desk.

"Frank, what a pleasant surprise." Her voice was softly modulated, throaty, her Spock-like diction the only hint of an accent. In her early thirties, with short, glossy black hair, faded jeans, and the face of a half-Oriental pixie, she always looked deceptively out of place in the midst of these rooms of musty Midwestern artifacts.

Truth was, she fit in perfectly.

A refugee from China's so called "Cultural Revolution," where books and newspapers had been destroyed and history itself rewritten, Laura had been virtually obsessed with the Historical Society from the moment she had come to Whitford. By the time Shirley Walters resigned the presidency two years later, Laura had convinced her and all the society members that she was the natural one to take over. Within a year, her enthusiasm and sincerity, not to mention talent, had begun to pay off. Donations and matching state and federal grants started rolling in at a rate Shirley had never dreamed of, including funds for Laura's pet project, the microfilming of the *Gazette*. She had even gotten funds enough to turn the presidency into a full-time, paying job.

The only sour note was her husband, civics teacher Wayne Young. From the start, he'd been less than thrilled with all the time she spent on the Society, and the situation had only grown more strained as her success grew. They'd met and impulsively married in San Francisco during one of his summer vacation trips there, but, according even to some of Young's friends, he'd misread her entirely during the brief "courtship." He'd mistaken her natural warmth and constant politeness for something else. Maybe he hadn't expected her to be his own personal Geisha, but apparently he had expected more "obedience" than he had gotten. Rumors of a potential breakup had been floating around—and being denied—for months now, and Frank found himself now and then hoping—guiltily—that they were true. But until that day came, if it ever did...

"It is nice to see you," Laura said, smiling as Frank waved and began picking his way toward her through the maze of artifacts and display cases. "What can I do for you?"

"I need to find out a few things about yesterday afternoon," he said. "I suppose it was really busy, what with the museum being the main event on the mayor's agenda for the English?"

"Indeed," she said, the smile becoming a grin. "I believe they were all here at one time or another, but they were not the only ones. Ever since Louis Cameron uncovered the original visit, and Mr. Richardson and Mayor Hardesty began publicizing it, we have had twice as many visitors as normal. And now that the English are actually here, and every story that is printed about them mentions the original visit and how it was discovered purely by accident right here in the museum, the spotlight shines even more brightly.''

"I suppose Lou's been the center of attention.''

She laughed softly, eyes sparkling. "And loving every minute of it.''

"He was here yesterday, as usual?''

"Of course. I do not think he has missed a single Sunday for the past three months, and he would certainly not miss the day that our English friends were scheduled for their tour. But he has not been in today,'' she added. "Did you wish to speak with him?''

"There's nothing I'd like better. But tell me about yesterday. What, exactly, did Lou do?''

Another small laugh. "The same as the rest of us, only perhaps with more enthusiasm. As I'm sure you know, we answer questions for the most part. 'How does that peculiar-looking machine there work?''' she illustrated, pointing at the hand-cranked floor model Victrola next to her desk. "'Where did you get that? It looks just like something my Aunt Gertrude used to have.' And there are always questions about the newspaper, particularly yesterday. All the English wanted to see the original article, of course.''

"Then Lou wasn't doing anything special yesterday? No new project he was working on?''

"None of which I am aware. Why? Is something wrong? You look concerned, and these questions you ask…?''

"As a matter of fact, there is something wrong, Laura,'' he admitted. "Lou Cameron is missing. He—''

"Missing? Do you mean something has happened to him?'' Her almond eyes widened, her smile vanishing into concerned solemnity.

"I don't know. I hope not. But that's why I'm asking questions."

"Of course, of course. Whatever you wish to ask, I will be most pleased to answer."

"For a start, do you know of any papers Lou might've been working on? Anything at all?"

She shook her head again, looking sad that she couldn't answer his very first question. "He and Mr. Wintergreen are still working on the index, but I doubt that either of them would have been working on it yesterday."

"I don't think it would've been the index. Lou's daughter Sheila said he had some papers in a manila envelope when he came home yesterday afternoon. And that he was—well, she said he seemed excited."

"I am sorry, but I cannot imagine what it could be. You are welcome to look through the desk that he uses." She waved at a desk a few yards beyond the one she had been sitting at. It wasn't a roll top like hers, but it looked almost as old, its massive wooden top scratched in a dozen places but cleaned and polished nonetheless.

"If you don't mind," he said, walking back to the desk.

"Of course I do not mind. But everyone uses it, so what it contains would not necessarily belong to Louis Cameron."

But there was nothing, at least nothing beyond the normal junk that shared desks collect, including one or two of almost every item that could be found in a stationery store. And dozens of packets of blank file cards for the index.

When Frank looked up, Laura was watching him hopefully, but he shook his head. "What about a file cabinet?" he asked.

"Of course." She led him to an ancient quartet of gray, four-drawer cabinets hidden in a corner between two display cases.

"I don't suppose there's any way of telling if any files are missing?"

"Perhaps," she said, pulling open the top drawer of one and taking a loose-leaf binder from the front. "This is a listing of all the file headings, so it is possible to see if a file has been taken away.''

No files were missing, they found, but they had no way of telling if each individual file was complete. Glancing at his watch, Frank saw that it was nearly two, and he still hadn't accomplished a damned thing toward finding Lou Cameron.

''I understand Lou came back to the museum last night, probably around seven or seven-thirty. Do you have any idea why?''

''None, I am afraid. He has his own keys and is free to come and go as he wishes.''

''He didn't talk to you about anything special yesterday? Didn't say anything about what he was working on?''

''Actually, I saw very little of Louis,'' she said apologetically. ''I spent most of my time here, in the main room. He was in the Wetherston Room. That is where the microfiche viewer is set up.''

Other than the statue in the park, the Wetherston Room was the town's major memorial to Nathaniel's grandfather, Leander Wetherston. Leander's widow had for sixty years preserved her husband's office in the family home, and when she died, her will gave the entire contents of the room to the museum, along with a healthy trust fund for upkeep, all with the understanding that the office would be recreated and maintained as a public exhibit in the museum. That had been in the middle nineteen-forties. The Leander Wetherston Room had outlasted two museums as well as a dozen Historical Society presidents and was now in its third home, what had once been the shop teacher's office and workroom.

Laura led the way through the room with the canopied bed into a small, open-doored room beyond. The first thing that caught his eye was a typewriter even more ancient than those in the other room. It sat on a small table in one corner, everything but the keyboard covered by what looked like an inverted fish tank. According to a placard fastened to the table, the tank was not a dust cover but a ''device to render the machine virtually noiseless in its operation." Most of the placard, however, was devoted to explaining how the "forward-looking" Leander had been one of the pioneers in the business use of the machine, the efficiency of which "contributed in no small measure to the unprecedented success of his bold endeavors."

But it was the ornate and massive desk that dominated the room. The microfiche viewer sitting on a pad in the middle of the desk looked both small and anachronistic. Next to it was a box of microfiche cards, one month of the *Gazette* on each card, over thirteen hundred cards. The August 1883 card was still in place, so that, when Frank flipped the switch, the article about the original English visitors appeared on the pale green screen.

After glancing at the article—he'd read it last winter when it had first been found and reprinted—he switched the viewer off and stood looking around the room, wondering, his thoughts growing darker by the moment.

Lou Cameron had spent Sunday afternoon here. He had gone home in a good mood, even an "excited" mood. Then he had come back here, presumably still in the same good mood.

And vanished.

The next morning, he was accused of embezzling an undisclosed amount of money and of deserting his family. Accused by Nathaniel Wetherston, who not only didn't want Cameron caught and prosecuted but who was being implausibly generous with Cameron's family.

It didn't make sense, Frank thought irritably, no matter how you looked at it.

For starters, it didn't make sense that Lou Cameron could be an embezzler. And even if he was an embezzler, it didn't make sense that he'd be "excited" about the prospect of deserting his family.

It didn't make sense that he'd say he was returning to the museum and then hide out until three or four in the morning before dropping a note through his own mail slot. During the hour or two while Jennie was at the party, before she started looking for him, he would've had plenty of time to leave a note on the kitchen table, pack some clothes, and drive away. Even assuming he had stolen the money and had it all in his pocket—in thousand dollar bills?—he should've taken something, if only a change of clothes and a razor and toothbrush.

Only one way would it make sense, Frank thought grimly. And that was if Lou Cameron had not left of his own free will.

FIVE

As HE CRANKED DOWN the windows and got the car moving, Frank debated what to do next.

Laura had given him the names of everyone who had been on duty as well as a Xerox of the last five pages of the visitors' register. Almost two hundred people had signed in Sunday afternoon. Talking to them all would be a long, tedious job that would probably put him not one inch closer to Lou Cameron.

No, the Wetherstons were the ones saying Lou was a thief, and the Wetherstons were the ones who knew a hell of a lot more than they were telling. Certainly more than any of the people Lou might have talked to casually Sunday afternoon. But Nathaniel had given him nothing but lies. And questioning Allen, unless the younger Wetherston had changed drastically during his long absence, would be even more futile.

Which left Garrick, the hard-working, low-profile Wetherston, and the one who, as business manager, should know at least as much about Allied and its allegedly missing money as his "retired" father.

Normally, the elder Wetherston brother would have been in his office across Twelfth Street from the bank, but not today. Nor was he, surprisingly, at the Allied office down the block. He was, his soft-spoken secretary said, at Lakeview Estates, the mobile home park Nathaniel had started in the fifties.

"The manager quit a week ago," she explained in a disapproving tone. "Mr. Garrick is trying to find a replacement.

In the meantime, he has his hands full straightening out the mess Mr. Daugherty left behind.''

Lakeview Estates, despite the name, did not have a view of Carlton or any other lake, though it was within shrieking distance of Whitford's municipal swimming pool. The name was derived from the street on which the park fronted, Lakeview Road, which did give a view of the lake—a winding mile and a half further on. For that matter, the ''Estates'' half of the name didn't strike Frank as all that appropriate either, not for the checkerboard of narrow, dusty access roads and parched ''lawns'' even smaller than the trailers themselves.

Frank found Garrick Wetherston in the office, a one-room bunker-like building just inside the entrance, in the shade of one of the few trees on the property.

Garrick was sitting behind the room's single desk, sorting through untidy stacks of papers. His jacket and tie lay on the arm of a small couch, the only furniture aside from the desk and office chair he occupied. Sleeves rolled up over long, slender forearms, he twisted his narrow, almost gaunt features into a scowl as he looked from paper to paper. When Frank pushed open the plate glass door, Wetherston was running bony fingers through his still-dark but thinning hair. From the disheveled look of it, it wasn't the first time.

Wetherston looked up from the papers, the scowl fading into a forced neutrality as he recognized Frank.

''Good afternoon, Sheriff,'' he said. ''What can I do for you?'' His voice sounded tired, but Frank could detect no obvious emotion in the tight syllables.

''I have a few questions,'' Frank said. ''You can probably guess what they're about. Mind if I sit down?''

''Be my guest,'' Wetherston said, indicating the couch with a restrained, or perhaps wary, nod. Despite the air conditioning, his forehead glistened with sweat.

''I assume you know about Lou Cameron,'' Frank said.

Wetherston nodded again, a motion so slight as to be almost invisible. ''Father said you would probably wish to speak with me, although I doubt that I'll be able to tell you anything you haven't already learned from him.'' His lips pressed briefly together before he added, ''In fact, I'm quite certain that I won't.''

''I'm just wasting my time, then? And yours? Is that what you're saying?''

Wetherston shrugged, a gesture as minuscule as his nods.

''I might as well get on with it then,'' Frank said. ''For a start, since you're the one in charge of Allied, do you agree with the way your father is handling the affair?''

''I am hardly in a position to disagree.''

''But you must have an opinion,'' Frank persisted.

''If I do, it has no effect on the real world.''

''You're saying that your father's still in charge? Or is it just this Cameron business you have no control over?''

Another almost invisible shrug.

''All right, let me put it another way,'' Frank said impatiently. ''Do you have any idea why your father's doing what he's doing? Why, for instance, is he being so generous to the family of someone he says is a thief?''

''Surely he told you that himself, Sheriff. He wants no more publicity than absolutely necessary.''

''I know. He's afraid someone else will do the same thing Lou Cameron did. He says.''

''You don't believe him, Sheriff?'' Wetherston asked, a touch of mockery entering his tired voice.

''Frankly, I don't. But, then, I don't believe Lou Cameron stole that money in the first place.''

''Oh?'' For the first time since Frank had entered the office, Garrick Wetherston actually looked interested. ''Do you mind if I ask you a question?''

''Feel free.''

''If Mr. Cameron didn't take the money, do you have any thoughts as to who the real culprit might be?''

''Maybe. But before we get into that, tell me about the missing money. From what your father said, it had been taken over a long period. How did you finally discover it had been taken?''

"I didn't, Sheriff. My father did." Garrick's nostrils flared slightly. "Surely he also told you that!"

Frank blinked, trying to recall exactly what Nathaniel Wetherston had said. "He told me the theft had been discovered, that's all. He didn't say by whom, or at least I don't remember it if he did. I guess I assumed it was discovered by you or Bill O'Blennis."

A faint smile pulled at Garrick Wetherston's pale lips. "The so-called president or the office manager. That would be a logical assumption, wouldn't it?"

"But it's wrong?"

Wetherston nodded, gripping the arms of his chair as he leaned back. "I learned of it—" He paused and glanced at his watch. "—approximately six hours ago. Father called me at eight this morning with the news."

"And you told O'Blennis?"

"Precisely. And Mr. O'Blennis was, I may say, surprised. Astonished, even."

"All right, then. How did your father discover the money was missing?"

Wetherston shrugged, the gesture almost full size now. "I fear I am not privy to such information."

"Then I don't suppose you know the amount, either?"

"Sorry. The matter is, according to Father, 'under investigation.'"

"He has someone going over the books?"

"In a manner of speaking. He is investigating the matter 'personally.' This morning he took what he called 'all pertinent records' from the Allied office. If you wish to know more, you will have to inquire of my father."

"I have, but he wasn't very forthcoming," Frank said, prompting Garrick to a faint smile. "But maybe I'll try again."

"You do that, Sheriff. I wouldn't mind learning somewhat

more about the matter myself. But you implied that you have a suspect other than Mr. Cameron in mind. I don't suppose you would care to share your suspicion?''

Frank hesitated, but only a moment. "At this point, all I have are hunches. And the first hunch I had when your father said he wanted to see me was that, whatever the trouble was, it probably had something to do with your brother."

Wetherston's brows arched above his hollow eyes. "Ah, yes, dear Allen. You do know he's back, then?"

"I haven't spoken to him, but I've seen him around town in his—what is it? A Mercedes?"

Garrick nodded. "He left his Jaguar in California."

"He's been here a couple of months, hasn't he?"

"Fifty-nine days and three hours, if you want the precise figure. But let me get this straight, Sheriff." Garrick leaned back and gazed at Frank from beneath lowered lids. "Are you saying you feel that my dear brother Allen, a member of the illustrious Wetherston clan, the pride of Whitford, is more likely to have stolen our money than the lowborn but perhaps more admirable Mr. Cameron?"

"Much more likely."

A faint smile appeared on Wetherston's face again, this time more tired than mocking. "And would it surprise you," he asked, "if I were to say I felt the same?"

"It might have a few minutes ago, but not now. You sound a little cynical, Mr. Wetherston. Or should I say bitter?"

"Now what could possibly make you think me bitter, Sheriff?" Garrick's eyebrows rose. "Nonetheless, I fear that I do agree with your assessment of my brother's criminal potential."

"And your father? What does he think of your brother?"

Wetherston shrugged. "Probably much the same as he has for the last twenty years. My brother is officially a member of the family, after all, and not a lot can be done about it. But tell me, do you have any notion just what dear Allen could have been up to that could have resulted in this bizarre situation?''

Frank hesitated again, then shook his head. ''Unfortunately, no. But I sure as hell would like to hear a suggestion or two. I don't suppose you happen to have a workable theory?''

''Nothing specific or provable, I'm afraid.'' Wetherston fell silent, his eyes seeming to go blank. For several seconds he sat that way while Frank watched, frowning. Then he blinked and straightened himself in the chair, as if his mind had just returned from some long and not altogether pleasant journey.

''No, nothing specific or provable,'' Wetherston repeated. ''However, would you care to hear a story? A long, sad story, I should warn you, that could best be appreciated with a background of melancholy gypsy violins?''

Abruptly, Wetherston interrupted himself with a harsh, barking laugh. ''And you thought I sounded bitter before,'' he said with a grimace.

Frank, not wanting to abort Wetherston's talkative mood, said nothing, only tried to look as interested as he felt.

After a brief pause, Garrick continued. ''But I'll leave it to your judgment, Sheriff, as to whether bitterness is appropriate to my situation, or if I am merely being petty, as I am sure some would say. Now, the story. Are you still listening, Sheriff?''

''Hanging on your every word.''

''Good. Very good. I doubt that I can bring myself to tell it twice to an 'outsider,' even one as sympathetic and official as yourself. Not that I haven't rehearsed it often enough, mind you, at least mentally. But tell me first, Sheriff, what do you know about my dear brother?''

''Not a lot.''

''Come, come, Sheriff, you must know something! You've just said you believe him capable of thievery at the very least. That belief must be based on some knowledge.''

''All right.'' Frank sighed. ''I know—or I've heard rumors—that your father bought him out of several scrapes when he was growing up. And probably even more after he'd grown up. And he hasn't been in Whitford for several years. I've heard that your father had something to do with that, too."

"A good start, Sheriff, a very good start, and quite accurate. But do you know what he has been doing all those years— ten years and nine months, to be exact—since leaving hearth and home? No? I thought not. He has been doing nothing. And I mean that quite literally, Sheriff. Unless, of course, you count as 'something' such activities as lolling about California beaches and having endless affairs and smashing up cars and gambling and maintaining an almost continuous high. Unless you count any of those as 'something', he has been doing absolutely nothing, just as he did absolutely nothing while he was here.

"And how does he support himself, you ask? Well you may." Garrick leaned his chin on his clasped hands, much as his father had that morning. "Well you may. To put it as succinctly as possible, my dear brother does not support himself. He has an allowance, a generous, even lavish allowance. And all he is required to do in return for that allowance— Would you care to venture a guess as to what he is required to do in return for this constant supply of non-taxable cash, Sheriff?"

"Stay out of trouble?"

Garrick laughed and shook his head. "There isn't enough money in the world to persuade dear Allen to stay out of trouble. No, he is required merely to stay out of Whitford, certainly out of Farrell County, preferably out of the entire state. Not that this is an unusual or even untraditional arrangement. On the contrary, it is quite traditional, even old fashioned. You could hardly expect the Wetherstons to do something that wasn't traditional, now, could you? In the last century, there was even a name for what my brother is. 'Remittance man.' You may have come across it in Victorian novels. No? A common literary device, drawn from all too real life: a wealthy and aristocratic family sends the black sheep out of the country, paying him handsomely to stay away and not disgrace them any more than he already has. In those days, India was the popular destination. California now appears to be the 'in' place.''

"But he's back," Frank prompted quietly when Wetherston fell silent.

Wetherston sighed. "Yes, he's back. And I fear I am to blame. Because of me, he's back. But I meant well, truly I did. Ironically, I was merely attempting, as I have attempted for some years, to get him off our financial backs. You may have guessed that I resent my brother. Anybody with the intelligence of a tree frog might guess that I resent my brother, and yours is considerably higher, I believe.''

"Thanks," Frank said.

Wetherston might not have heard him. "I have always resented my brother, but never more than when, each month, I see another check start on its way to wherever he wants it sent.'' He closed his eyes for a moment, wiping at the perspiration clinging to his face with a well-used handkerchief.

"In case you hadn't realized it, Sheriff Decker," he went on, "I have had to work like hell those same very nearly eleven years that dear Allen has spent in idle and luxurious exile. It may not be the kind of physical labor that builds mighty sinews," he said, holding a slender arm up for inspection, "though at times I would have preferred something of that sort. That, at least, would come to an end each evening. A whistle would blow or a buzzer would sound, and I would be free for a few hours.''

Wetherston paused, drawing in a deep breath as he slowly stood up. He was only an inch or two shorter than Frank's six-five but couldn't weigh more than one-fifty. Stiffly, he moved out from the cramped space behind the desk and picked his jacket off the arm of the couch. Pulling a small bottle of chalky liquid from a pocket, he unscrewed the cap, put it to his lips and swallowed, grimacing and then shuddering.

"God!" he said. "Eight years and I'm still not used to it."

He slipped the bottle back into the jacket pocket, returned to his chair, and slumped into it, leaning back and stretching his legs straight out under the desk. His face was even sweatier than before, and for several seconds he was silent, breathing hard.

"An ulcer, in case you hadn't guessed from the symptoms and the remedy," Wetherston said. "It hasn't started bleeding yet, but any day now, according to the best physicians money can buy. To tell the absolute truth, I hope it does. Then, just possibly, they'll decide it's necessary to operate. Hack out half the old gullet and see how I get along on the half they leave behind."

"I'm sorry," Frank said into a silence.

Wetherston waved a hand, almost airily. "Hardly your fault, Sheriff, so there's no need for apologies. It's just that I don't stand up to stress all that well, apparently. Nor does my wife, which perhaps explains why she spends so much time 'vacationing.' This summer she's on her third—or is it fourth?—tour of Europe. Not that Father minds, of course, as long as there's nothing so indecent as a divorce."

Wetherston paused and shook his head wonderingly. "Do you have any idea, Sheriff, how lucky you are? Just like that—" He snapped his fingers. "—you were free. Tell me, how did it feel?"

"Not all that good, if you must know," Frank told him. "But I'm here to talk about your family, not my divorce."

"Now, now, Sheriff, I've been spilling my metaphoric guts to you. Don't you think it only civilized to return the favor? Really, I'm truly interested in how non-Wetherstons go about their lives. I have so little experience along those lines."

"Mostly, we go about them with much less money."

Wetherston chuckled, the first genuine-seeming emotion he'd shown. "True, very true. But there's more to life than money. Freedom, for instance, or so I've heard. Tell me about yours, Sheriff, how you obtained it.''

Frank scowled. ''There's not much to tell that didn't get thrown around in the campaign. My wife didn't like the idea of me quitting my job as an electronics tech at Leverentz to go in with Jerry Peterson in his repair shop.''

''But you went ahead anyway. You did what you wanted.'' Wetherston spoke softly, sounding genuinely envious.

''I did. And she divorced me. End of story.''

''Surely not. Now you're the sheriff. You're a powerful man, even in so small a county as Farrell. You could have her back.''

Frank scowled. ''It doesn't work that way, Wetherston, not in the non-Wetherston world. In the first place, I don't want her back. In the second, she liked the idea of me being sheriff even less than she liked it when I went into business with Jerry. In the third, she married a used car salesman and moved up in the world. Now can we get back to your family? And the 'long sad story' you were telling me. Or is it over?''

''Unfortunately, no. But you're right. I was explaining about this,'' he said, tapping his stomach and wincing. ''To get this, you multiply that repair shop of yours and Peterson's by thirty or forty, which is the number of Wetherston enterprises I'm supposed to 'keep an eye on,' and then you put my father on a perch just above and behind your right shoulder, where he can see what you're doing and snarl in your ear whenever you make the slightest mistake. You put him there, second-guessing you at every turn and then, after all his 'suggestions' you have him say, 'but it's your decision, son. After all, I did turn the reins over to you.' ''

Wetherston paused again, as if reorganizing his thoughts. ''But that isn't the story I started to tell. I seem to have interrupted myself more than I thought. No, what I started to tell you was why dear, carefree, ulcerless Allen is back in Whitford. As I believe I said, it's largely my own fault. For years I've been trying to convince Father that the sensible course would be to cut Allen loose and let him sink or swim, although personally I doubt he could even tread water. Well, three months ago I read about the centennial visit of the English, and it reminded me that 1983 was also the centennial of the founding of the Wetherston fortune. And it reminded me of the contrast between someone like Leander, who made a fortune out of nothing, and my dear brother, who has been doing his damnedest to deplete that fortune most of his life. In any event, the inspiration must have made me particularly eloquent, because, for the first time ever, Father agreed—or almost agreed, I should say—to cut Allen off. He wouldn't do it instantly, of course. Far too much of a shock to Allen's delicate constitution. Who knows what kind of disgraceful behavior he might then feel obliged to engage in? No, he would be called back home so Father could face him directly and issue an ultimatum. Or so I thought."

Again, Wetherston chuckled. This time Frank heard no amusement in the sound. "'Shape up or ship out,' so to speak," he went on. "So the summons was duly issued, and Allen and his unearned Mercedes eventually arrived at the old plantation. That was, as I said, fifty-nine memorable days ago, coming up on sixty. But things do not seem to have worked out quite the way I had hoped. Not only have the checks not stopped, but dear Allen appears to have taken up permanent residence with our father."

"What happened?" Frank prompted when Wetherston again fell silent. "I assume you're not suggesting that your brother 'shaped up.'"

Wetherston laughed. "I'll admit, I haven't seen much of Allen recently, but I seriously doubt that 'shaping up' is in his nature. No, he's done something, but whatever it is, it certainly has nothing to do with 'shaping up.'"

"What is it, then? Any idea?"

"None, unfortunately. I do know there has been no, repeat no more talk of cutting anyone off—unless, of course, they have been talking about cutting me off. The only time I've seen Allen was when he dropped by my home a few weeks ago, apparently to verbally thumb his nose at me. He was then, and has been since, in disgustingly high spirits.''

"And you think it's all connected? Your father's turn-around with Allen? The missing money? Lou Cameron's disappearance?''

Wetherston stared at him, his mouth grim. "I don't, off-hand, see what the connection could possibly be," he said slowly. "But the coincidence is really rather striking, don't you think?''

SIX

IRENE'S CAR, a red Pinto, was in the drive when Frank stopped in front of her Willow Brook Heights split level. The note he had left taped to the front door earlier was gone, but she hadn't called him. Surprise!

More than a minute after he rang the bell, she appeared and opened the inner door. She left the screen door latched and eyed him coldly. With her red, curling hair and green eyes, she was physically as attractive as she had ever been, but her spiteful look turned her rounded features into a pinched, angry mask that thoroughly disguised her beauty.

"What can I do for you, *Sheriff?*" she asked.

The same derisive emphasis, he thought with a mental scowl, that she had put on it when he had first told her he was thinking of running for the job. "You?" she had said with an incredulous laugh. "Sheriff? My God, Frank, be serious!"

"Is Beth home yet?" he asked.

"No, but I'll tell her you were here. Again."

"It's you I want to talk to. May I come in?"

Shrugging, she unlocked the screen and stood back.

Inside, everything was what fashionable—and expensive—furniture dealers called "earth tones." As far as Frank could tell, they were nothing more than browns and tans, the total effect being only slightly less depressing than bare concrete.

"Your husband's still at Krueger's?" he asked.

"It's still part of the working day for people with real jobs.

Not everyone can wander around whenever and wherever they please and have the taxpayers foot the bill.''

Frank suppressed a sigh. This was going to be even harder than he had feared. Normally, at least for the first few minutes, she put up a screen of courtesy, but this time she was spoiling for a fight even before she had any idea what he wanted.

''I have to talk to you about Beth,'' he said. ''She—''

''If it's that custody nonsense again, don't bother. I haven't changed my mind and I never will.''

''Beth called me this morning,'' he said stiffly. ''She wanted to see me. She was more than a little upset.''

''What about?'' Instant suspicion narrowed her eyes.

''For a start, she's worried about her stepbrother. And the fact that she doesn't have a lock on the door to her room.''

''I might have known she'd run right to you!''

''You knew something was wrong, then?''

''There's nothing wrong, for God's sake! She's just in a snit, that's all. She's been in one from the day we moved in here.''

''Didn't it ever occur to you that she might have a good reason for being 'in a snit'?''

''What the hell is that supposed to mean?'' Irene demanded. ''She just hasn't given Gordon or David a chance. She barely talks to them, and even when she does, she doesn't bother to be polite. I don't know what's gotten into her, I really don't! If anyone has a right to complain, it's them. And me! She drives me to distraction.''

As usual, Frank thought.

''They've gone out of their way to be nice to her, they really have,'' Irene went on, aggrieved, ''but she just won't meet them half way.'' She paused. Beneath the angry bluster, he was startled to hear something else, perhaps a defiant pleading to be believed. ''What did she tell you, anyway?''

''That David is always barging into her room, uninvited. And without even knocking.''

''That's hardly a major crime.''

"Maybe not, but she's worried, at least a little. She wouldn't have come to me if she wasn't. And so am I. She said that when she tried to keep him out—"

"She jammed a chair under the knob, for God's sake. Tried to barricade the door! Like she was afraid of us."

"You think it's all right, then, for the boy to barge into her room, no matter when?"

"I didn't say that," she flared. "You're overreacting, the same way she does. David doesn't mean anything by it. He just forgets now and then, that's all. After all, it had been his room for as long as he could remember."

"Maybe so, but after three months—"

"You sound just like her! What did you do, spend the day coaching each other?"

"If I sound like Beth, it's because I'm worried about the same things she is," he snapped. "When a sixteen-year-old boy continually barges into a fourteen-year-old girl's room—"

"He's her brother, for God's sake, not some criminal in your jail."

"Her stepbrother, Irene, her stepbrother!"

She flinched at the sudden intensity in his voice. For a moment she was silent, her face frozen in an unreadable expression, maybe puzzlement, maybe fear. Then, as quickly as it had gone, the anger was back. "I will not listen to this, Frank Decker. David's a good boy. He wouldn't in a million years do the disgusting sort of things you're insinuating!"

"He probably wouldn't, I agree, but he certainly could. It does happen, you know. Every day, even in small towns like Whitford. And it's time you admitted it, before it's too late."

Her lips were clamped together now, in a defiant, bloodless line, although, again, there was a hint of something else in her eyes. "I don't know what you hope to accomplish with this—this obscene slander. But whatever it is, it won't work. It will not work! Now get out. Just get out!"

Swallowing his own anger, Frank withdrew. He paused on

the step just outside the door and said quietly, "I don't know what's going on here, Irene, but whatever it is, I don't like it. I'm going to talk to Beth again, and I'll tell her that if she wants to, she can come to live with her grandmother and me, no matter what you or that tame judge of yours says. From what I've heard today—from both of you—a lawyer wouldn't have any trouble getting—"

The slam of the door cut his words off.

Back in the sweltering squad car, he realized he hadn't gotten around to even mentioning the mis-used college fund.

BETH WAS STILL at the Hylands', reading a paperback on the couch, even though Carrie Hyland had returned home nearly an hour before and was in the back bedroom taking a nap. Her reaction to his suggestion was a huge grin and a hug and a promise to be at the jail to move in that same evening.

"When you're ready, I'll come pick you up," Frank said as Beth unchained her bicycle from the lamp post, "or your grandmother will, if I'm tied up. Okay?"

"Okay? All right!" she said, tossing the chain in the basket and speeding off down the driveway and into the street.

FRANK EASED the squad car into the parking strip along the west wall of the jail. Later, the trees across the street in front of the Lutheran church would cast some shade, but for now the strip was baking in the sun. The jail itself, a boxy, two-story building of whitewashed brick, got shade only from passing clouds.

The other squad was gone: Phil must be out on a call, or patrolling.

Frank let the windowless main door clank shut behind him as he clacked up the metal-edged concrete steps to the main floor. To the left at the head of the stairs, behind a second metal door—this one with a small, wire-reinforced window— a short corridor led to the main block of cells, current population three. Straight ahead, behind a similar door, were the isolation cells and drunk tank, none currently occupied. To the right was an ordinary open corridor. A pair of vending machines—soft drinks and candy bars—stood backed against one dull green wall, while at the far end of the corridor was the blank wooden door to the living quarters. Next to the vending machines was the door to a large room with the lockers and desks the deputies shared, while opposite them were the radio room and, beyond that, Frank's office with its cluttered desk and bookshelves and the wooden straight back chair visitors were forced to use if they didn't want to stand.

As Frank reached the top of the steps he saw Del Richardson leaning against the doorframe of the radio room talking to his mother. As always at this time of day, Del had his first-off-the-presses copy of the *Gazette* folded under his arm.

"Job must agree with you, Ellie," he was saying. "You're lookin' better every time I see you."

"I thank you kindly, but I still don't know any more than I did a minute ago. Frank? That you?"

"Yes, it is."

Richardson, middle-aged and balding with a decided paunch, turned toward him, waving the paper as Frank's mother eased past him into the hall.

"Did you talk to Beth?" she asked.

"I did. She may be coming over this evening. Might stay overnight."

His mother's face blossomed into a smile. "You can answer the phones, can't you, son? If Beth will be here for supper, I have some shopping to do."

"Mother, I'm not sure if—"

But she was already pushing through the door to the living quarters, presumably on her way to her purse and then to the supermarket.

"She is looking better, Frank," Richardson said, chuckling as the door clicked shut behind her. "Must be a relief for you," he added soberly. "You were afraid for a while there she'd never get over your dad's dyin' that way. What was it, two years ago?''

Frank nodded. "Almost."

The *Gazette*'s editor was right. Working as matron, a job traditionally reserved for the sheriff's wife but open to whomever the sheriff recommended, did agree with her. For over a year after his father's heart attack, she had dragged around listlessly, looking every one of her sixty-three years and more, but today, bustling about in new slacks that almost matched his own uniform trousers, her graying hair in a new short, casual style, she could easily have passed for someone in her mid or early fifties. Frank didn't know exactly what had brought the change about, but he had long ago quit looking that particular gift horse in the mouth. Could be moving into new quarters, out of the house she'd lived in for thirty years. Or being thrust into the routine of planning and cooking meals for the prisoners and looking after the occasional females and juveniles. Might even be the radio and telephone. After all, she had had a police scanner on her kitchen counter at home for years, silent ninety-nine percent of the time, spewing out terse, static-filled exchanges the other one percent. "Better than back fence gossip any day," she had often said, and now she was a major participant in the "gossip."

Frank motioned the newsman into the office. "What's up?" he asked.

"You tell me." Though the hallway was empty, Richardson shut the door behind him as he entered. "What's this I hear about Lou Cameron?"

So much for Nathaniel's cover-up. Frank raised his brows and slouched into his swivel chair. "I don't know, Del, what do you hear about Lou?"

"Aha! You never did have a poker face worth a plugged nickel, Frank. What's the story?"

"You tell me, Del. You're the one brought it up."

"All right, be that way about it. I hear Lou Cameron is missing, along with a lot of money. Money that belongs to

Allied Insurance, which I don't have to tell you belongs to the Wetherston clan. And I hear that you were summoned into the Great One's presence this morning.''

''Where did you hear all that?''

''The summons, from your mother,'' Richardson said with a grin. ''And I also heard—from her—that the summons had to do with Lou Cameron. True?''

''You haven't told me where you heard about the missing money. That you did not hear about from my mother.''

''Then it is true?''

''I didn't say that,'' Frank snapped. ''Damn it, Del, I asked where you heard about the money.''

Richardson hesitated, then shrugged. ''To tell the truth, I don't have a clue. Somebody that sounded like he had a sock in his mouth phoned half an hour ago and told me Lou Cameron had absconded with some money he'd managed to filch from Allied.'' Richardson paused, shaking his head with a rueful grin. ''I never got one of those before, you know? Anonymous tip, I mean. Sounded ridiculous, but I figured I'd better check it out. I hoped you might have some idea who the caller was.''

Before Frank could answer, the phone rang.

''Maybe I'd better warn you,'' Richardson said quickly as Frank reached for the phone. ''My 'checking it out' included a call to Old Man Wetherston.''

''And?'' Frank prodded, his hand on the receiver but not picking it up.

''He muttered something about a 'goddamned loudmouth sheriff,' and denied the whole thing. Said he didn't know what the hell I was talking about or where I could be getting such crazy ideas. Said it very loudly, too,'' Richardson added with a crooked grin.

Frank picked up the receiver. ''Sheriff's office, Decker speaking. What can I do for you?''

''You have done quite enough already, thank you,'' Nathaniel Wetherston's voice crackled.

"I beg your pardon?"

"As well you should. Too late for that now! Thanks to your loose tongue, the whole Louis Cameron episode is common knowledge. Delbert Richardson called me a few minutes ago, and he seems to know the entire story."

"What makes you think I'm responsible?"

"You can't imagine that I told anyone. And the other people involved have assured me that they haven't either. I don't know why you are doing this, Sheriff, but let me tell you—"

"Let me tell you," Frank interrupted. "I don't believe Lou Cameron is guilty. And I have not told anyone about your accusations—yet. I suggest you look closer to home for your leak, no matter what the 'others involved' have told you."

"And what is that supposed to mean?"

"You're an intelligent man, Mr. Wetherston. I think you can figure it out. My investigation—"

"Investigation? I told you, as far as I am concerned, no crime has been committed. I desire no investigation of any kind! I thought I made that clear."

"You did, but it's not up to you." Frank glanced at Richardson, who was still leaning against the door, listening intently. "It is not your decision, Mr. Wetherston," he went on. "Robbery or no robbery, there is a missing person, and that's quite enough for me. So you go ahead and do whatever you want about the missing—the allegedly missing—money. I am going to look for the missing person."

"Decker!" Wetherston sputtered, but before he could go further, Frank said a sharp "good-bye" and slammed the receiver down.

"Anything else you'd like to know, Del?" he asked sourly.

SEVEN

RICHARDSON LEFT to talk to Jennie Cameron, and Frank phoned the state police with a description of Lou and his car, an aging AMC Pacer.

He had waited too long already, never mind the rule that you had to wait forty-eight hours before declaring someone officially missing. He should have done it the minute he heard Wetherston's cock and bull story. At the very latest, right after talking to Jennie and Sheila. Not that it would do any real good, though, no matter when the call was made. No state-wide manhunt, not for someone as low on the priority totem pole as Lou Cameron. The license number would be added to a list, a long list, and that would probably be the end of it. If a state trooper saw Lou's car and happened to notice the license number and then happened to remember that it was on the list, he'd report it, but that was a lot of if's.

He was just finishing the call, which had gone about as expected, when Beth, sweaty from the mile-plus bicycle ride from Willow Brook Heights, appeared at his office door. Frank grinned: her red hair was even more of a tangle than usual.

"Hi, Daddy," she said, standing tentatively in the doorway.

"Hi, Pint Size," he said. "How'd it go at home? Any problems?"

"Well..." Her voice trailed off. Her eyes, he noticed, weren't meeting his.

"Something wrong?" He stood up and moved around the desk toward her.

"Not really, but—" She stopped and looked up at him. "I was thinking, maybe I should wait a little longer, you know, to move over here. If that's okay with you?"

"Oh? You sounded like a young lady with her mind all made up the last time I saw you."

"I'm sorry, it's just—"

"It's okay," he said quickly. "I'm just curious, that's all. I want to be sure you're all right, that nobody's forcing you into anything. And that includes me, Pint Size."

"I know, Daddy, and, well, I really would like to come live with you and Grandma, you know that. And that creepy David does bug me a lot and all that, but…" Her voice trailed off again.

"But…?" he prompted gently, touching her shoulder. "We're still friends, aren't we?"

"Oh, sure." She shrugged. "It's just, well, I talked to Mom about all this, I even asked her about that money for school, and she said she'd take care of it, but when I told her about moving out—"

The girl stopped, her clear green eyes flicking up to meet his, then lowering again. "Well, she was just so shook up. I mean, she didn't yell or anything like she usually does. She just went blank for a second, and then she was almost crying, and all of a sudden I felt like I was running out on her, you know what I mean? And she did promise she'd make sure David stayed out of my room, and she even said she'd have a lock put on my door if I really wanted it, and, well, I got to thinking maybe it wouldn't be too horrible if I stuck around a little longer. And Mom…"

Frank was silent a moment, then squeezed her shoulders and released them. "Okay, Pint Size, if that's what you want. Remember, though, if things don't work out, I'm right here, and so's your grandmother. If ever you need anything, or just want to talk…"

She gave him a quick, jerky hug and pulled back. "Thanks, Daddy. See you," she said, and then she was clattering down the steps.

As he heard the street door clank shut behind her, Frank felt an odd mixture of pride and uneasiness—pride that his daughter, not fifteen for another month, could come up with more compassion for her mother than he himself had mustered recently, but uneasiness, too. What if that compassion was misplaced, even dangerous?

FRANK'S MOTHER was visibly disappointed that Beth wouldn't be there for supper, but he distracted her with a full-scale briefing on the Cameron affair. At her suggestion, after supper, he drove over to see how Jennie was holding up after Del Richardson had quizzed her. The man was not, his mother pointed out tartly, known for excessive tact.

Jennie was considerably better than she had been that morning. Dr. Edwards' pills had worn off, allowing her anger at Wetherston's accusations to surface, and the anger was a powerful source of strength. Also, Sheila had called her younger brother early in the morning, and Jennie was looking forward to his arrival later that night.

Frank was tempted, but he said nothing about his conversation with Garrick Wetherston. Though Jennie might feel better knowing that one of the Wetherstons didn't believe Lou guilty either, it might also get her to thinking about the alternatives.

And the alternatives were not good.

If the accusations were true, Lou was at least alive, starting a new life somewhere with Wetherston's money. But if the accusations weren't true, then an undiscovered accident, with Lou surviving but trapped in the car, was the best he could hope for. In this part of the state, with its hills and dangerously winding roads, a roadside ravine could easily conceal a wrecked car. But with just two squad cars and a grand total of three deputies for all shifts—one of whom, Wally Granger, was on vacation—there was no way they could conduct a thorough search. But he could talk to the rural mail carriers, have them keep an eye out, not just for Lou's Pacer but for broken fences or crushed weeds or anything indicating a car might've gone off the road. And the drivers that delivered the *Gazette* every evening, too.

But first, back to the jail. He'd give the list of museum visitors to Steve to call, and while the night deputy was on the phone, Frank would head for the park. Mayor Hardesty's softball game was this evening, and half the people from the museum would probably be out there, either playing or watching. And maybe, just maybe, one of them would have some idea what Lou had been so "excited" about and why he had gone back to the closed museum after supper.

FRANK'S SPIRITS lifted as he pulled away from the jail and noticed a huge bank of clouds along the western horizon. The cool front Channel 7 had been promising must be getting closer. Sunday morning, they'd said first, but the front had stalled two states away and hadn't budged for two days.

And the display on the court house lawn still showed a temperature in the upper eighties and a hundred-plus "discomfort index."

Grimacing, he recalled a movie he'd seen on TV two or three years before—a fifties monster movie, but a good one, where the monster from outer space turned out not to be a monster at all. But what he had just recalled was not the monster but the sheriff, who had had a theory that more crimes took place at one particular temperature. What had it been? Ninety-two degrees? Something like that. Hot enough to make people irritable, the movie sheriff had said, but not hot enough to make them want to sack out in the shade. In the bone-dry air of the desert, maybe, where the movie had taken place. Personally, Frank would have put the magic number somewhere in the eighties, at least here in the Midwest, where the air periodically turned into a swamp. Humidity counts.

Cloud bank or no cloud bank, it would be another hour before the sun dropped into it, and the air that eddied through the windows as he drove felt as sticky as ever and seemed to grow even thicker as he pulled into the tree-filled park and rolled to a stop on the grass at the end of a ragged line of thirty or forty other cars. Old bronze Leander, a half dozen trees to the north, looked cooler and less pigeon-spotted than usual, he noticed. Someone must've hosed him off recently.

From the ball field fifty yards beyond the last of the cars, Frank could hear shouting, though he couldn't make out words, only the enthusiasm. The game should be well under way, if not nearly over. The English team was theoretically learning the rules as they played. Tomorrow the Brits were scheduled for revenge: Soccer.

Not everyone was watching the game and cheering the teams on, however. A group of a dozen or so, including one of the English couples, had a ragged net strung up in the picnic area in front of the cars and were playing volleyball. A couple of the locals waved to Frank between attempts to swat the ball, and when Frank waved back, one of them— Garland Sims—ducked out of the borderless court and trotted toward him.

"Hey, Frank, how's things going?" Sims called, still a dozen yards away.

"Pretty good, considering the weather," Frank said, waiting as Sims approached, sweat running down his pudgy face and soaking huge portions of his flowered shirt.

"Yeah, a real bitch, ain't it? But, hey, what's the scoop on Lou Cameron? I mean, my Harriet's supposed to be in one of his classes this fall, and—well, you know."

"No, I don't know, Mr. Sims," Frank said, frowning and wondering if there was anyone in the county who hadn't heard about Wetherston's wild accusations. "What sort of scoop did you have in mind?"

"You mean you don't know?" Sims said loudly, ignoring the frown. "Hell, the guy took off with half the insurance company, way I heard it. Ran off with a woman, somebody said."

"Where did you hear that?"

"Couple guys told me. The money part, anyway. To tell the truth, that's what's worrying me. Lou sold me some insurance a few years back, and, well, I trusted him because he was a teacher and all that, but now this crap comes up. I'd sure hate to think there was something wrong with that policy I bought. I paid him a hefty chunk of change."

"There's nothing to worry about," Frank said, unable to keep the irritation out of his tone. "As far as I know, nobody's run off with any money or anyone's wife, and even if they had, it wouldn't have any effect on your insurance."

Sims blinked, looking more disappointed than relieved. "You mean nothing's happened?"

"Nothing like what you're talking about. Lou's missing, but that's all. Far as I know, he's the only person missing."

"No woman, huh? Too bad for Lou. The money, now, that's something else. These guys I talked to were pretty sure about that part of it."

Frank's frown deepened. "Who are these people? And how the hell did they hear so much?"

Sims shrugged. "Jack Barnes, for one. He's over there watching the game," he said, waving a hand toward the ball field. "And he said he'd heard it right from the horse's mouth."

"And who's the horse's mouth, Mr. Sims?"

"No need to get touchy about it, Frank," Sims said, finally noticing Frank's irritation. "Somebody that works for the insurance company, that's who. Said he'd heard it right from O'Blennis himself, the office manager. If the guy that runs the place doesn't know what's going on, who does?"

O'Blennis! Frank thought. He'd probably been Del Richardson's anonymous caller, too! But why? Was O'Blennis mad at Wetherston for some reason and trying to get back at him by spreading the story against the old man's orders?

"If Mr. O'Blennis says money is missing, it must be missing," Frank said. "But as for Lou Cameron taking it—that's another matter."

Sims grinned triumphantly. "So it's true! I'll be damned! Hell, I should've known yesterday something funny was going on."

Suddenly alert, Frank frowned down at Sims. "Yesterday? What about yesterday?"

Sims continued grinning, unfazed. "Flora and I were at the museum, see? My brother Art—that's him over there, striking out—is putting up one of those English couples, so he talked us into going. Told us all about this hundred-year-old article and all, how Lou's the one that found it last winter. Well, I hardly ever read the local rag so I hadn't heard much of anything about it, but it sounded kind of interesting, so I decided, what the hell, I wasn't doing anything else, and it is a little cooler in the museum. Anyway, we get there, and Art takes me and those two house guests of his around, showing the place off, but when he gets around to where Lou is supposed to be, he's not there. Now I didn't think anything about it then, even if Art did think it was sort of funny, what with Lou being so involved and all. But now, with him missing, and the money, too—I suppose he took off Friday evening, so he'd have the whole weekend for a head start before they realized anything was missing, huh?"

"I was told Cameron was at the museum yesterday," Frank said, hiding his surprise. "Are you sure about this?"

Sims laughed. "You think I don't know Lou Cameron when I don't see him? Hell, no, he wasn't there."

"What time was this?"

"Oh, three-thirty or so. See, I went out for a quick nine holes right after lunch, didn't get back till almost three, and Flora said Art had called and it sounded like fun and so on.

Anyway, whenever it was, there was no Lou Cameron there, and I remember Art thought it was funny, like I said.''

"Maybe he'd just stepped out for a minute.''

Sims shook his head. "He just wasn't there. Ask Art. Or Sam Wilson over there,'' he added, flicking a thumb in the direction of the ball field again. "Sam was doing Lou's job.''

Sam Wilson, ten years younger than Cameron, was also a teacher—math and science. He, too, was a history bug, though not as much so as Cameron, and he'd occasionally helped out on the *Gazette* indexing. Right now, Wilson was standing behind the high, chain-link backstop behind home plate, leaning on a bat, watching Mayor Hardesty waggle his bat—and his ample behind—as he waited for the next pitch.

"Thanks for the information, Mr. Sims,'' Frank said.

"Any time, Frank, any time. You gonna talk to Sam, then? Think he knows what happened to Lou?''

"It's possible,'' Frank said, moving away. "Thanks again,'' he added, wondering if he was going to have to tell Sims to stay put so he could talk to Wilson alone.

To Frank's relief, only Sims's eyes followed as he walked over and leaned against the backstop next to Wilson. Turning at the metallic jangle of the backstop, Wilson grinned. His sweat-dampened hair barely at Frank's chin level, he was wearing a soggy T-shirt with "Teachers Do It With Class'' stenciled across the front.

"Sheriff, we were afraid you weren't going to make it. Only a couple of innings left, and we could use a pinch hitter.''

"Don't tell me you're losing?'' Frank said, raising his eyebrows in mock shock. At the party Sunday night, everyone—including the English—had assumed the game would be a total wipeout, Yanks winning.

"Tied five to five,'' Wilson said, laughing. "I think those limeys put in a ringer. See that skinny looking kid in left field? He's been knocking it out of the park every time he comes to bat. We'd be in real trouble if they could get anybody on base ahead of him."

A crack of the bat and a loud cheer jerked their attention back to the field. Mayor Hardesty puffed and sweated his way to first while the right fielder caught, bobbled, then picked up and threw the ball unsteadily to second. Hardesty, almost tripping as he rounded first, lurched to a halt and hastily backed up. Safe on the bag, he doffed his cap and waved his arms to acknowledge the three or four whoops from the sidelines.

"First time Hizzoner's been on base," Wilson said, laughing again. "If we win, he'll probably claim he did it single-handed next time he runs for election."

"You got a minute?" Frank asked as Wilson started to move away.

Wilson stopped and turned back to face Frank. "Sure. What's up?"

"It's about yesterday, Sam. I understand you took Lou Cameron's place at the museum?"

"That's right. Most of the afternoon."

"How come?"

"Because he asked me to." Wilson paused, shaking his head again, chuckling. "I've never seen Lou in a state like that. He was really worked up. If I didn't know better, I'd think he'd been smoking something he shouldn't have."

"He was acting funny?"

Wilson shrugged. "Not really, not for Lou. But you know how he's been ever since he found out about that trip."

"Enthusiastic, you mean?"

Wilson nodded, chuckling again. "Right. Enthusiastic. That's what he was yesterday, in spades."

"What was different?"

"Search me. You'll have to ask him."

"He didn't say what had him so pumped up?"

"Not a thing, but he was really going. Looked like he'd just won the lottery and couldn't wait to tell someone about it. Came running over the second he saw me come in. Could

I fill in for him for a while, he wanted to know. And when I said sure, he was off. You don't have any idea what he was up to, either?''

"Not yet. But did you notice if he had anything with him? Any papers for instance?''

Wilson pursed his lips thoughtfully for a moment. "I'm not sure,'' he said finally, "but I think he had something in his hand. A folder, or maybe an envelope. No idea what it was, though. Why? Is it important?''

"Could be. Was he alone?''

"When he came running up to me, yes. But there was someone in the Wetherston Room when I followed him back there. One of the English.''

"You remember which one?''

"Not by name. Lou didn't introduce me, he was in such a hurry, but I'd recognize him. I remember his picture in the paper when this trip was first set up, and I saw him come into the museum with the group, but I never got a chance to talk to him.''

"And he was with Lou? They left the museum together?''

"He was with Lou, yes. Lou was talking his ear off. Not sure if they left together or not, though. Why don't you just ask Lou?''

"Nothing I'd like better, but I can't. He's missing.''

"Missing? You mean like in 'missing person'? What happened?''

"That's what I'm trying to find out. So far, I'm as much in the dark as anyone.''

"You don't think that Englishman had anything to do with it, do you?''

"I doubt it, but I'd sure like to talk to the guy.'' Frank looked out at the players on the field. "Which one is he?''

"None of those.'' Wilson paused, frowning thoughtfully. "Matter of fact, now that I think about it, I haven't seen him today.''

"I don't suppose you know which family he's staying with?"

Wilson shook his head. "Sorry. I should know his name, but you know how I am. Numbers are my game, not names. Takes me half the semester to get the names of the kids in my classes straight."

"What's he look like?"

"Older than most of the others. Fifties, probably. Thick gray hair, pretty long, combed straight back, curly if he'd give it a chance. A little on the heavy side, but not quite as much of a pot as Hizzoner."

"That should be good enough."

"Sure, just ask around when they come up to bat." Sam paused, wincing as Walt Overton, the middle-aged manager of Overton's Pharmacy, went down swinging, prompting a half dozen good-natured cat calls from the sidelines. "Which should be any second now. You're sure you don't want to pinch hit for someone? Like me? It could still be arranged."

"No, thanks, Sam. What I'd really like to do is talk to your mysterious Englishman."

"Yes, I'd be interested in that, too." Wilson paused, shaking his head. "Lou Cameron missing, huh? What about—"

"Hey!" a voice broke in. "Sam! You're up!"

"That's me," he said quickly, glancing at the diamond. "Guess they didn't pick *Hizzoner* off after all. But look, if you find out anything about Lou—"

"I'll let you know."

"And stick around. I'm the third out, so those guys should be coming in any second now."

True to his word, Sam Wilson was a quick out, going down swinging wildly at a ball at least a foot on the far side of the plate. As the teams changed places, Frank moved out from behind the backstop and waited. One man, the right fielder, hung back from the rest, looking nervous enough to catch Frank's attention. He had thinning red hair, freckles, and a neatly trimmed, sandy beard. Frank had seen him somewhere recently, but he couldn't remember where.

After a few seconds, the man pulled in a breath and continued his walk in from the outfield. Irritated by his inability to place him, Frank waited as the man approached, hesitated nervously, then straightened his shoulders and crossed the last few yards separating them.

"You wished to see me, Sheriff?" he asked apprehensively, his accent more subdued than some of the others Frank had heard, more like Masterpiece Theater than the Cockney comedies he'd seen on late night TV now and then.

"If you've got a minute, Mr....?" Frank's voice trailed off into a question.

"Wellman. Carl Wellman," he said, and then hurried on, "I really must apologize for my driving this morning, Sheriff. I assure you that I will be more careful in the future."

Frank blinked and then laughed. "I thought you looked familiar. You're the one on the wrong side of the street this morning."

"I fear I am, but—"

"It's okay," Frank interrupted. "This has nothing to do with your driving. I just wanted to ask you—any of your group, actually—a question or two."

Wellman let his breath out in a sigh of relief. "That is very good of you, Sheriff. I certainly do not wish to run afoul of your laws, even inadvertently. What do you wish to know?"

"Actually, I'm looking for one of your friends, one of the group."

"Of course. Who is it you wish to see?"

"That's the trouble. I don't know his name, just what he looks like. He's in his fifties, gray hair, with—"

"That would be Mr. Ardly," Wellman interrupted, looking pleased with himself. "He's the only one in the group in that age range."

"Ardly?"

"Willis Ardly, yes."

"Is he here this evening?"

"I haven't seen him." Wellman stopped, his brow wrinkling in thought. "In fact, I haven't seen him all day, which is rather odd."

A sinking feeling hit Frank's stomach. "When," he asked softly, "did you last see him?"

"I have to think…" Wellman's voice trailed off as he concentrated. "He was at the party last night, or I believe he was." He paused again, chewing on his lower lip, his eyes half closed in thought. "Yes, he was definitely at the party. I remember now, we had all gathered for a photograph, and I recall that they had some trouble finding Mr. Ardly. Off in a corner chatting with someone, I believe, but they did locate him."

"You don't know who he was talking with, do you?"

"I fear not. One of you Yanks, that's all I know."

"And you haven't seen him at all today?"

"No, I am quite sure I haven't."

"And his wife—have you seen her?"

Wellman shook his head. "Mr. Ardly is not married, so far as I know. Unlike the rest of us, he is traveling alone."

"Do you know what family he's staying with?"

Wellman shook his head again. "The man you need to speak to is Mr. Drivas over there," he said, pointing to a large, balding man who looked a bit like the stereotype of a British dock worker. "I believe he has the names of all the host families. He is our mayor, and it was he who made the arrangements for our journey."

"Thanks," Frank said, and made his way toward Drivas, who was standing near the backstop, hands on hips, waiting for his turn at bat.

"Mayor Drivas?" Frank said, noticing as he stopped next to the man that Drivas was within an inch of his own six-five and weighed probably two-fifty.

"Yes? Oh, Sheriff Decker, it's good to see you." Drivas'

voice was thin, sounding more as if it should belong to someone Wellman's size.

"I hope you're enjoying your visit."

"Oh, very much. Very much indeed." He paused, drawing
in a deep breath and stretching his arms out to the sides. "I
must say, your climate is most invigorating. I do enjoy
warmth."

Frank suppressed a grimace. "Then you certainly came at
the right time. But Mr. Drivas, the reason I wanted to talk to
you—I'm looking for Willis Ardly. Have you seen him this
evening?"

Drivas shook his head. "Not that I recall. But, then, Mr.
Ardly isn't a bloke who goes in for group activities. Keeps
very much to himself, in fact."

"What about yesterday?"

"He was at your museum, of course, at least for a time.
Though I don't recall seeing much of him after we all arrived."

"He left with someone around three, I've been told. But
what about before yesterday? You arrived last week."

Drivas shook his head again, a touch of apology in his eyes
this time. "As I said, he keeps very much to himself. I have
often had the feeling that he has his own agenda for this trip."

"But he never said what that agenda was?"

"Not to me, certainly."

"I see. What about the family he was staying with? Maybe
he talked to them. I understand you would know who they
were."

"Ah, yes, I do have a list of all the host families, but not
with me. However, I'm sure I can remember the name you
wish. Mr. Ardly joined our group fairly late, you know..."
His voice trailed off into a thoughtful frown, and then he
nodded. "Yes, their name is Haliday. John and Audrey Haliday. I recall their remarking on the similarity of names, Ardly
and Audrey."

Frank didn't recognize the names. "Are they here this evening, do you know?"

Drivas shook his head. "I'm not that good at remembering faces. Much better at names. But if Mr. Ardly is not here, I rather doubt that his hosts are here, either. Perhaps they have gone somewhere together. Some of our people have been doing that, and as I have said, Mr. Ardly is not overly enamored of group activities, particularly sports. His age perhaps."

"All right, Mayor Drivas. Thank you."

"Not at all. But is there some difficulty? You do appear a trifle on edge, if you don't mind my commenting on the fact."

"Nothing to worry about," Frank said. *Not yet, at any rate,* he added to himself as he turned to leave.

Fifteen minutes later, he had radioed his office to get the Halidays' address and was walking across the lawn toward their front door. But there was no car in the drive, and knocking loudly on both front and back doors confirmed what he had already begun to fear—that the Halidays, like Lou Cameron and Willis Ardly, were nowhere to be found.

EIGHT

FRANK RESISTED THE URGE to force a lock and conduct an illegal search of the Haliday residence. Instead, he settled for leaving notes taped to both front and back doors.

He lumbered back to the car, his face oozing sweat just from the walk around the house. Evidently the clouds he'd noticed off to the west before sundown had nothing to do with the promised cold front. In the car, he switched on the scanner and listened distractedly as the National Weather Service announcer confirmed his guess. A few showers fifty miles west, in the Springfield area, but that was all. The upper air winds had shifted yet again, now blowing parallel to the front and not moving it at all. Cooler air was still a state and a half away.

Back at the office, he joined Steve on the phones, alternating between calls to Sunday's museum visitors and the Halidays' answering machine. As the evening wore on, the hope of learning anything worthwhile—let alone encouraging— steadily faded. The hollow feeling in Frank's stomach grew stronger.

Of the forty people who remembered seeing Lou Cameron at the museum early Sunday afternoon, only a dozen had talked to him. No one recalled any special excitement or nervousness on Lou's part; certainly nothing like Sam Wilson had described. Lou had been, as one of his fellow teachers put it, "his usual history-freaking self."

And no one had seen him after Wilson had taken his place in the Wetherston Room, not even at the party Sunday evening, although a couple of people who had hung around the museum until its five-o'clock closing time thought they had seen his Pacer pull into the parking lot as they were leaving. No one could swear that Lou was driving, however, or had noticed if anyone else was in the car.

As for Willis Ardly, he had apparently vanished just as completely as had Lou Cameron. A score of people, including the English themselves, recalled seeing him at the party. At one point he had been talking earnestly to someone Frank at last identified as Bill Englehardt, a lawyer. But by that time Englehardt had already spent more than enough time at the bar and now could barely remember Ardly, let alone what they had talked about.

"Something about international law, I think," he said, "but don't quote me on that. I could be remembering it that way just because I'm a lawyer and he had an English accent. It could've been nuclear disarmament, or maybe I was even talking to someone else."

And that was it. After one last encounter with the Halidays' answering machine, Frank abandoned the phone, returned to the living quarters, took a much-needed shower, cranked his bedroom air conditioner up another notch, and went to bed.

About one a.m., Steve buzzed him from the office. "John Haliday," the deputy said as Frank fumbled the phone to his ear. "Says he just got back and found your messages. I figured you'd want to talk to him."

"Thanks. Put him on." The phone clicked erratically while Steve transferred the call. Frank sighed through his teeth. At least the Halidays weren't missing, too. He heard breathing on the other end of the line. "Mr. Haliday?"

"That's right," a somewhat reserved voice said. "Sheriff Decker?"

"Yes. Thank you for calling. I—"

"Audrey and I were at Brewster's Playhouse, you know, near Carrothers, and we found your notes when we got back. To tell the truth, I thought it might be someone's idea of a joke, but Audrey felt we should make sure, particularly after we listened to the messages you left on our machine.''

"I'm very glad you called, Mr. Haliday. I'm trying to locate Willis Ardly. I understand he's staying with you."

"Why, yes, he was, but not anymore."

"Oh?" The visit had another two weeks to run. "You didn't have any trouble with him, did you?"

"Goodness, no," Haliday said hastily. "Mr. Ardly was the ideal house guest. We were sorry to see him go."

"When did he leave?"

"Sometime last night."

"Where did he go? Back to England?"

"I couldn't say for certain."

"He didn't tell you?"

"Not a word. The whole episode was rather bizarre, if you ask me."

"Bizarre?" Frank echoed. "In what way?"

"He just slipped out in the middle of the night!" Haliday said. "Not a word to either of us. We got up this morning and he was gone, without so much as leaving a note. Enough to make Audrey count the spoons."

A shiver prickled at Frank's spine. "In the middle of the night? Look, Mr. Haliday, this is important. Would you mind if I came over so you could give me the details?"

"Now? But Sheriff—"

"I know it's late. It's very important."

"Well, if you think— Very well." Haliday chuckled. "Actually, after this conversation, I doubt I'd be able to sleep tonight anyway."

BOTH HALIDAYS WERE waiting at the door when Frank crossed the fading lawn. They were in their fifties, John dark-haired but balding; Audrey short and stocky, beginning to gray. Both were still dressed for the playhouse, though John had loosened his tie. Despite a lack of air conditioning in the house, neither was even sweating, Frank noticed enviously.

Frank forestalled their questions with one raised palm. "I'll tell you everything I can," he said, "but it'll be better if you tell me about Ardly first. Whatever you can remember."

John Haliday motioned Frank into the living room. "Whatever you want," he agreed. "But I must say, I have no idea what's going on."

"Neither do I, Mr. Haliday," Frank admitted. "I'm trying to find out. Now please, just tell me about Ardly's leaving. The middle of the night, you said?"

"Exactly." He glanced at his wife, who was standing uneasily by. "As I told you, we didn't even know he was gone until this morning."

Just like Lou Cameron, Frank thought, but he only nodded. "Tell me about it."

"He was acting oddly," Audrey Haliday put in. "Very— what would you call it, dear? Preoccupied?"

"Yes. Definitely preoccupied," Haliday agreed. "Starting when he made a phone call. After that, well, I don't know where his mind was, but it wasn't too well attached to the rest of him."

"Phone call?"

"When he came home Sunday afternoon the first thing he did was make a phone call. Long distance, and he didn't even find out what the charges were. Not that we minded, of course," Haliday added. "He was our guest, after all. It struck me as strange, though. Out of character."

"Who did he call?"

"He didn't say, and of course we didn't ask. Or listen in, if that's your next question. He used the phone in our bedroom—for privacy, I suppose. Afterwards, he hardly said a word, and then he went off to that party. Which was another surprise, wasn't it, dear?" He glanced at his wife, but gave her no time to answer before he continued. "He hadn't been planning to go, I'm sure, but after that phone call, he was eager."

"And then…?" Frank prompted.

"Then—well, someone phoned while he was at the party. Do you recall who it was, dear?"

"It was a man, but he didn't give a name," Audrey supplied.

"An English accent?" Frank asked.

She shrugged. "Not that I could tell. Nothing like Mr. Ardly's."

"Could it have been Lou Cameron?"

"The teacher? Possible, I suppose. I don't know that I'd recognize his voice. He sold us some insurance years ago, but— Why Lou Cameron?"

Frank ignored the question. "What did he want?"

"He didn't say. He just asked for Mr. Ardly, and when I told him Ardly wasn't here, he hung up."

"And then?"

"Then—nothing," John Haliday said, shrugging, "until Mr. Ardly came back from the party."

"Did he say anything about the party? About anything that happened there?"

Haliday shook his head. "No. In fact, he seemed even more preoccupied than he had before."

"There was another phone call," Mrs. Haliday supplied. "I don't know what time it was, but John and I were asleep, which means it was at least midnight. It gave me quite a start." She smiled uncertainly. "You just know a phone call that late has to be bad news. Mr. Ardly must have been waiting by the phone in the living room—he picked it up on one ring."

"I don't suppose you know what that call was about?" Frank asked.

Both shook their heads. "As Audrey said, we were asleep," Haliday told him. "I picked up the phone when I woke, but whoever called was already hanging up. Five or ten minutes later, a car stopped outside, and Mr. Ardly was out the door like a shot. We heard a car door slam, and then the car drove away." He paused, turning up his hands. "And that's the last we saw of Mr. Ardly. When we got up this morning, he'd packed up and left. Not even a note. Just the house key we'd given him, left on the kitchen table.''

"You didn't see the car that picked him up?"

"Sorry," Haliday said. "By the time I decided to get up and take a peek, it was gone."

"But Ardly did pack, you said. He took everything, all his clothes?"

"As far as we can tell."

"You don't mind if I take a look myself?"

"Of course not, Sheriff, but there's nothing there."

They trooped upstairs, and Frank searched. Empty bureau drawers, a closet barer than any he had ever seen in an inhabited house. Not so much as a scrap of paper in the wastebasket. Frank, his hands shoved into his back pockets, surveyed the room one last time. Either Ardly had been exceptionally neat throughout his brief stay, or he had cleaned the room thoroughly.

So that was that—except, Frank recalled abruptly, the phone call Ardly had made.

"Mind if I use your phone?" he asked.

"Of course not, Sheriff," Audrey Haliday said. "Go right ahead."

"Thank you." Picking up the receiver, he dialed the operator and identified himself. "A long distance call was made from this number Sunday afternoon. I'd like the number that was called."

"Do you wish the charges?"

"No, thank you, just the number."

He could hear the clicks and hums as she consulted the computer. "That was an overseas call, to Whitford, England," she said after a minute, and then gave him the number.

So he called home, Frank thought, or at least someone in his hometown. *Whatever the hell that means.*

BACK AT THE OFFICE, with Steve Waymore watching curiously, Frank dialed the number that Ardly had called. He wasn't up on his time zones, but it would have to be at least seven or eight in the morning in England. Well after dawn, at any rate. He just hoped it wasn't so late that whoever the number belonged to had left for work for the day. After nearly a dozen rings, a curt voice said, "Yes?"

"Who is this?" Frank asked.

"I beg your pardon? Who are you?" the voice came back.

"My name is Frank Decker. I'm the sheriff of Farrell County, and I'm calling from Whitford, in the United States. Who—"

"Sheriff?" The annoyance in the anonymous voice shifted suddenly to apprehension. "Has something happened to Dad?"

"Dad? Who's your dad?"

"Willis Ardly!" the voice snapped impatiently.

"You're Willis Ardly's son?"

"Didn't I just say that? Now what's 'appened to him?"

"I don't know that anything has, but—"

"Then why the bloody hell did you ring me up?"

"I'm sorry if I alarmed you, Mr. Ardly. Your name is Ardly, isn't it?"

"Of course! Clayton Ardly! Now what—"

"It's like this, Mr. Ardly. Your father left his host family's home without a word of explanation, in the middle of Sunday night, and hasn't been seen since. According to the phone records, he called you not long before he left, so we were wondering what he said. Was he maybe returning home early?"

"Coming home? No," the younger Ardly said, now sounding fully alarmed. "Bloody hell! What's happened?"

"All I know is what I've told you. Late Sunday night, your father packed his bags and left the home of the people he was staying with, the Halidays."

"To go where?"

"I hoped you might know."

"Oh, Christ," the voice said under its breath.

"What did he say when he called you?" Frank asked.

"He—he wanted something sent to him."

"Sent here? To Whitford?"

"In care of your Post Office, yes, so he obviously wasn't planning on going anywhere. I posted it yesterday morning, airmail. Pricey, I don't mind telling you, but he wanted it two weeks ago Thursday."

"What was it?"

"A photo album."

"A photo album?" Frank echoed. "Why was he so anxious to get a photo album?"

With a brief sigh, Ardly said, "I don't know! It's something to do with some ancestor of ours."

"I'm afraid I don't understand."

"That's two of us, Sheriff. I don't share Dad's, uh, fascination with the past."

"Your father's an historian?"

"An 'istorian!" A short bark of laughter came through the satellite relay. "'E's a lorry driver! Look, if you want, I'll tell you what I know. Though it ain't much."

"Any information at all could be helpful," Frank said.

"Right—here goes. Dad's had his knickers in a twist over this as long as I remember. As I understand it—which, I told you, really I don't—some great-grampa of ours went to your Whitford a hundred years ago and never came home. Planned to start a business on your side of the pond, I think, but he died before he could bring the family over, no one knows exactly why. And there you've got it. When Dad heard about this tour, he joined up. 'Go right to the spot,' he said, 'and find out.' He probably would've done before, but the costs—you know how that is."

"Of course," Frank agreed, thinking of the long-distance charge. "But this ancestor—was his name Ardly, too?"

"Dunno. Dad would know for certain. He found some papers in somebody's trunk, ages ago. Letters, I think, though I never paid them much mind, myself.''

''Could you find these papers?''

''Dad's got them with him, I think.''

''I see,'' Frank sighed. ''And the photo album—why did he want that?''

''Something to do with this great-grampa, I'll wager. He found it in that same old trunk.''

''He didn't tell you why he wanted it?''

''No, but I can't say I blame him. Overseas calls cost, you know? And what's it to me?''

''Is there anyone who might know more? Any of your father's friends? Or Mrs. Ardly?''

''Mum's been gone for years. As for Dad's chums, yes, some might know more'n I do. They couldn't know much less. D'you want names, then?''

Frank hesitated. ''No, not right now. But I'd appreciate it if you could talk to them yourself.''

''I could do,'' Ardly said reluctantly. ''If you think it's important.''

''I can't be positive, but it certainly could be important. And if you could take a look for those papers you mentioned, just in case your father didn't take them all with him, that could be a big help, too.''

''No probs. He wanted me to look 'round his flat every day or two anyway. Water the bloody ivy, feed the cat.''

''Good. I'd appreciate that. What about the group he was traveling with? Would he have talked to them about this ancestor, do you think?''

''I'd guess not. Dad ain't the most talkative bloke in the world, not with those he don't know.''

''He didn't have any friends in the group, then?''

''All strangers, far as I know.''

''This ancestor—you said he came over here a hundred years ago?''

''Something like that. Could've been a hundred and fifty.''

"He didn't come with a tour group, too, did he? In eighteen-eighty-three?"

"A tour group?" Ardly asked blankly.

Hurriedly, Frank explained. "That original group," he finished, "was the reason for this new group that your father came with."

"Now that you mention it, I do remember Dad going on about something like that."

"Then your ancestor might've been part of that first group?"

"He could've been, I suppose. Does it make a difference?"

"It may. Do you think you'd recognize his name if you heard it?"

"Maybe. I know Dad has said it, but, well..."

"Let me find the names and read them to you, just in case."

"Right-oh."

"When you locate those papers, or if you remember anything else, anything at all, you call me," Frank said, giving Ardly the number. "Call collect, any time, day or night. Or if you hear from your father, tell him to get in touch with me immediately."

When he hung up, Frank had the distinctly queasy feeling that Ardly would not be hearing from his father any sooner than he would be hearing from Lou Cameron.

NINE

TO HIS SURPRISE, Frank managed to get to sleep fairly quickly, though he found himself wide awake again before six. While his mother fixed breakfast, he filled her in on what he had learned the night before.

After breakfast, before Phil showed up, Frank called the Halidays but learned little.

"No," Audrey Haliday said, "he didn't once mention any 'research' or any ancestor. Did he, dear?" That last off the phone, to her husband. "Although he did ask how to find the *Gazette* office. I suppose he might've thought that was the place to begin."

"When was that?"

She thought a second, consulted with John, and finally decided it had been sometime Friday. "But if he learned anything, he didn't say a word to either of us. Did he, dear?"

After that, Frank began calling the host families, asking their guests about Ardly and his "research." As the son had suspected, Ardly hadn't spoken to any of them about it, any more than he had to the Halidays. None of them, in fact, knew much about Ardly at all, except that he kept largely to himself. "An unsociable bugger," one of the more plainspoken ones said.

When Phil arrived, Frank gave strict instructions that if Ardly or his son called, collect or by carrier pigeon, they should accept the call and contact him immediately. Then, grimacing as he stepped out into the morning heat—it was already eighty-three on the temperature display across the street on the courthouse lawn—he headed for the post office to talk to the mail carriers and to ask the postmaster to notify him the instant anything arrived for Willis Ardly.

A half hour later he was at the *Gazette* office, telling a fascinated Del Richardson and his staff about the ancestor and the research. Then, from the group picture in Thursday's edition, Sarah Parker, who took care of the classifieds and anyone who wandered in off the street, easily identified Ardly as "that English guy" who'd come in Friday afternoon wanting to look at the August 1884 issues of the *Gazette*. She remembered because she had at first assumed he wanted the 1883 issues, since those were the ones that had been getting all the publicity, but he'd insisted it was 1884 he wanted. When he returned Saturday morning, he wanted the whole year, plus the second half of 1883.

"And he had his nose in the machine right from the minute I handed him the cards until we closed," Sarah said with a shrug. "If we didn't close early on Saturdays I think he would've been here all day."

"But he didn't say what he was looking for?" Frank asked. "Or what he found, if anything?"

Sarah shook her head. "Not a peep. Didn't even tell me who he was. He just sat there with his nose in the viewer. He'd stop to read something every so often and scribble some notes, but that was all."

"How was he acting? Did he look excited? Angry? What?"

"His face didn't talk a whole lot more than his mouth," Sarah said with another shrug. "I saw him frown like crazy a couple of times, but that was all. And he was sort of grouchy looking when he left, but I figured that was because we were closing and he had to leave."

"Did you tell him about the museum?"

"That they have a set of the *Gazette*, too? No. I was going to, but when I told him we were closing and he'd have to come back Monday, he gave me such a look, like it was all my fault, and went stomping out. So I figured he could just wait.''

For a moment, Frank was tempted to ask for the August '84 card as well, but without some idea what he was looking for, it would be pointless. Instead, he got the August '83 card, located the tour group article, and copied down the names of everyone in the group and took them back to the office so they'd be there if the younger Ardly called.

A few minutes before nine, Frank was at Jennie Cameron's door again. This time Ray, the fourteen-year-old son, answered. The boy's eyes widened as he saw Frank.

"Is your mother home?" Frank asked.

"Sure. Have you found out anything about Dad?"

"Not much, I'm afraid. Mind if I come in?"

The boy stepped back hastily. "No, of course not. Come on in."

Tensely wordless, the boy led the way through the hall and kitchen and out into the back yard, where Jennie Cameron was on her knees, sweating profusely as she pulled weeds from a six-by-six patch of vegetables. Just something to keep herself occupied, Frank guessed, noting the painstakingly deliberate way she worked. A half dozen garden tools, none of which appeared to have seen much use today, were laid out next to one edge of the patch like operating instruments next to a surgical table. His own mother had often worked in the yard and around the house in much the same way those first few months after his father had died. She had spent at least as much time making preparations, laying out tools and cleaning and putting them away as she had actually working.

Jennie looked up when she heard the back screen door click shut.

"Oh, Frank," she said, climbing hastily to her feet, brushing her hands on her faded jeans, "I'm glad to see you. Have you learned anything about Lou yet?"

"Nothing all that helpful," he admitted. "He spent some time talking to one of the English visitors Sunday afternoon, a man named Willis Ardly. Did he ever mention the name to you?''

She shook her head. "Not that I recall. What were they talking about?''

"I've got a good guess, but that's about all.''

"What does Mr. Ardly say?''

"He's missing, too," Frank said, and went on to explain what he had learned from Ardly's son about the mysterious ancestor.

"It looks as if they might've driven off together Sunday night," he finished, trying to put the best face possible on the situation, "if we assume it was Lou driving the car the Halidays heard.''

Jennie had looked doubtful at first, but the last couple of minutes had seen her nodding, a reminiscent smile, maybe even some hope, on her face.

"Yes, I can see Lou getting involved in something like that," she said. "It certainly makes more sense than those ridiculous things Nathaniel Wetherston is saying. Lou *would* head out somewhere in the middle of the night, so wrapped up in what he was doing that he never thought to tell anyone where he was going.'' She paused, the half smile still pulling at her full lips as she brushed a strand of sweat-damp hair back from her forehead, leaving a smudge of garden dirt in its place.

"Mr. Ardly's mysterious ancestor certainly would have—well, intrigued him," she went on. "And it would explain why he was acting the way he was Sunday afternoon. It's the way he is whenever he finds—well, some new puzzle to work on.''

She smiled, her eyes taking on a dreamy, faraway look. "Just after we were married, he got involved in something—well, not quite like this puzzle of Mr. Ardly's, but a puzzle. We couldn't afford new furniture, so we picked everything up at second hand shops. Well, one of the pieces we bought was a desk. Oh, it was in terrible shape! Someone must have stored it in a damp basement. The drawers would hardly open, and there were water spots all over it, but it was good and solid. Anyway, when Lou pried the drawers open, he found a letter, fallen behind one of the drawers. It was more than thirty years old."

She chuckled. "Lou was in seventh heaven, as if he'd found a buried treasure. Which is just what it was, for him. For us. The letter itself was, well, really rather sad. It was a love letter, a woman writing to a man, talking about wanting to leave her husband, I don't even remember the names anymore, though I'm sure Lou remembers every detail. He spent hours trying to find out who the desk had belonged to, trying to find someone who would know who these people were, how it had all turned out. Then one Saturday, when he should have been grading papers, he talked someone in the courthouse into opening up the files for him, and we both went down there and spent the whole day looking for names that matched the ones in the letter. Finally we found one of the names, the woman's—it was unusual, that I remember—but she had died almost ten years before, still married to the same man, the only one she had ever married. But one of her children, born just a few months after the letter was dated, had the same middle name as the man the letter had been written to."

She pulled in a sighing breath. "So, yes," she went on after a time, "if Mr. Ardly came to Lou with a story about a mysterious ancestor who died here a hundred years ago, he couldn't've come to a better person."

She paused, swallowing audibly. "He couldn't've come to a better person," she repeated slowly. Frank's throat tightened as he saw a tear trickle from the corner of one eye and realized she was talking about her whole life with Lou, not just his fascination with puzzles from the past.

"I'm sorry, Frank." Jennie produced an unsteady smile and wiped at her eyes with a still-dirt-smudged finger. "It's just that—that he's my best friend in the whole damned world and I'm scared to death I've lost him.''

For a moment despite the lump in his throat, Frank couldn't squash the envy that suddenly and unexpectedly twisted at him. Even at the best of times, Irene would never have said anything remotely like that about him, nor he about her. If it weren't for Beth, he would have fervently wished that he and his wife had never met. He and Irene had never been friends, not the way Jennie meant, maybe not the way anybody meant. Irene had come to work on the assembly line at Leverentz and started flashing a lot of leg at him, and the next thing he knew they were dating. And then sleeping together. And then they were married. And for the life of him, he had never known exactly how it had come about. It had "seemed like a good idea at the time," as the old joke went, but that was all he could remember. Hell, he had been twenty-one years old and should've known what he was doing, but obviously—

Shaking his head sharply, he forcibly yanked his thoughts free of that emotional whirlpool and focused on Jennie Cameron's tear-stained face.

"You don't have a damned thing to be sorry about," he said, barely able to keep his voice steady. "And I'll find Lou, I swear."

Abruptly, he turned to go, before he could find himself compelled to turn his vow into a lie by promising to find Lou Cameron alive.

JENNIE CAMERON'S WORDS were still repeating themselves in Frank's mind as he pushed through the swinging doors to the museum annex fifteen minutes later, but he had at least been able to squash the painful and irrational surge of envy that had ripped at him. Even so, the very thought of being envious of a friend's happiness—especially a happiness that had in all likelihood now ended in tragedy—made him feel ashamed. And even more determined to find out what had happened to

Lou and to clear him of Wetherston's ridiculous and insulting charges!

Laura looked up from the assortment of recent donations she was cataloging as he stopped just inside the doors. Her eyes widened as she saw him. "What have you learned about Louis Cameron?" she asked anxiously.

"Nothing all that helpful," he said, moving to meet her, "but it looks as if he's not the only one who disappeared Sunday."

Hurriedly, he explained about Ardly's being seen talking to Cameron, his subsequent disappearance, and his search for an unnamed ancestor. "I don't suppose you know of anyone who'd fit the role of Ardly's ancestor?" he finished.

Laura, obviously fascinated by his story, shook her head slowly. "I am certain that none of the members of the 1883 tour stayed behind, and I am reasonably positive that none returned to Whitford later. At least Louis never mentioned discovering any such return in the *Gazette*."

"Then he didn't find anything," Frank said with a sigh. "If he had, he'd've been telling anyone who'd listen. And no one else you know of came here from England and tried to—to set up a business of some kind?"

"No, but that is the same period when Leander Wetherston was starting the first of the Wetherston enterprises. It is possible that this ancestor, whom you say enjoyed lesser success, or perhaps failed altogether, was lost in Leander's shadow."

"You mean someone could've gone broke and died without anyone noticing?"

"I'm certain there would have been an obituary when such a person died, but his other activities, if neither successful nor spectacular, might well have been overlooked. Although," she added with a frown, "I would think that if he were fresh from England, that alone would have been reason for reporting his activities."

Frank nodded. "I'd think so, too. I hope so, anyway." He glanced in the direction of the Leander Wetherston Room and the microfiche reader still set up on the desk. "The problem will be finding it. I could really use a native guide."

"Come," Laura said, smiling as she turned and moved toward the Wetherston Room, "we will look."

They started with the boxes of file cards that would someday, when arranged and transcribed, become an index. In their current state, Frank quickly realized, they were a massive and largely useless collection of names, dates, page numbers and headlines, presumably stored in the order in which Lou Cameron and the others had written them, which was largely but not completely chronological. In addition, there were no descriptions of the articles under the headlines, only lists of names, occupations, and businesses mentioned. To learn what was said about any of the names, the microfilm itself would have to be consulted.

For the next five hours, then, they stayed at the microfiche reader, except for a brief lunch break and a half dozen calls from the jail, none of which were urgent enough to require more than a quick "You handle it however you want." Starting with yet another re-reading of the original article, they skimmed through every issue of the *Gazette* from July through the end of 1883, reading at least the headline of every story and often the lead paragraph. The sole mention of the group after their one day and night in Whitford was a brief item more than a month later telling of their departure for England from New York.

Nor could Frank spot anything that gave even the slightest hint as to the identity of Ardly's ancestor, or what had happened back then that could have resulted in the disappearance of two men a hundred years later.

Even the obituaries gave them nothing. They checked every one, looking not only for a name from the tour group but for anyone who had recently arrived from England or, for that matter, from anywhere else.

On the other hand, true to Laura's word, one person definitely had come to Whitford in 1883: Leander Wetherston.

His arrival was noted not once but a half dozen times, but it was noted just as often that he had come from New England, by way of Chicago, not England.

"New Arrival to Wed," a December headline said. A fast worker in more ways than one, Frank thought when he read it. He had known that the original Wetherston's rise was rapid, but this was the first time he had ever seen any dates. In town three months, and he already had a bride and was, according to the last paragraph of the article, "firmly established in the local business community." Firmly established, the article went on to say, by the founding of the Farmers and Merchants Bank, Wetherston's first enterprise and the seed from which everything else had grown.

Finally, his vision blurred by the shifting green images, Frank found himself staring again at the original article about the tour. He almost had it memorized, he had seen it so many times: The visitors' names; their gracious words about the town and its people; the impromptu nature of their visit; the fact that, while stopping at Carrothers, forty miles to the northeast in what was now Granger County, they'd inadvertently learned of this Whitford's existence and had decided they had to see it, even if the detour did make them a day late for their next stop at Springfield.

Did Carrothers have a newspaper in 1883? he wondered. If it had, it probably covered the visitors just as the *Gazette* had, and maybe, just maybe, the coverage would have something the *Gazette* didn't. Could that even be where Lou and Ardly had gone? He wouldn't put it past Lou, in his enthusiasm for solving a mystery, to haul the editor away from Sunday dinner—or drag him out of bed—to get him to open the files.

He thought briefly of asking Laura about the existence of a Carrothers paper, but he quickly decided that Carrothers could wait until tomorrow, or maybe forever. Most likely, Ardly's son had simply gotten his information about the ancestor wrong. After all, he'd admitted that anything his father had said about it went in one ear and out the other. It would be little wonder, then, if what he had told Frank was as garbled as Frank's own mind was getting to be.

Weary and frustrated, entertaining ever darker thoughts about Lou Cameron's fate, Frank thanked Laura and headed for the post office to check with the returning mail carriers.

TEN

To NO ONE'S SURPRISE, none of the mail carriers had found any indication that Lou's Pacer or any other car had gone off the road unnoticed.

Back at the jail, Frank's mood changed to irritated impatience: Ardly the younger hadn't called. Not caring what time it was in England or whether or not he woke the boy up, he made the call himself. Ardly hadn't located his father's papers yet, the boy said. And when Frank read him the names of the people in the hundred-year-old tour group, Ardly didn't recognize any of them. Yet another dead end.

Around supper time, when the people Frank and his deputy had talked to the night before began seeing the new edition of the *Gazette* with its front page account of Lou Cameron's disappearance and Wetherston's accusations, the phone started ringing. Most of the callers were indignant that he and Steve had been holding out on them during the questioning. However, now that they'd "had a chance to think about it," they nearly all realized that Lou had been "acting funny," not just Sunday afternoon but, some callers thought, for years. Unfortunately, no one could remember anything specific about how either Cameron or Ardly the elder had spent Sunday afternoon and evening. They seemed equally divided as to whether or not they thought Lou Cameron could possibly be a thief.

As for Frank, the more he thought and talked about it, the more ridiculous the accusation seemed. And, sheer ridiculousness aside, there was far too much coincidence involved for his taste. Ardly shows up, involves Cameron in his search for a hundred-years-dead ancestor, and within days both Ardly and Cameron disappear. There had to be a connection.

Even by itself, the embezzling story didn't make sense. Taken in conjunction with the rest, particularly Cameron's high spirits as testified to by his family and Sam Wilson and a half dozen others, it was simply ludicrous. There had to be another explanation, another set of answers.

But what? How could some unnamed and long dead ancestor of Ardly's cause two people to disappear and inspire Wetherston to come up with such an outlandish story? What could Ardly's digging have uncovered that, after a hundred years, would still be powerful enough to cause this kind of havoc?

Could it have something to do with the fact that Leander Wetherston had arrived at about the same time Ardly's ancestor was supposed to have arrived? Could the two have been connected in some way?

Would it do any good, Frank wondered, to tackle the Wetherstons again? He hadn't talked to Allen yet, hadn't even seen him since this whole thing started. After all, instinct—and memory of past escapades—pointed to Allen as the culprit in any nastiness involving the Wetherstons.

But what could Frank ask, and how could he force a natural liar like Allen to answer? Instinct—or prejudice—was hardly grounds for arrest, or even a search warrant. Butterfield, with his bluster and intimidation, probably would've tried it, might even have gotten away with it, but Frank couldn't see himself in Butterfield's role. He would end up with egg on his face— or, more likely, with the biggest lawsuit in the history of the county. Or a Wetherston-financed recall election. People like the Wetherstons might not be above the law altogether, but they could surely levitate over small town sheriffs with very little strain.

The remains of his phone-interrupted supper consigned to the garbage disposal, Frank drove to the city park to watch the last few minutes of the soccer match. The English won handily, after having eventually lost last night's softball game eight to seven. Returning to the jail's living quarters, he sat staring unseeingly at the TV program his mother was watching while his mind continued to chew at the same unyielding problems, like a dog trying to get at the marrow in a concrete bone.

The ten-o'clock news was just ending when the intercom crackled to life. "Someone out here I think you'll want to see, Frank," Steve Waymore's tinny voice told him.

Glad for any interruption, Frank shoved himself to his feet and pushed through the door between the living quarters and the jail area. In the corridor outside his office, he was confronted with a disheveled but triumphant Dale Arvin.

Well into his sixties but muscular and crew cut, Arvin was the retired manager of Whitford Construction, another of Wetherston's many enterprises. He gestured at a figure slumped sullenly on the wooden bench next to the candy machine. A kid, fifteen at the most.

"Here's the little son of a bitch you've been looking for, Frank," Arvin said. "The one that's been wrecking the damn town!"

A sudden mixture of elation and anger swept through him. Frank looked down at the boy. Blood spattered the kid's shirt front.

"What happened, Dale?" Frank asked uneasily.

"I caught the little weasel red-handed, that's what happened! Must've thought I wasn't home or something. I was down in the basement, staining that cabinet I made for Sally Peters, and I guess he didn't see the light, or maybe he figured a senior citizen like me'd be afraid to come out and take him on. All I know is, I heard this crash, and I come running up the stairs, and there's this son of a bitch on the back porch with a brick in his hand. He'd already pitched one through the window. I grabbed him before he knew what hit him, and that was that. So I hauled his lousy ass down here, and now he's yours. Do whatever you want with him, the worse the better!"

"What about the blood, Dale?"

"The little bastard tripped while I was dragging him to the car. I didn't beat him up, if that's what you're thinking. Not that he didn't have it coming, mind you."

"Okay, Dale, thanks. I assume you want to press charges?"

"You're damned right I want to press charges! As many and as hard as I can! Damn punk!"

Frank made shushing motions with both hands. "Just go home for now, okay? I'll take care of it." Turning to Steve Waymore in the door of the radio room, he said, "Steve, you better get hold of Doc Starret. Have him come by and take a look, make sure there's nothing serious."

"Now just a minute—" Arvin began, but Frank cut him off.

"Just go home, Dale. Come down tomorrow and you can sign a juvenile report. It was a big help, you bringing him in, and I appreciate it more than you can imagine, but I'll take care of things from here on out."

Arvin stood silently for a long moment, his eyes shifting from Frank to the boy and back. "Okay, Frank, if you say so. I'm not going to argue with the law. But you better take care of things right! I caught this little shitface red-handed, no questions, no nothing!"

"Fine. You can testify at the hearing. But for now, just go home."

Reluctantly, Arvin nodded at Frank. With a final glare and a muttered "Damn punk!" he disappeared noisily down the stairs.

"Get a wash cloth, Steve," Frank said as Steve emerged from the radio room again. "Looks like it might be just a nosebleed if we're lucky."

Dropping to his haunches in front of the boy, he looked more closely at the face. No bruises that he could see, but there was a trickle of blood on his lips and chin.

"What's your name, son?" Frank asked.

"Screw you!" the boy muttered, not taking his eyes from the floor.

At the sound of the voice, instantly and infuriatingly familiar from the taunting phone calls, Frank's fists clenched. The boy cringed against the wall despite his sullen show of indifference.

I hope Arvin smashed a few teeth loose, Frank thought.

No, dammit! He'd better hope the injury wasn't serious. Not for the boy's sake, but for Arvin's. If it was serious, it didn't matter what the boy had done. Even Whitford had lawyers who would jump on a case like that in a second, screaming "Vigilante!" at the top of their ambulance-chasing lungs.

"Here ya go, Frank," Steve said, returning with a washcloth.

Carefully, gripping the boy's head with one massive hand, Frank wiped away the blood. He breathed a sigh of relief as he saw that it was, indeed, just a nosebleed. No obvious bruises, no split lip or broken teeth.

"All right," Frank said, "let's see who you are."

A quick search of the boy's pockets yielded only a soiled handkerchief, some loose change, and a key ring. The boy maintained a sullen silence.

"Hang onto him, Steve," Frank said, stalking toward the door to the living quarters. "I know how to find out."

A minute later he was back, carrying a pair of slender, eight-by-ten leatherette-bound books. He handed one to Steve. "Beth's last two yearbooks," he said. "Our friend here doesn't look much older, so he'll probably be in one of them."

The boy glanced up with a new scowl but said nothing. Five minutes later, as Dr. Starret was clumping up the stairs to the office, Frank located the boy's picture. He and Steve waited patiently while Starret checked the boy over and pronounced him "healthy but surly." When neither Frank nor Steve volunteered any information, Starret shrugged and left. "I know when I'm not wanted," he said over his shoulder, "and just for that, you don't get the special law enforcement discount for house calls this time."

"Thanks, Doc," Frank called after him. When he heard the

street door clank shut, he looked down at the boy. "You're Willard Shriver," he said. "Bob Shriver's boy."

The boy snorted loudly. "If you say so."

Frank slowly and deliberately explained the boy's rights to him. When he had finished, the boy applauded silently, derisively, and refused to answer when Frank demanded to know if he understood them.

"Now I have to call your parents," Frank said finally. "Do you know if they're home?"

The boy only shrugged broadly and slumped further down on the bench, his body taking on a boneless look.

"Keep an eye on him, Steve," Frank said over his shoulder as he turned and strode into his office.

He found Shriver's number and dialed. On the fourth ring, a man's voice, gruff and gravelly, answered. "Hello?"

"Mr. Shriver? Robert Shriver?"

"That's right. Who's this?"

"This is Sheriff Decker, Mr. Shriver. We have your son Willard here at the jail. You'd better come down."

For several seconds there was only silence.

"Did you hear me, Mr. Shriver? I said, we have your son Willard here at the jail."

"Yes, I heard you. It's just that— Yes, I heard you."

"Can you come down, then?"

Another silence, and then. "Come down. Yes, I suppose I can. Right now, you mean?"

"Right now would be a help."

"All right. I'll be— What did he do?"

"We can talk about it when you get here."

Yet another long silence, and then, "All right. I'll come down. Right away."

They waited, the boy saying nothing. When they heard the clank of the door and then footsteps on the stairs, the boy looked up for the first time. Shriver, with a close-cropped beard and lank, brownish hair like the boy's, stopped at the head of the stairs and looked hesitantly down the corridor. For several seconds, he didn't move or make a sound.

"What happened, Sheriff?" he asked finally, an unexpected uncertainty in his voice. Frank had had to deal with the parents of a dozen or more juveniles since he'd taken office, and this was the first time one had reacted this way. Normally, whichever parent came down was angry, either at the juvenile for getting in trouble or at Frank for "picking up the wrong kid." A couple of times, a parent had been embarrassed or apologetic, but Frank had never seen this particular brand of nervous uncertainty before—like the reaction he sometimes got when he showed up unexpectedly at someone's door to serve a warrant.

"Willard was caught tossing a brick through a window," Frank said, after he had repeated the boy's rights for the father's benefit. "And we think he's responsible for several other incidents of vandalism in the last few weeks, most lately Harry Truitt's flower garden Sunday night."

"I see," Shriver said, swallowing. "He's under arrest, then?"

"Technically, no, since he's a juvenile, but that's what it amounts to."

"Has he—has he admitted that he did these things?"

"He hasn't even admitted that he's Willard Shriver. But Dale Arvin caught him standing just outside a broken window with a brick in his hand."

Another nervous swallow. "Will he have to stay in jail?"

"Not if you'll assume responsibility for him. He'll have to see a judge in the morning. You or his mother will have to come with him, of course."

"I see." Shriver looked sideways at the boy, who was staring back under lowered lids. "I don't suppose if I—uh, if I paid Mr. Arvin for the damage…"

"I doubt it. Mr. Arvin wants very much to press charges. You can talk to him if you want to, see what he says." Frank looked at the boy for a moment. "For that matter, if Willard here wants to confess to all the other incidents, you could talk to those people, too. But for tonight—"

"But if I paid—I'm sure I could get the money somehow, and then maybe he wouldn't have to—"

Suddenly, the boy was on his feet, his fists knotted at his sides. "That's right!" he shouted furiously, his voice an octave shriller. "Get another goddamn handout! Just tell them their goddamn poor relation fucked up again, and they'll dump a few more lousy dollars on you. Just tell them and they'll—"

"Son, please—"

"Don't call me that. I'm not your goddamn son and we both know it! You've been sucking up to those bastards all your life, and—" The boy broke off, laughing harshly. "'Those bastards!' We all know who the real bastard is, don't we?"

"He doesn't know what he's saying," Shriver said, almost pleading. "I don't know what he's talking about. He's never—"

"The hell you don't. What's the matter? You afraid if the truth comes out, your little gravy train will end? You afraid they won't pay you for me any more? Is that it, 'Father'?" The last word dripped with sarcasm.

"What do I have to do before I can take him home?" Shriver asked, looking around frantically.

"No, thanks!" the boy interrupted harshly. "I think I'll stay. Or maybe I'll call my real family myself and make my own deal. You think they paid a lot to keep me a secret before, just see what they'll pay now. Now that I can really smear the family name!"

With each angry sentence, Shriver cringed and seemed to physically shrink. His eyes closed. His entire body trembled.

"Well?" the boy asked, his high-pitched voice now filled with angry defiance. "How much do you think they'd pay to keep this quiet?"

When there was no answer, he turned to face Frank.

"I did it," he said. "I smashed the goddamn window and tore up the flowers and threw the paint through Old Lady Harper's window and—and everything! I did it all. But they'll get paid for it, and that'll be the end of it. And he'll get paid for it and you'll get paid for it, and we'll all be one big happy family again.''

Then the boy paused and looked at Shriver. "Isn't that right, 'Father'?"

"Who—" Frank began, but the boy's shrill voice cut him off.

"Shall I tell him, 'Father'? Shall I?"

"You don't understand, son," Shriver moaned. "You don't understand what you're doing."

The boy snorted derisively. "Then you haven't done a very good job of explaining it, have you?" He dropped back onto the bench in a boneless slump. "Just call them, Sheriff," he said, his voice lifeless. "Just call them. You should be able to hit them up for a few grand yourself if you play your cards right. Unless they own you already."

"Call who, Willard?" Frank asked.

Anther derisive snort. "Who the hell do you think? Who else could throw that kind of money around?"

"The Wetherstons?"

"You got it," the boy said with a thin laugh. "You fucking got it."

A HALF-HOUR LATER, Robert Shriver sat miserably on the straight back chair in Frank's office, his eyes downcast. Steve had just left to drive a still sullen but unresisting Willard Shriver home to his mother.

"You have to understand, Sheriff," Shriver mumbled miserably. "You have to understand."

"I'm trying, Mr. Shriver. Believe me, I'm trying. Why not start from the beginning?"

"The boy's right about one thing," Shriver almost whispered. "They would pay a bundle to keep everything quiet."

"I suggest you limit yourself to explaining how the Wetherstons fit into all this, unless you want to be arrested for attempted bribery yourself."

"I didn't mean—" Shriver yelped, his eyes jerking up to Frank's face.

"I know what you meant," Frank cut him off. "Just explain. And when you finish explaining, maybe we'll go see the Wetherstons."

Shriver gave a shuddering sigh. "There's nothing wrong with what I did. Nothing at all."

"I didn't say there was. I just want to know what you did. Or what the Wetherstons did. For starters, Willard's really—whose? Allen Wetherston's son?"

Shriver nodded.

"And his mother?"

"Irma. My wife."

"Allen had an affair with her?"

"No!" Shriver jerked upright, his voice indignant. "Nothing like that!"

"Then what did happen?"

"Before we were married…Allen—you know how he was."

"I've heard rumors."

Shriver nodded, looking at the floor in front of Frank's desk. "Probably all true. I worked for Mr. Wetherston—Nathaniel Wetherston. I was a—a custodian, a janitor at the foundry. It wasn't much of a job, but…" Shriver's voice trailed off, as if the gate in his mind were trying to force itself closed again.

"And what happened?" Frank prompted. "With your wife and Allen Wetherston?"

"I told you, she wasn't my wife, not then. I—I knew her, but that was all. We'd had a date or two in high school, but she didn't want anything more to do—"

He broke off, taking a deep breath to brace himself. "One day my boss at the foundry said the manager wanted to see me, and when I went in to see him, he said I should take the rest of the day off and go see Mr. Wetherston. Mr. Nathaniel Wetherston. At his house. I should go home and wash up and put on clean clothes and go to Mr. Wetherston's house. Said

I wouldn't even be docked for the time I was gone. He'd punch out for me himself. At the end of the shift.''

Shriver shrugged. "If somebody like that tells you to do something, you do it. You do it. So I went. Mr. Wetherston himself let me in and took me into the—I guess the living room. Enough furniture for a whole house for someone like me. Anyway, he asked me if I wanted to marry Irma—Irma Hazleton, her name was then. I practically fell over. I hadn't even talked to her for months, and here he was— 'What makes you think she'd ever marry me?' I asked right out.

"'Because I'd tell her to,' he said. Those were his exact words, I swear. I'll never forget them as long as I live. 'Because I'd tell her to.'

"I asked him why he would tell her to do something like that, why he would tell her to marry me, and he just shook his head. 'Don't worry about it,' he said. 'All you need to know is that she will marry you—if you want her to.'

"Well of course I wanted her to. Anyone with a pair—" He broke off, wincing. "Anyone in his right mind would've," he went on. "But then he told me what the catch was. She was going to have a baby. He never came right out and said it was Allen's kid, but it must've been. My guess is, she'd refused to have an abortion. I heard a couple other girls had done that for him, but Irma just plain refused. Wanted more. Probably wanted Allen and the Wetherston name, but—"

Shriver paused, closing his eyes altogether. "So since he couldn't buy her an abortion, he bought her a husband. Me. He bought me for her. And since she couldn't have Allen, she took me, along with a lot of promises from Mr. Wetherston. For a start, he gave me a better job, in his construction company. Had me trained to operate a bulldozer and a backhoe, so he could raise my wages. And—and he's been slippin' us something under the table every month since.''

"Cash?"

"Cash. No records. No taxes. Nothin'.''

"And Willard found out?"

Shriver nodded miserably. "When Allen came home a few

weeks back. He come over to the house one night, and—well, to hear him tell it, he was in some kind of trouble with his father. His father was gonna cut off his money and kick him out or something, and he didn't like it one little bit.''

"But why would he come to you about it?''

"He wanted to know all about Irma and me, and about Willard. I sort of thought he knew all along, but I guess he didn't, at least not the whole thing, not about the money his father'd been slippin' me, anyway. And when I got done tellin' him, he just sort of grinned and said something like, 'This should get the old skinflint off my back.''''

"How?''

"He didn't say. Just said things would be fine now, and that I didn't have anything to worry about. And I guess things were fine, for him. Old Man Wetherston didn't kick him out, anyway, like he was expecting.''

"But Willard overheard you and Allen talking?''

Shriver nodded again. "I tried to explain, but he just wouldn't understand. He just wouldn't understand. I guess he thinks the Wetherstons ought to own up and tell everyone he's really one of them and put him in their wills or something like that. I told him, that sort of stuff just happens in fairy tales, but he won't listen. In real life, you got to take what you can get, like his mother did, like I did. You got to take what people will give you and not go around stirring up trouble.''

Shriver was silent for several seconds, his eyes almost closed, but finally he looked up at Frank, and for the first time since he'd entered the office, there were just the beginnings of a faint, if rueful, smile. "But I guess things are pretty stirred up now, huh, Sheriff?''

ELEVEN

FROM THE HEAVY FEEL of the air as Frank climbed into the squad car the next morning, Wednesday promised to be no different from Tuesday or any of the last half dozen days. The promised cold front, according to the National Weather Service, was now officially a stationary front three hundred miles to the northwest and would so remain until the upper air winds shifted. Current computer projections suggested no such change until Thursday evening at the earliest, possibly not until Saturday.

Already sweating, Frank cranked the windows down and pulled out onto Twelfth.

Three miles later, he turned off the winding blacktop road into the steep, oak-shaded drive that led to the hundred-year-old Wetherston mansion. He parked under the oak nearest to the house and took the curving flagstone walk to the broad front door. A hundred yards beyond the house, visible through a thick stand of oaks and birches and willows, the blue lake looked deceptively cool.

The housekeeper reluctantly let Frank in. Her name was Martha Winters, and her bun of graying hair was pulled so tight it almost erased the frown lines from her forehead. Before Wetherston had hired her last year, she had been a supervisor at Sunset Manor. Nurse Ratched, Carrie Hyland had called her after she saw *One Flew Over the Cuckoo's Nest*. The fact that Martha had left the Manor was one of the reasons Carrie had gone back to cooking there after the baby was born.

Trailing the housekeeper through the house, Frank found Wetherston swimming doggedly back and forth in the glass-enclosed pool attached to the back of the house. The old man's arms and shoulders were stringy, but he was in good shape for someone in his seventies. Spotting Frank, Wetherston scowled briefly and continued to stroke the water, at an even more energetic pace. After another half dozen laps, he pulled himself from the pool and wrapped a luxuriantly thick robe around himself.

"Decker," he said sharply, "I told you Monday, I have nothing more to say to you."

"I remember, Mr. Wetherston. But I have something to say to you."

"As you wish, but be quick about it. I don't have all day to waste."

"I'm sure you don't," Frank said. "We could save time if Allen were here, too."

"I beg your pardon?"

"What I have to say involves both you and Allen. Why don't you call him down?"

"Just say what you have to say," Wetherston ordered. "I will inform my son."

"I'll have to talk to Allen, anyway."

"About what?"

"Yes," a new voice said from behind Frank, "about what?"

Turning, Frank saw Allen Wetherston standing—posing?—in the open doors of the house. Like his brother Garrick, he was slender, though a couple of inches shorter, and his hair, a lackluster brown, was thick and extravagantly—probably artificially—curly. He was wrapped in a silk dressing gown, the first one Frank could remember seeing outside of nineteen-thirties movies on the late show.

"Allen!" his father snapped. "I've told you to get dressed before coming down!"

"I'm as dressed as you are, Father dear," Allen said, eying his father's robe.

"There is a difference between dressing appropriately for exercising and simply not dressing."

"You know I don't approve of exercise," Allen said languidly, as if he were in a movie to match his dressing gown. Frank suspected Allen's tone, his dress, everything he did was intentional—something he knew would pull the old man's chain.

Nathaniel's lips tightened. After a tense moment, he turned to Frank.

"You said you had something to say to us." His voice was stiff, his stare the sort you give to something you're considering stepping on.

"I've discovered who's responsible for the vandalism the last few weeks, and I have a pretty good idea of the reasons," Frank said.

"You said this had something to do with my son," the old man snapped.

"It does. Allen's son, your grandson, is the one responsible."

"Allen has no son."

"None that he acknowledges, maybe, but he does have one. Willard Shriver."

Nathaniel's features froze for a second. Then the scowl deepened. "What is this, Decker?"

"It's obvious, isn't it, Father?" Allen laughed. "You have just acquired another mouth to feed. How much, Sheriff?"

"I'm not after money, Wetherston. Just information."

Allen's eyes widened in mock surprise. "Only information? How fortunate for us, and how refreshing!" He glanced at his father, then looked back at Frank. "We have more information than we really know what to do with, anyway. What would you like to know?"

Shallow sarcasm must run in the family, Frank thought,

recalling his exchange with Garrick. Briefly, he outlined his conversation with Shriver the night before.

"Now, if I've got it straight," Frank concluded, his eyes locking with Allen's, "you threatened to go public with the whole affair, including the under-the-table payments, unless your father continued your allowance."

Allen nodded admiringly. "That's really quite good, Sheriff." He sighed dramatically. "I suppose the truth is going to have to come out now, what with the boy being arrested."

"Probably," Frank said, "unless you can talk all the victims into dropping the charges—which I suppose is a possibility, since they all worked for a Wetherston business at one time or another. I'm guessing, by the way, that that's why the boy picked on them."

"I see." Allen turned to his father, who had been listening silently, his face a taut mask. "That shouldn't be a problem, should it, Father?"

Wetherston waved the question away. "I assume, Decker, that you have a reason for telling us these things. Aside from convincing me I should generously reimburse the victims, that is. Which of course I will do."

"It's all true, then?"

"Substantially."

"Including the payments?"

"Including the payments!" Wetherston grated impatiently. "What is this preoccupation you have with payments? Is my son right? Are you here to sell your silence? If so, name your price and have done with it!"

"No price, Mr. Wetherston," Frank said, "except the truth about Lou Cameron."

"Which you already have! If you would remove the rose-colored glasses you view Cameron through—"

"The truth, Wetherston!" Frank grated. "The truth!"

But he wasn't going to get it, he realized as he saw the old man's face turn to granite. Not here, not today. Blackmail money, yes. The truth, no.

Abruptly, he turned and stalked from the room.

DRIVING BACK TOWARD Whitford, Frank wondered futilely what the truth really was. Could the money Wetherston was accusing Cameron of embezzling be the money paid to Shriver? Were the accusations just the old man's way of covering up the payments? But why now? The payments had been going on for fifteen years. Could this whole mess have been triggered by Allen's return? By his threats?

Frank shook his head, baffled. No matter why they suddenly needed a cover-up, why such a preposterous story? And what about Lou's euphoria before he disappeared, not to mention the simultaneous disappearance of Willis Ardly?

Frank decided to visit Garrick Wetherston again. Garrick might or might not know about Willard and the hush money paid to Shriver, but he almost certainly did not know how Allen had used it to keep from being kicked out.

And when he found out—

Garrick would surely stir things up in the Wetherston clan, even more than Frank just had. And the more things were stirred up, the better the chances that some piece of the truth would float to the top.

Not a scientific principle of detection, maybe, Frank thought, but better than nothing. And it did remind him of the classic solution to stubborn problems in a TV set. A good hard bang on the chassis couldn't make things that much worse, and it might just jar loose whatever was causing the problem.

Glancing at the dashboard clock, he decided he had plenty of time to deliver one more jolt to the Wetherston clan before ten-thirty, when he had to be in court for the Shriver hearing.

THE RESULTS were even better than Frank had hoped.

Garrick Wetherston, once again seated behind the cluttered desk in the Lakeview Estates trailer park office, listened silently as Frank outlined Allen's machinations. Gradually, the sardonic smile he had greeted Frank with faded. His hands, at first resting lightly on the arms of his chair, gripped them tightly. Even the family penchant for sarcasm seemed to have been driven out of him when he finally spoke.

"That bastard!" he exploded. "So that's how he managed to pull it off! He's blackmailing our father with what he himself did!" Garrick shook his head, not in disbelief but in fury. "'If you don't continue to support me in the grand style to which I've become undeservedly accustomed, I'll tell the world what a low down son of a bitch I've been and what you've done to cover it up for me!' My God, the gall! Well, two can play that game!"

Garrick stood up so fast the chair banged against the wall behind him. Snatching his crumpled jacket from the arm of the couch, he shoved out into the heat without waiting for Frank to leave or locking the door behind him and threw himself behind the wheel of the gray Lincoln parked next to the squad car. As the Lincoln sprayed gravel, Frank saw Garrick fumbling in his jacket with his free hand. Just before he ran the stop sign and lurched out onto Lakeview Road, Nathaniel Wetherston's eldest son extricated a bottle of chalky liquid from a pocket and lifted it to his lips.

BACK AT THE JAIL, Frank got a surprise. Not one question from his mother! Instead, she hastily turned the phone and radio over to Phil Biggs and headed for the living quarters, motioning for Frank to follow.

She hesitated in the middle of the living room and then, not looking at him, walked to the curtained window and stood looking out at the courthouse square across the street.

"Something wrong, Mom?"

"No, nothing." Her voice was as oddly tense as her behavior. He couldn't remember her ever sounding or acting exactly like this. Could the depression be back?

Worried, annoyed, he asked, "What is it?" and when she

didn't answer, added, "You didn't drag me back here to watch you stare out the window."

Still holding the curtain aside with one finger, she finally spoke, sounding almost as if she were talking to herself, not Frank. "I'm only sixty-three, you know."

"I know."

"That's not really old."

"Of course not, but—"

"Just because I've been a grandmother for almost fifteen years and a widow for two doesn't mean I have to stop living."

"No one's said it does, Mom," he said patiently. "Haven't Joyce and I spent the last two years telling you exactly that?"

"I loved your father, you know. We didn't put on a show the way a lot of them do today, holding hands on the street and such. But we did love each other."

"I know you did," he assured her as he wondered what on earth she could be leading up to.

"And I love you and your sister. And Beth."

"I know. And I'm sure Beth knows it, too."

"I wouldn't do anything to make you ashamed of me, any of you."

"You couldn't if you wanted to," Frank said, beginning to be worried as well as puzzled by her words.

"I mean it, son," she said. "There's no need to humor me."

"I'm sorry, I didn't mean to."

For several seconds he could hear only his own breathing. Then his mother asked abruptly, "How would you feel if I went out on a date?"

For a moment, the words didn't register, as if she'd made a sudden right turn and he'd shot on past the intersection. But then, suddenly, he found himself grinning broadly.

"That's terrific! Who's the lucky man?"

"Harry Truitt," she said, smiling suddenly herself, suddenly looking even younger than before. "He came down

yesterday to make his statement about his garden, the ̖ ̖
man, and we got to talking. And this morning he called to
ask if I wanted to go to a movie over in Wallace tomorrow
evening.''

''You told him you'd go, I hope.''

''I said I'd let him know.''

''So let him know. Go call him. Now!''

''You're sure?''

''I'm sure! You want a signed affidavit? I could call the
courthouse and arrange it.''

Apparently satisfied, she went to the phone, but pointedly
waited until Frank left the room before dialing.

WILLARD SHRIVER WAS released into the custody of his parents, pending a formal hearing. All the defiance had drained
out of him overnight. The boy even showed signs of remorse,
or at least embarrassment, when, leaving the courtroom, he
came face to face with Estelle Coutts, at eighty the oldest of
his victims.

The rest of Frank's morning was taken up with the routine
of a two-car smashup out on the bypass, the third at the same
intersection in less than two years. There were no fatalities
but both cars were totaled. Del Richardson, who had arrived
with Chris Fredericks, the *Gazette* photographer, before the
wreckage could be cleared away, was already planning yet
another blistering editorial calling for a complete redesign and
rebuilding of the intersection.

When Frank finally wheeled into the jail parking strip early
in the afternoon, he saw Gordon Bailey leaning against the
whitewashed brick wall next to the door.

''Sheriff Decker,'' he said, hurrying forward before Frank
could climb out. ''I'm Gordon Bailey. Got a minute to talk?''
Irene's new husband was short, maybe five-eight, with thinning blonde hair done up in bushy curls that, like Allen Wetherston's, might or might not have been natural. He had on a

light blue sport jacket and a yellow tie, loose around a half-open collar.

"Sure," Frank said. "Come on up. I've been wanting to talk to you."

"I can imagine," Bailey said, with a nervous laugh. "But could we talk out here? Or in my car?" He gestured toward a red Cougar in the visitors' section of the parking area. "I was upstairs a few minutes ago, and I got the distinct impression your mother would as soon clap me in irons as look at me."

"What do you want to see me about?"

"I—I just thought it was about time we had a talk, and, well, got to know each other a little better."

"That's all?"

A nervous swallow, and then: "Well, no, not entirely. It's—well, I don't know what all you've heard about me, but probably nothing good. Right? Like how I'm stealing Beth's college money?"

Frank felt himself tense. "Something like that, yes."

"I figured as much. Irene—well, she gave me a good going over last night, I'll tell you true. I talked to Beth, too. I think we understand each other a little better now. And she knows the money will be there when she needs it."

"Then you did take it?"

Bailey grimaced. "I borrowed it. But I had to do something. See, I don't get a salary from Krueger, just a commission. Of course I never told Irene. You must know how she is. She's always going on about how you quit your 'good steady job' to go in with Jerry in that 'fly-by-night' repair shop, so you can imagine how she'd react if she ever found out my 'steady job' depends one hundred percent on the whims of car buyers. Now normally all that's okay by me. I do better than most, and Irene's never suspected a thing. But these last few months, what with Ronnie's economy going to hell, things have been pretty grim. A lot of bills have to be paid no matter how many cars I do or don't sell. Just can't be put off. You can only cut so many corners.''

''I see you're cutting them to the bone,'' Frank said, glancing at the Cougar.

''Not mine, I'm afraid. That's—well, Krueger owns it, like he does everything else on the lot. He just lets me use it. Sort of a billboard on wheels. See the bumper stickers? Krueger's name and number.''

He shrugged. ''I guess I'm lucky I don't have one of those strap-on signs on the roof. And it's good only for around town. We go anyplace outside our 'primary customer area,' we have to drive our own. Anyway, it was borrow a couple hundred from the college money or let them take the house.'' He gave a bitter laugh. ''Foreclosure city, and I've been paying on the damn thing for over ten years. I made up some story about Krueger being in a temporary financial bind and not being able to pay all of our salaries for a couple of months, and Irene went along with the idea of borrowing the money. At least she did until Monday, when I guess Beth went to see you. Actually, that's what I really wanted to talk to you about anyway, about Beth.''

''What about her?''

''She really does want to stay with you.''

''That's hardly a secret,'' Frank said cautiously.

''No, I guess it's not. And it's no secret that you want her, either. Or that the problem is Irene.''

''You're saying you'd prefer Beth to live with me, too?''

Bailey nodded. ''It's not that I want to get rid of Beth. She's a good kid, don't get me wrong, and I like her, but she'd sooner be with you. And David—well, you know how kids are when someone moves in and they have to give up things they've always thought of as their own.''

''Like his room?''

''You got it. Like his room. And he has been giving her a hard time. I know that. I've told him to lay off, but like I said, you know how kids are, especially when they're used to being the only kid in the house."

"I assume you're leading up to something, Mr. Bailey," Frank said when the other man fell silent.

"More or less," Bailey admitted, as if relieved to have been asked. "See, I've just been letting things slide. I figured it was up to Beth and you and Irene. I told Irene how I felt right at the start, and she didn't take it very well. Practically snapped my head off, if you want to know. Would've been our 'first fight' if I hadn't backed off, fast."

"And now?" Frank prompted.

"And now, well, I tell you true, she's getting a little scary. Just your name's enough to set her off. Or practically any little thing. Like last night, David made some crack about how he'd thought he was going to get his room back. I guess Beth must've said something to him before she talked to Irene and changed her mind about moving out. Anyway, it was a dumb thing to say, I'm not denying it, but Beth took it okay. It was Irene who went off the deep end, screaming at him. And at me. Like I said, she's starting to scare me. So what I thought—I know Beth was all set to move out Monday, but Irene talked her out of it. I even know what you said about getting an emergency legal something-or-other, and I understand. David's not that kind of kid," Bailey babbled on. "He'd never do anything like that, but there's no way you can know that, so I understand. I can see where you're coming from, I really can. I've read about crap like that happening, and not just in the sinful big city. Anyway, what I thought was—well, considering the way anything about you seems to set Irene off, having you talk to her would only make her dig her heels in all the harder. But if you could maybe talk to Beth again instead, and maybe get her to go ahead with the move to your place, the way she started to a couple days ago, maybe we could just present Irene with a—what's it called? A *fait accompli?* But you know what I mean. It would be all over and done with, and nothing Irene could do to stop it.

She could yell at me, maybe yell at you, and get it all out of her system, and then maybe we could get back to more or less normal, once she got it through her head that the matter really was settled once and for all. And Beth—well, she'd obviously be better off with you, since that's where she wants to be anyway.''

With a whoosh of breath, Bailey stood back. ''Well,'' he said, briskly dusting his hands together, ''I guess that's everything I wanted to say. Now it's up to you.'' He glanced at his watch. ''Now, if you'll excuse me, I got to get back to the lot, or I'll be in trouble there, too. Not to mention missing the late lunch walk-in trade.''

Without waiting for an answer, he was in the Cougar and roaring away.

TWELVE

"I DON'T KNOW, Daddy," Beth said, when Frank told her about his conversation with her stepfather. "I'll have to think about it. I know you mean well, and I guess maybe Gordon does, too, but Mom..." Her voice trailed off into a worried shake of her head.

Frank returned to his office, hoping things would be better between Beth and her stepfather now that they'd talked. He thought briefly about talking to Irene, but Bailey was probably right. It would only make the situation worse. Irene had always had a paranoid streak. Back at Leverentz, she used to think the foreman and half the women on the line had it in for her.

After she quit to have Beth, Irene had turned into the stereotype of a jealous wife, accusing him constantly of having an affair with one or another of the women she'd once worked with. Now she must really feel ganged up on, with everyone telling her Beth would be better off with Frank. No, for him to try to push the matter would only confirm her suspicions. Maybe later, when she'd had a chance to calm down—

The raucous buzz of the phone snapped him back to the present. "I got it, Phil," he called out to the deputy, who was in the hall by the vending machines. Swiveling around in his chair, Frank snatched the receiver from his desk. "Sheriff's office," he said.

"Frank?"

"That's right. Who's this?"

"Mel Gruenwald, out on Route Two."

"Yes, Mel. Something I can do for you?"

"Actually," Gruenwald said, "it's my kid, Marty. He—well, he come runnin' in here a minute ago, sayin' he'd found— Now mind you, Frank, I ain't checked it out myself, but he says he found Lou Cameron's car."

Frank jerked upright. "Where?"

"Now that's why I ain't checked it out, and why I figured I better give you a call, just in case. I mean, I saw the story in the paper and all, and Joe, when he dropped off the mail yesterday, he told me you'd asked all the carriers to keep an eye out."

"That's right," Frank said impatiently. "Where's the car?"

"You know the old gravel pit?"

"Sure, about a half mile from your place. Is that where the car is?"

"Sort of. According to Marty, it's clear down at the bottom, forty or fifty feet under water."

THE GRAVEL PIT had been abandoned as long as Frank could remember, at least since the early fifties. The nearest county road, narrow and neglected, ran a quarter mile to the east. The "road" that led to the pit itself was little more than a memory—a weed-covered path among the trees, used at night by couples who preferred the great outdoors. Daytimes, youngsters who found the supervised water of the lake and the municipal swimming pool too tame found better adventures in the depths of the pit, despite the "NO TRESPASSING" signs on what had once been a gate across the access road, and despite the *Gazette*'s periodic cautionary tales about drownings in similar pits around the state.

Frank parked next to Del Richardson's car, a dozen yards back from the edge of the pit. Del and Chris Fredericks, camera in hand, stood looking cautiously down at the water, at least forty feet below them. To the left, a path wound downward to where the trucks had taken on their last loads a third of a century before and where, now, swimmers were able to scramble out of the water. But it was from up here, from the tree-shrouded bluff that overlooked the entire pit, that they dived in.

It was twenty years since Frank had last dived in, but his entire body recalled the feel as he climbed from the squad car. Working up the nerve to jump had been half the fun. Then two or three terrifying seconds of free fall that seemed like forever, and finally the shock of the water. In spring, when it hadn't yet warmed to decent swimming temperature, the effect was like being swatted in the stomach with an icy two-by-four.

But the biggest adventure had always been for those who had the guts and the breath control to make it all the way to the bottom. Almost everyone tried it, but most—including Frank—stalled out halfway down, and broke the surface a few seconds later trying desperately not to look any more panicked than they could help. Those who made it to the bottom had to bring back proof, even if it was nothing more than a pebble.

A couple hours ago, Marty Gruenwald had come up with proof a lot more dramatic than a pebble.

Half a dozen boys were standing near the edge, their bicycles scattered under the trees. Frank spotted Marty instantly, not because he knew him but because the other five were standing around him in a ragged semi-circle and he was talking a blue streak. With the slam of the squad car door, the boy wheeled around. A second later he was pelting through the trees toward Frank.

"Sheriff Decker!" the boy shouted. "I'm the one that found it. It's right over there." Marty halted in front of Frank. He was a whippet-thin kid of twelve or thirteen, his ribs plainly visible, his waterlogged black hair only now beginning to dry.

Richardson turned and waved at Frank. "Why the hell can't you do things right, Frank?" he called. "Don't you know you're supposed to find bodies before we go to press?"

"I'll try to do better when I find yours," Frank returned, not quite able to muster a smile. He looked down at the boy. "You're Marty, right?"

"Yessir. I'm Marty Gruenwald, and I found Mr. Cameron's car."

All but grabbing Frank's hand to tug him along, the boy led the way to the edge of the pit, a few feet from where Richardson and his photographer still stood. The water didn't look quite as far down as Frank remembered, but it was far enough to make him wonder at his sanity all those times he had made the leap. The other boys edged away from him and Marty.

"It's right down there," the boy said, pointing at a spot twenty-five or thirty feet out, "like I told Mr. Richardson. It's just sitting there, right on the bottom. See, I was trying for the bottom—not trying, actually, 'cause I've already been down a couple times, so I knew I could do it. Anyway, I was almost all the way down when I saw this big shape off to the side. Sort of scared me at first. Like I say, I've been down there before and I hadn't seen anything like that, but—"

Eyeing Frank, he broke off and went on, "Anyway, I got a sort of a look at it, but I had to come up for air, and then I went down again, only I couldn't make it all the way because I didn't have the head start you get when you dive in from up here, so I had to come all the way up here and jump in again, and this time I aimed right for it, and there it was, plain as anything, I almost touched it I was so close, but when I came out these guys wouldn't believe me so they had to all go look, too, only they couldn't get near as close, and I took off to tell Dad because I knew you were looking for Mr. Cameron's car and—"

"Why are you so sure it's Mr. Cameron's car?" Frank asked, bringing the boy's breathless story to a halt.

"I'd know it anywhere. It's that junky looking Pacer, you know, with the dumb looking rear end with all that glass. I had a flat tire a couple months ago, and Mr. Cameron picked me up and drove me home, and he put my bike in the back, so I remember what kind of car he had, and anyway, there's that parking sticker for school on the bumper, that big orange sticker the teachers all have.''

"Could you see anything inside?"

"Gee, I didn't—you mean like a body or something? You think— Hey, I could go back down and look. It only takes a minute, and—"

"No, you stay up here. All of you," he added, glancing at the others, still standing around in jittery silence. "Jake Rowland's coming out with his scuba gear, and some people from the state crime lab, and I don't want anyone touching anything. Okay?" A large crane from a nearby construction site—the same company that Shriver worked for—was also on its ponderous way over, in hopes it could lift the car up to where a tow truck could take over.

"I could take another look anyway. I mean, I wouldn't touch anything, and if there really is a body—" The boy stopped, his jaw dropping. "You think maybe Mr. Cameron's in the car?"

"It's possible," Frank admitted reluctantly.

Frank could see the boy fighting to look sad at the thought that there might be a dead man—a man he knew—in the car, but the excitement of discovery won out. He turned and ran over to the other boys. "Hey, guys!" he said. "There might be a body down there! The sheriff said so!"

A moment's silence, and then they were all talking at once. Frank watched for a few seconds before returning to the squad car to wait for Rowland. He couldn't blame the kids. He probably would've acted the same at their age. Discovering a car at the bottom of the gravel pit was exciting, and so was the possibility of a body in the car, as long as the body wasn't that of a friend or relative.

Like a husband or father, he thought, his stomach knotting. Someone would have to tell Jennie and the children. He would have to tell them.

He would, at the very least, have to tell them that Lou's car had been found, and he was very much afraid he would have to tell them that Lou had been found, too.

APPREHENSION TWISTED at Frank's gut as he stood, hands on hips, watching Jake Rowland lever himself out of the quarry and onto the rock ledge. For a long moment he sat with his flippered feet dangling in the water, shoulders slumped, his head bowed, water dripping from the tank strapped to his back.

"What did you find, Jake?" Frank asked.

Jake lifted the breathing mask onto his forehead and looked over his shoulder at Frank. "There's a body all right," he said.

"Whose?" Richardson asked, before Frank could work up the courage.

"Damned if I know." Jake grimaced. "It's all puffed up like a balloon. Tell the truth, I didn't look all that close."

"Lou Cameron, you think?" Richardson asked.

Jake turned his face back to the quarry. "No way."

Relief flooded through Frank. "It's not Lou?"

"Not unless he grew a whole new head of hair since I had him in history class." Jake shuddered. "I must've stirred up the water when I was moving around, looking in the windows—they're all open, by the way. Anyway, the hair was floating around like it was alive, and there was a hell of a lot more than Lou Cameron ever had."

For a moment, the feeling of relief held, but then it faded. While the body might not be Lou Cameron's, it was in Lou Cameron's car. Probably Willis Ardly, the Englishman Lou had been seen with Sunday, the Englishman with the long hair and the mysterious ancestor.

And if it was Ardly, and if Ardly had indeed been murdered, as seemed obvious, then there was no reason Frank could think of to believe that anything better had happened to Lou.

FRANK TURNED AWAY from the waterlogged car, leaving it
and the body to the two technicians from the state crime lab
and to a queasy looking Chris Fredericks and his camera.
Jake's description hadn't done the body justice. Pale as a slug,
it was so bloated it looked as if it would pop if someone stuck
it with a pin. The right side of the short-sleeved shirt was
covered with a dark stain, presumably blood. Not as grisly as
the walking corpses in horror movies, maybe, but even more
grotesque. And real. Even supposing Chris managed to hold
his lunch down long enough to get his pictures, they'd never
dare print them in the *Gazette*. A supermarket tabloid, maybe,
or a forensic medicine text, but not the *Gazette*. The kids,
who had waited patiently for the car to clear the surface, had
lost all eagerness at their first glimpse of its contents, most of
them turning nearly as pale as the body itself.

As Jake had said, the hair—thick and long and gray—
proved that it wasn't Lou Cameron.

Ardly? Probably. But positive identification would have to
wait, one of the technicians had said, until they could check
fingerprints. Or dental records.

Ardly's suitcases, with the initials WA on both, had been
in the car. His clothes had been hastily stuffed inside, along
with a half dozen rocks. "Here we go," said one of the technicians. "Piece of cake."

Frank cleared his throat as the technician held up a British
passport, in a waterproof case, which had been tucked into a
zipper compartment of one of the suitcases. "Got his fingerprints right here," the man said with satisfaction. "All we
have to do is get them to the lab."

Nothing that belonged to Lou Cameron had been in the car,
other than the usual odds and ends in the glove compartment
and, possibly, the spade jammed in behind the back seat.

How the car had gotten into the pit was clear enough. As
Jake had remarked, the windows had been rolled down. The
accelerator had been weighted down with a badly scratched
and scuffed wooden gun case fastened clumsily in place by a

half dozen rubber bands, another half dozen of which still lay loose in the glove compartment where Lou had probably tossed them months ago. In the case was the apparent murder weapon, an old twenty-two caliber target pistol.

The body itself was in the driver's seat. The killer had clamped the steering wheel loosely in place by running the shoulder and lap belt through it, wrapping it around the rim a couple of times, and fastening the buckle.

He must have then started the engine, rubber-banded the gun case to the accelerator, gotten out, reached in past the body, put the automatic transmission in drive, and jumped free to watch the car accelerate to the cliff edge and arc into the water.

With the technicians still at work and the crane being loaded back on the huge flatbed that had brought it, Frank returned to town, where Jennie Cameron took the news with seeming stoicism. The children, particularly Sheila, reacted more violently.

"He didn't steal that money and he didn't kill anyone!" Sheila shouted, fighting back tears. "That's just dumb, and if you think he did, then you're even dumber!"

When Jennie started to apologize for the girl, Frank shook his head. "It's okay. I know how she feels." He looked at Sheila. "I feel the same way myself, believe me. Anyone who thinks your father did those things is dumb."

As Jennie walked with him to the squad car a few minutes later, he asked about the spade that had been found in the car. "Could it have been yours?"

"One of those old fashioned ones with the long handles?" she asked, frowning. "Not square, but sort of rounded with a point?"

"That's right."

"We had one like that, down in the basement, with the garden tools, but yesterday—" Her frown deepened. "It wasn't there. I remember wondering about it when I was putting things away, but I—I didn't think anything about it," she finished, her voice once again taking on an apologetic tone.

Frank nodded, remembering the single-minded effort she had been putting into the garden when he had come to see her the day before. "No reason you should have," he assured her. "But if you feel up to it, maybe you should check and see if you can spot anything else that might be missing, anything at all."

BACK AT THE OFFICE, Frank delayed the necessary call to Ardly's son by calling Laura.

"I didn't want you to hear it on the evening news," he said and went on to tell her about finding Ardly.

"You hold out no hope for Louis, then," she said when he finished, her voice almost inaudible.

"I can't be certain of anything," he said, "but no, I guess I don't."

"I will call on Jennie," she said flatly.

"Good. I'm sure she'll appreciate it."

Hanging up, he braced himself to make the call to England. Police in larger cities, he'd heard, were given instructions, if not entire classes, in how to notify the next of kin in cases of unexpected death. He had nothing to go by but his own instincts, which told him, simply, that straight out is best. The reality of death can be dealt with more easily without that period of anxiety and terror and blind hope that "breaking it gently" brings, just as the reality of a pulled tooth can be dealt with more easily without the hour in the dentist's waiting room.

Clayton Ardly answered the phone on the third ring. "If you're calling about those papers, no, I haven't searched them out yet," he said when Frank identified himself.

"That's not why I called." Frank closed his eyes. He had the same half-queasy feeling in his stomach he used to get while working up the nerve to make the jump into the water in the gravel pit. "I called about your father. He's been found, and—"

"Where did he take himself to?" Ardly asked sharply.

"I'm sorry," Frank said, pushing the words out now by physical force, "but he's dead. He's been killed." He had made the jump, he thought. He was in the air waiting for the icy blow of the water. Finally, it came.

"What?" Ardly's voice was unnaturally soft, almost expressionless. "What did you say?"

"I said, your father has been killed." The words came easier this time.

"That's absurd!" Ardly snapped, the softness gone as quickly as it had come. "You said he'd gone somewhere."

"I'm sorry, Mr. Ardly, but it's true. We found his body this afternoon. It appears he was murdered."

"What? My father didn't even know anyone over there! Who the bloody hell would want to kill him?"

"I don't know, Mr. Ardly. I hope we can find out. And those papers you said he took with him—knowing what they were might be a big help."

"Those papers were a hundred years old! What could they possibly have to do with—" Ardly broke off, sounding bewildered.

"Are you all right, Mr. Ardly?" Frank asked, after several seconds of the faint hiss of the satellite connection. "Mr. Ardly?"

He heard a sigh, and then, "I'm all right, Sheriff." Ardly's voice was more nearly normal now, neither irritated nor empty. "I realize you're just doing your job, and it can't be easy, God knows. If it's any help, my father and I aren't— weren't all that close. Haven't been for years. It's a shock, hearing this, but, well, I'm not about to collapse."

Frank resisted a sudden impulse to laugh as he realized that he was being comforted by the deceased's next of kin.

"You're sure you're all right?" Frank asked.

"Right enough, considering. I suppose— Do you know how this should be handled? Getting the body back home?"

"I can find out for you. The requirements at this end, anyway. It may be a day or two before the body is released, however. There'll have to be an autopsy."

"Oh, a post mortem. Yes, of course."

"And, well, we'll need time to confirm the identity." Frank hesitated, not really wanting to say any more than necessary about the condition of the body.

"Can't someone in the tour group identify him? I know he joined the group late, but they must be able to recognize him."

"I'm sure they could ordinarily, but—"

"But what?" A sharpness, not of anger but of something else, edged Ardly's voice.

"It's just that the body was under water for three or four days. The appearance is, well, altered considerably."

There was another silence of several seconds, and then, "He was drowned, then?"

"No, he was shot."

Yet another brief silence. "Sheriff, please. Just tell me the whole story."

Frank winced, realizing he had, despite his determination, been doing precisely what he had vowed not to do: making Ardly pull the information from him. "I'm sorry, Mr. Ardly," he said, and went on to outline everything that had happened since Sunday. The meeting with Cameron, Cameron's seeming high spirits, the disappearance of both men, even the fact that Cameron had been accused of embezzling from his employer.

"So you see," Frank finished, "why I'm so interested in those papers your father brought with him, and the photo album he had you send. I can't imagine what was in them that could have caused his murder, but I can't help but feel it's all connected. It's just too much of a coincidence otherwise."

"I quite understand, Sheriff. And I've been thinking while

you talked. Maybe I should come over myself, if only to bring the body back. I can work it out. And if you think those papers could possibly shed some light, I can bring what I find with me. I think I know where to lay my hands on them. It's just that, until now—"

There was another pause, and the sound of an indrawn breath. "Besides, even if we weren't as close as we should have been, I was closer to him than any of those bloody tourists."

THE DISCOVERY OF Ardly's body got less than thirty seconds on the six-o'clock news on the Springfield channel, but by six-thirty Frank's phone was ringing continuously. Half the people in Farrell County wanted to talk to him. Unfortunately, like the dozen or so reporters who had called from around the state right after Del put the story on the wires, they wanted to get information rather than give it. After the last call, he was no closer than before to finding out what the hell had happened Sunday, or what Ardly had found in the *Gazette*, either 1883 or 1884—if he had found anything at all.

Later, he visited the Halidays and once again went through the room Ardly had used. He also talked to the other British visitors, but all he really discovered was that the English were just as fascinated by murder as any bloodthirsty Yank.

THIRTEEN

THURSDAY MORNING, after less than five hours of fitful sleep, Frank woke thinking about Carrothers and the 1883 tour group's stop there. If he could find nothing in Whitford, maybe he should finally take a look at Carrothers?

At first he resisted the temptation to waste the time and gas to drive forty miles on the off chance that the Carrothers paper—if one had even existed then—would contain anything the *Gazette* did not.

A note from the night deputy told him that Clayton Ardly had called at five-twenty a.m. He would be arriving at the Springfield airport at eight-fifteen that evening, and he would be obliged if someone would meet the plane.

He called the state crime lab and received an annoyed assurance that they would get to work on his case ASAP and would let him know as soon as they had anything "worth the cost of a phone call."

For two hours, then, he cleared his desk of an accumulation of paperwork. Several hours remained before Ardly was due to arrive.

Finally, he called Del Richardson, who gave him the name of the Carrothers newspaper—the *News Sentinel*—and its current editor—Norb Devlin—along with the opinion that the *Sentinel* had probably begun publication about the same time as the *Gazette*.

That did it. Climbing into his squad car to drive to Carrothers, Frank appeased his conscience with the thought—rationalization—that finding something worthwhile in the next county was no more unlikely than any number of other things he had stumbled into, including his current job. Until one Friday afternoon late last spring, when he'd gone to the jail to debug the Department's new transmitter, the idea of becoming sheriff had never crossed his mind. While he was there, however, a pair of angry farmers had stormed in, each demanding the other be arrested for something to do with some livestock that had broken through an allegedly faulty fence. Sheriff Butterfield was away, but Frank, half fearing the pair might come to blows and damage the expensive new transmitter, had managed to calm them down while Phil Biggs watched admiringly.

The next day, Phil and another deputy, Wally Granger, paid Frank a furtive visit at the repair shop. Both liked their jobs, they explained, but Butterfield's ham-handed tactics were making so many enemies that their uniforms were getting downright unpopular. So they wondered if, in the interests of keeping Butterfield from being elected to an unopposed second term, Frank might consider running for the job himself?

"You'd be perfect," Wally said. "What with the TV shop—and the football you played back in high school— you've got the name recognition thing beat before you start. You don't have any enemies worth mentioning, except maybe your ex-wife, and the way you handled those two hotheads yesterday—well, Phil here used to be a teacher, so he knows good mediation when he sees it. See, that's what a sheriff does, a good one, anyway. Settles arguments, shoots the breeze, throws a little bull, and lets everyone know he's around when he's needed—and looks like he'd do a little good when he does show up, which should be easy enough for a goddamn giant like you. You'd probably have it knocked without ever having to raise a finger."

Frank's first reaction had been "You've got to be kidding!" But the deputies had been persistent, almost as persistent as the coach who'd conned him into football in high school. By the time they left, he was actually giving the idea serious consideration, especially after they assured him there was no reason for him to abandon the repair shop. Even if he couldn't work there himself, he'd still own half of it, and becoming sheriff would be good for business. Butterfield's laundromat, they pointed out, had added a half dozen machines since his election.

So, he had run and, to his surprise, won handily, which was, he told himself as he merged into expressway traffic and headed north, no stranger than hoping to find enlightenment in a hundred-year-old newspaper in Carrothers.

SHORTLY BEFORE NOON, Frank found Norb Devlin, middle-aged and paunchy like Del Richardson, having a quick lunch at the Dairy Queen in downtown Carrothers, a block from the *Sentinel* office. After quickly downing a chili dog and ordering a larger milk shake than he should have even considered, Frank approached Devlin where he sat on a concrete bench, finishing a packet of French fries as he idly watched the noon-time strollers and shoppers across the street. When Frank introduced himself, however, Devlin leaped to his feet, dropping the packet and its remaining half dozen shriveled fries into the wire trash barrel next to the bench.

"Happy as hell to meet you, Sheriff," Devlin said, reaching out to pump Frank's hand. "I heard about what's been happening down in your neck of the woods. Even managed to put together a few column-inches for today's edition, but all I've really got to work with is what I've been picking up off the wire. Thought about calling you, but I figured you probably had more on your plate already than you wanted. But now that you're here and there's still time to slip a couple new paragraphs in, I hope you won't mind answering a few questions."

"Not at all, but I want to ask you a few first."

"Shoot. Anything I can do to help, though I can't imagine what it could be. Like I said, all I know is what we've ripped off the wire. Look, why don't we head back to the office?"

"Glad to, especially if it's air conditioned."

"Couldn't survive without it." Devlin mopped his brow as he started up the sidewalk at a brisk pace, Frank grabbing the shake and hurrying after him. "Where's that weather control business everyone was predicting fifty years ago? Sure as hell could use some, a summer like this."

At the long, narrow building that housed the *Sentinel*, Devlin held the door open and gestured Frank inside. He led on through a gate in the counter that separated the "news room" from the "lobby" and past a half dozen cluttered but now vacant desks. A young girl, probably in her late teens, was behind the counter, carefully printing on a form what a gray-haired man on the other side of the counter was dictating.

"Right back here," Devlin said, ushering Frank into the tiny, glassed-in cubicle that served as his office. Frank dumped the now-empty milk shake container in the waste-basket. "Now, what are those questions?"

"First, I understand the *News Sentinel* was being published in eighteen-eighty-three. Is that right?"

Devlin blinked. "I beg your pardon?"

"I said, I was told that your paper was being published in Carrothers in eighteen-eighty-three."

"I thought that's what you said." Devlin shrugged expansively. "As a matter of fact, it was. First issue of the *Sentinel* came out in eighteen-seventy-eight. May twenty-third, to be exact. I remember because we did a hundredth anniversary issue five years ago, and the thing's still framed out there on the wall." He gestured over his shoulder toward the combination news room and lobby. Frank saw the glassed-over paper hanging on the wall just behind the counter.

"You must have copies of the eighteen-eighty-three issues, then."

"More or less. They're kind of ragged around the edges. We really ought to get them microfilmed one of these years. I heard about what you people did with your *Gazette,* but our historical society doesn't have a go-getter to front for it like yours does. That Young woman has got our bunch turning green.''

''Tell your bunch to come down and talk to her some-time,'' Frank said, grinning. ''Laura'd be happy to give them some advice, anyway. But right now, could I see your August 'eighty-three issues?''

Devlin blinked. ''Sure, if you tell me why. I don't mind saying, you've got my curiosity bump all bent out of shape.''

Frank explained about the eighteen-eighty-three tour as Devlin led him down a narrow staircase to the basement, where, by the light of an incandescent bulb swinging from a frayed cord, he searched through sagging shelves of massive, dusty and sometimes crumbling volumes.

''I'll be damned,'' Devlin said, shaking his head. ''Damnedest thing I ever heard. You really think something that happened a hundred years ago might've gotten that Brit killed?''

Frank shrugged. ''I'll never find out if I don't look.''

''That's for sure,'' Devlin agreed. ''Well, here's 'eighty-three.''

A cloud of dust swirled as he blew energetically on the spine of one of the two- and three-inch thick volumes that filled yard after yard of shelves. ''Just be careful how you turn the pages,'' he warned as he hauled it out and laid it with a thud on a rough, wooden table directly under the bare bulb. ''I'll be back in a few minutes,'' he added, turning and heading for the stairs, ''as soon as I figure a way to work this hundred-year-old connection into what we've already got.''

Gingerly, Frank opened the featureless black volume, wincing as bits of paper flaked off under his fingers. The brittle, brownish pages were in far worse shape than the *Gazette* had been. He would definitely have to tell Laura about this. If the Carrothers Historical Society didn't contact her, she would probably want to contact them—if only to give the local group ideas on how to raise money for microfilming.

But with care the pages could be turned, and, except for occasional missing corners, everything was there and legible.

The main story on August fifteenth, a Wednesday, was not about the tourists but about the sudden death from "heart failure" of one of the county's leading citizens, one Jeremiah Ingram. A similar but smaller story, he remembered, had been in the *Gazette*, since some of Ingram's survivors had lived around Whitford. The visitors, however, ran Ingram's demise a close second.

"City Impresses Trans-Atlantic Visitors," a headline proclaimed, and the article went on to run three relatively bland quotes, one of which expressed appreciation of the "clean and spacious grounds" that surrounded the county courthouse. All three sounded suspiciously similar in both tone and substance to the comments quoted in the *Gazette* about Whitford two days later. The *News Sentinel*, however, outdid the *Gazette* by running a pencil sketch of someone identified as Mayor Claibourne presenting a key to the city to an extremely dignified looking group, all standing on what must have been the "clean and spacious grounds" of the courthouse.

The article itself was longer than the one in the *Gazette*, but it covered the same ground, only in wordier prose, like two versions of the same press release: The reasons for the group getting together, their impressions of the colonies, etc., etc. Frank almost quit reading halfway through. Only the fact that he had driven forty miles to look at the article kept him going.

As he came to the last paragraph, he stiffened. "Find something?" asked Devlin, who had reappeared and had been looking over his shoulder the last few minutes.

Frank pulled in a breath. "It sure as hell looks like it," he said. "If it means what I think it does, it answers one major question, maybe even two, but it raises a whole bunch more. Here, take a look."

Leaning back so that his bulk didn't block Devlin's view, Frank indicated the final paragraph in the article. It was a list of the names of the English visitors. A similar list had appeared in the *Gazette*.

Similar, but not identical. In the *Gazette,* there had been twelve names. Here there were thirteen.

Thirteen.

And the thirteenth name was Leander Wetherston.

BACK IN WHITFORD, Frank went directly to the museum. If anyone outside the Wetherston family had any idea what his discovery in the *Sentinel* meant, it would be Laura. She was at her desk, speaking earnestly into the phone as she shuffled a series of multi-carbon forms spread out amid the clutter on her desk. Spotting him as he threaded his way through the maze of displays, she smiled and returned his wave of greeting, but continued talking into the phone. At the same time, though, she collected the forms and consigned them to the back corner of the desk.

Hanging up as Frank reached the desk, she looked up at him. "Have you learned anything about Louis Cameron? After Mr. Ardly's body was found—"

He shook his head. "Nothing for sure. But I just got back from Carrothers, and I found the damndest thing in their paper. You know how that tour group was at Carrothers just before they came to Whitford? Well, the Carrothers paper ran basically the same article the *Gazette* did, including a list of the members of the tour group. But their list—"

The jangle of the phone cut him off. Laura grabbed the receiver. "Historical Society," she said, her voice soft and pleasant despite her grimace at the interruption, "Laura Young speaking."

Listening, she frowned, glancing toward Frank. "Yes, the sheriff is here," she said, much of the softness gone from her voice. "Do you wish to speak with him?"

Puzzled, Frank gave her a questioning look as she held the receiver out to him. From several inches away, he could hear a woman's voice shouting, almost screaming. Good God! It was Irene! Bailey had been right about her yesterday, he thought. She was acting "downright scary."

"Irene," he broke in, his tone as soothing as he could manage under the circumstances, "I'm on the line now. What do you want?"

Silence, except for the sound of Irene's raspy breathing and the creaking of the desk chair as Laura stood up. His hair began to rise.

"I know what you're up to, the two of you," Irene resumed icily, her voice as venomous as when, a decade ago, she had confronted him about his nonexistent affairs, and for one heartstopping moment he was afraid she was doing it again and was referring to him and Laura. That was one subject he didn't want to get into, particularly not with Laura standing next to him. The last thing he wanted to do was say something that would wreck their friendship now or—and he felt both guilty and foolish just for thinking about it—kill any chance he might have with her in the future, when and if the breakup rumors about her and Wayne proved true.

"What's the trouble, Irene?" he asked, somehow managing to keep the nervousness out of his voice. "And what do you mean, the 'two of us'?"

"You know damned well what the trouble is, Frank Decker! You think because you've got that badge, you can get away with anything you please, but I'm warning you, it won't work!"

"Irene, I honestly don't know what you're talking about."

"All right, play dumb! Just remember what I'm telling you, Sheriff! I know all about how you hauled Gordon down to your jail and threatened him into helping with your cheap schemes. I know, and don't you forget it!"

Oh, God, he thought, with a mixture of relief and exasperation. She'd found out that Bailey had been down to see him, and she was twisting the incident all out of shape.

"I talked to Gordon, yes," he said, "but I didn't 'haul him down to jail.' He came to see me, and if you must know, it was because he's worried about you."

"Have it your way," she snapped. "You always did any-

way. But just remember, Frank Decker, you just remember—
Beth is my daughter, and Judge Hastings isn't going to let the
two of you steal her from me that easily! Just you remember
that!''

Before he could say more, the line went dead.

For a moment he thought of calling her back but decided
against it. He'd have to have another talk with Bailey—and
with Beth, preferably the two of them together—before he
tried talking to Irene again. She was obviously in no mood to
believe anything he said, but if all three of them approached
her—

Looking around as he hung up, he saw that Laura had with-
drawn several feet, giving him privacy. "All clear," he said,
shaking his head, and added apologetically, "She's been under some strain lately. What was she saying to you, anyway?"

"It does not matter," Laura said and then added with an
uncertain smile, "For the most part, if you delete the colorful
editorializing, she was simply asking to speak to you. Now,
you were about to tell me what you found in Carrothers."

"Right. The list of names."

Watching Laura as he told her about the list, Frank could
imagine how Lou Cameron must have reacted when—if—he
had learned the same thing. Instant euphoria: the state he had
been in on Sunday afternoon, as described by Sam Wilson
and the others. Frank suspected Laura's reaction would have
been the same, if not for the grim knowledge of what had
happened to Ardly and probably to Lou Cameron.

Even so, excitement was obvious in her voice when, as he
finished, she said, "If Mr. Ardly's ancestor was Leander
Wetherston, that would certainly explain why he wanted to
look at the August 1884 editions of the *Gazette*."

"Oh?"

"I assumed— But, no, I forget that not everyone is the
Leander Wetherston scholar that I have become in recent
months. It was in August of that year that Mr. Wetherston

died. August the 29th. The obituary was in the next day's edition, Saturday, August 30th.''

Frank grimaced. ''It must've been quite a jolt for Ardly Friday, finding out his ancestor not only wasn't a financial failure but was a deserter and a bigamist to boot. But Saturday he came back to the *Gazette* looking for more information. From what everyone says, he was playing the whole thing pretty close to his vest. He didn't tell anyone what he'd found, not even his son, when he called him Sunday. But somewhere along the line he must've found out that Leander's descendants over here own half the county. Probably when he talked to Lou Sunday afternoon. That would explain why he was asking Bill Englehardt about international law at the party Sunday night. He must have been wondering if his branch of the family had any claim on anything after a hundred years.''

''But why is he dead?'' Laura asked when he fell silent.

''I don't have the faintest idea,'' Frank replied, not entirely truthfully. ''Look, how about making me an instant expert on Leander? I need an idea of what Ardly found—besides the obvious, that is.''

''Of course, Frank.'' Turning, she quickly led the way to the Wetherston room.

''That is Leander Wetherston's portrait,'' she said, pointing as they came to a stop in the doorway, ''as I am sure you know. On the left is his wife, Dora. The other one is their son Lawrence, painted when he was fifty, almost twenty years older than his father at his death.''

Concentrating on the paintings that dominated the wall behind the massive, ornately decorated desk, Frank realized that, though he had seen them a dozen times, he had never actually looked at them before this.

Leander Wetherston had been strikingly handsome. His thick, shining, deeply waved hair was parted precisely down the middle. The pointed tips of his small mustache tilted ever so slightly upward, as did the corners of his mouth. Now that he looked, Frank could see a resemblance to Allen Wether-

ston, particularly in the slender features and high cheekbones
and the contrasting full-lipped, sensuous smile. Allen was not
nearly as handsome as Leander had been—unless the portrait
painter had been paid not for accuracy but for flattery. Always
a possibility.

Dora Wetherston's portrait was another matter altogether.
No flattery money had exchanged hands here. She was, at
best, plain, with a long jaw and broad forehead. She had a
determined, almost belligerent look in her eyes, as if daring
the painter to do his worst. The jaw in particular, and possibly
the aquiline nose, reminded him more of a hard-edged version
of Garrick than of Allen. Lawrence, also rather plain, might
have shared the jaw, but a thick, graying beard made it impossible to tell.

"As for becoming a Leander expert," Laura said, turning,
"it will be best if you inspect for yourself the material we
have." She led him back to her desk in the other room.

"Don't you have a crash course of some kind? I mean, all
I got out of those articles I looked at yesterday is that he's
supposed to have grown up in some unspecified part of New
England, lived in Chicago a few years, and come here in
eighteen-eighty-three."

"I am afraid that is all there is to know about his life before
he came to Whitford," Laura said. "And based upon what
you found in Carrothers this afternoon, even that is apparently
false."

"What about Nathaniel? Would he know anything?"

"I doubt it. Research has been attempted at various times,
but with little result. The assumption is that any records of
Leander's life in Chicago were destroyed by the fire in eigh-
teen-seventy-nine, and no one has ever found any indication
as to what part of New England he was from."

"All of which would be a good cover, if he actually came
here directly from England."

Laura nodded. "That should not be too difficult to verify,
now that we know what we are looking for. If he, like the

others in the 1883 group, was from the English Whitford, there should be records there to be checked.''

"I know. In fact, that's exactly what I intend to do. If the papers Ardly's bringing don't shed a little light on the subject first, that is. In the meantime, there must be something you can tell me about what Leander did while he was here, in this Whitford. Besides what I read in the *Gazette* yesterday.''

"I will show you what we have,'' she said. "You see, his widow Dora not only preserved the furniture of her husband's office, but all of his papers as well. His correspondence, his business records, everything, and she added her own diary, not only for the months of their marriage but for two years after his death, together with copies of all newspaper articles about him, not only in the *Gazette* but elsewhere. But none of it, so far as I can remember, mentions his life prior to his arrival in Whitford. It is not likely to add any clarity to the situation you have uncovered.''

"It can't make it any more confusing. Or I hope not.'' Frank shook his head. "I assume Lou knew all about this treasure trove.''

"Of course, but not many other people do. I wasn't aware of the extent of the material myself until a few months ago, when I began doing research.''

"Research?''

"Last winter, Nathaniel Wetherston commissioned me—or the society, actually—to do a comprehensive article on Leander.''

"He just wanted to learn about Leander? Or what?''

Laura shrugged minutely. "He did not say. I assume that he was aware of most of the information since it came primarily from the collection his grandmother amassed. He said only that he wanted the article written, however long it turned out to be. He was willing to pay generously for my time, but he never said specifically what would be done with the results. I assumed he would run the article in the *Gazette* this winter to mark the hundredth anniversary of the founding of the bank. Or perhaps he was planning to have a small book printed, I do not know.''

''But where is all this material? I didn't see it in the Wetherston Room.''

''Most of it is in the files.'' She gestured toward the ancient file cabinets along one wall. ''I have copies of what I suspect are the most interesting and informative items in my desk. I have been working on the article in my spare moments since last winter.''

''Maybe if you showed me what you've done so far? I assume you've been keeping notes of some kind.''

She laughed. ''Of course. But unless you can read my unpatented mixture of shorthand and Chinese, they would be of little help. I have been intending to bring a typewriter in to transcribe them, but...

Her voice trailed off as she pulled open the large central drawer of her ancient desk and lifted out a pair of large manila envelopes and three faded, leather-bound volumes. ''These are Dora Wetherston's diaries,'' she said. ''And these envelopes contain copies of the newspaper articles as well as some of the more informative correspondence. The rest of the correspondence and the original newspaper articles are in the files. The business records—ledgers and the like—are in a box somewhere. They are too big to fit in a file drawer, but I can locate them for you, if you wish. Though I doubt they would tell you much without an accountant to be your guide,'' she added with a smile.

''No, this should be more than enough,'' Frank said, shaking his head. ''You don't suppose one of these could be the mysterious envelope that Lou took home with him Sunday afternoon, do you?''

''It is possible, of course, but I would doubt it very much. I am sure he would have told me if he were taking anything that he knew I was working on. His enthusiasm was matched only by his conscientiousness.''

Thanking her, he returned to the Wetherston room and

emptied the first of the envelopes carefully onto Leander's desk.

Wetherston, the articles said, had first visited Whitford on
September fifth, a Wednesday, less than three weeks after the
tour group had come through town. Like the tour group, he
had stayed at the town's only hotel, the Arlington, and during
his first three days, he consulted with virtually every busi-
nessman not only in Whitford but in most of the surrounding
towns. And almost everyone he talked to was liberally quoted
in the articles, most to the effect that Leander Wetherston, in
addition to being "comely," had a great deal of what, a hundred years later, would have been called charisma.

The following week, he had gathered together roughly forty
of the area's leading citizens, including the mayor and other
town and county officials, and announced that, if arrangements could be worked out, he would settle in Whitford per-
manently and "make a modest investment in its future." By
putting up his own "substantial capital" right at the start, he
easily convinced the others to put up lesser amounts toward
the establishment of a bank, which everyone agreed had been
sorely needed since the last one had failed nearly a decade
before.

Wetherston's charisma—or perhaps a little bribery, Frank
thought perversely—got him a state bank charter in short order. By November, the building once occupied by the failed
bank was being refurbished, and the new bank was open for
business before Christmas. By spring, it had become, according to the articles, "the financial hub of the county." Leander's "charisma" apparently drew in not only the initial investors but depositors of all sizes from all parts of the county
as well as neighboring counties, even some from as far away
as the state capital.

Meanwhile, he had met and courted Dora Clemons, the
daughter of one of the bank's biggest investors, Stanley Clemons. Their marriage took place in December at the Clemons
mansion on the south shore of Carlton Lake. During the spring

and summer of eighteen-eighty-four, he personally supervised the building of a home, a mansion the equal of that of his new father-in-law, on the west shore of the lake. In August, as the home was completed and he and his bride of eight months moved in, it was announced that Mrs. Wetherston would "present her successful and devoted husband with an heir" in December.

But then, as Laura had said, on August 29, one week short of a year after he first set foot in Whitford, less than a month after moving into his new home, Leander Wetherston drowned in a boating accident on the lake. He had stood up in the boat, according to his widow, and had slipped and fallen overboard, striking his head on an oarlock as he fell. Mrs. Wetherston, who could not swim, had been unable to save him. His body was recovered from twenty feet of water the following day.

And that was that. Those were all the facts known about Leander Wetherston. In the glowing and maudlin tributes that filled the *Gazette* for a week after his death, Frank read little but repeated lamentations over the incalculable loss to the community and rehashes of the great things that Leander Wetherston had accomplished in the "tragically abbreviated span allotted him."

About his widow, however, there was much more.

For a start, Dora Clemons Wetherston turned out to be at least as capable as Leander himself, despite her lack of "charisma." According to later articles in the envelopes, she had taken over the bank's operation shortly after the birth of the child, Nathaniel's father, Lawrence Wetherston. She had, one eighteen-ninety article said, "supervised that institution's workings as well as any man."

Though she lived to be well over eighty, she never remarried, and by the time she "stepped aside" and allowed Lawrence to take over in nineteen-twenty, she had gained control of more than a dozen other enterprises, a number of them through foreclosures by the bank. Nominally under

Lawrence's guidance, the Wetherston empire continued to grow, even during the Depression years, but—significantly—reached its peak shortly before Dora Wetherston's death, following which it had, at best, not backslid greatly. New ventures were started by Lawrence and by Nathaniel, but equally as many existing ones were sold or failed.

What caught Frank's eye, however, were Dora's assessments of Leander, not only those quoted in the various tributes but in page after page of her diaries. Leander Wetherston had been not only a financial genius but virtually a saint in every aspect of his existence, a perfect husband who never spoke a harsh word to his wife, who indulged her every whim, and who never so much as looked at another woman during their tragically brief marriage. He was also a public spirited man whose primary interest was not to make money for money's sake but to enable community life in Whitford to be improved. And he gave vast amounts to charities, though all donations were made only on the condition they remain anonymous—which they did, at least until his wife's diaries were made public well into the twentieth century.

Much too good to be true, of course, but it had taken a hundred years for even Leander's bigamy to be found out. Meanwhile, Dora had almost certainly held him up as a shining and untouchable example to both his son and grandson.

Cynically, Frank considered how such lavish praise heaped on Leander had affected Nathaniel. Dora Wetherston hadn't died until the nineteen-forties, so her grandson had probably been subjected to more than two decades of a constant litany of his grandfather's perfections—surely one of the reasons Nathaniel had gone in for so much public-spiritedness himself, despite not seeming to enjoy any of it. But what choice had he had after twenty or more years of the kind of brainwashing Dora had doubtless been capable of? None. Unless, like Allen, he decided to thumb his nose at the whole affair.

But he hadn't, obviously. He had bought his grandmother's

fiction one hundred percent and had done his best to live up to it for seventy years.

Until Lou Cameron and Willis Ardly came to him last Sunday with a decidedly different picture. If the information had shaken Willis Ardly and elated Lou Cameron, it must have devastated Nathaniel Wetherston.

Unless Nathaniel had already known? In which case the fact that someone else now knew would have been equally devastating. Either way, intolerable.

And when something is intolerable to a Wetherston, that something is suppressed.

Or removed.

FOURTEEN

"YOU'VE GOT a visitor, Frank," Phil Biggs said as he met Frank at the top of the jail stairs. The deputy was on his way back from the cells with a tray loaded with the remnants of the prisoners' suppers. "Garrick Wetherston. He's in your office, all antsy to see you."

"What's he want?"

"Wouldn't say. Won't talk to anyone but you."

"Okay, Phil, thanks."

"And your mother wants to know why you weren't home for supper," the deputy added with a grin. "She also said I should remind you she won't be around this evening because she's going to a movie with Harry Truitt."

"Tell her to have a good time, and I'll stick something in the microwave later. After I see what Wetherston wants."

Frank made his way past the vending machines to his office. He didn't want to talk to any of the Wetherston clan until he had gotten his suspicions confirmed by Clayton Ardly, but it couldn't be helped.

He paused at the office door. "Mr. Wetherston? What can I do for you?"

Garrick Wetherston, who had been standing facing the bookcase and the bulletin board above it, jerked around. "Could you close the door?" he asked, his voice as tense as his rail-thin body.

"Sure," Frank said, clicking the door shut behind him. "What's wrong?"

"You know very well what's wrong, Sheriff! Willis Ardly has been murdered!"

"That's hardly news. The body was found yesterday afternoon."

"I know. But I learned of it only this afternoon. In the *Gazette,* of all places! I don't have time to watch television, and no one bothered to tell me." Frank thought he caught a note of self-pity in Wetherston's tone.

"I see. But what could Ardly's murder possibly have to do with you?"

"He was found in Cameron's car! And the last anyone saw of the two of them, they were together!"

"That's not quite true. They were seen together Sunday afternoon, but Ardly was seen Sunday night, alone, several times. But so what? What does that have to do with you?"

Garrick scowled. "Is my memory failing? I seem to recall your expressing a rather firmly held opinion that my brother Allen may have stolen the money Cameron was accused of taking."

"Which leads you to think what?"

"Damn it, Decker, Ardly was obviously mixed up with Cameron, who you hinted must be mixed up with my brother, and now Ardly's been murdered! It isn't just some missing petty cash anymore!"

"I still don't see—"

"I didn't come here to play games, Decker!"

"Then stop playing them and tell me why you are here." Frank lowered himself into his swivel chair and motioned Garrick to the uncomfortable straight back chair reserved for visitors.

For several seconds, Wetherston stood silently, glaring at Frank. At last he forced some of the anger from his face, but instead of sitting down, he stood straighter, as if bracing himself.

"I came because I'm worried," he said quietly, then dredged up a shaky imitation of his usual sarcastic tone as he went on. "But let me tell you about yesterday, Sheriff. That may help you overcome your deliberate obtuseness. I'm sure you recall that I was a trifle upset when you informed me of my dear brother's latest adventure, that is, how he was apparently blackmailing our father with his—Allen's—own misdeeds."

"I remember. I also remember your saying something about two being able to play at that game."

"Precisely. As you may have guessed, my intention was to tell Father that unless he followed through on his original plan—our original plan—to cut off Allen's allowance, I would go public with the Shriver episode." He shrugged. "I assumed that, being a pragmatic sort, he would yield to the inexorable logic of the situation. If that particular skeleton was coming out of the family closet no matter which way he jumped, he wouldn't have anything to lose by kicking Allen out of the nest. He'd actually be better off, since he would then at least save the money he would otherwise be dumping down Allen's rat hole for the foreseeable future."

"But he didn't see it that way?"

"He most assuredly did not. He refused even to consider cutting Allen off. Absolutely refused. I'm sure you've seen that 'lord of the manor' look he gets! 'I can't do it,' he said to me, and all the while dear Allen was standing behind him, smirking over his shoulder. 'I simply cannot do it. So go ahead,' he told me. 'Do whatever you feel you must do. I cannot stop you.' And that was that, except for more gloating on my brother's part."

"But you haven't gone public yet. Or is that what you're doing now?"

Wetherston shook his head angrily, though the anger seemed directed more at himself than at Frank. "No, I haven't."

"Maybe he knew you wouldn't. Maybe that's why he hasn't gotten rid of Allen."

"No, he knew I meant it. It's something else. Allen has

another hold on him, a hold even stronger than this Shriver idiocy. God knows what it is, but Allen has something up his sleeve. He can make our father do whatever he wants. Including, I very much suspect, making him change his will so that Allen will inherit everything. Everything he wants to inherit, that is.''

''So what you're worried about is the possibility that you'll be disinherited.''

''Totally irrelevant!'' Wetherston snapped.

''Several million dollars is rarely irrelevant, Mr. Wetherston.''

Wetherston glared at Frank, but then sighed. ''Very well. If you must know, 'furious' would be closer to the truth than 'worried.' After the work I've put in, the crap I've put up with, the ulcers I've developed, I deserve to inherit every red cent. And if the day comes when I do inherit it, that's the day that Allen is cut off without a penny! But that's not why I'm here. I'm here because, while I may be furious about the possibility of being screwed out of what I have coming to me, I am worried about my father. I'm afraid that, once the will is changed—if it hasn't been changed already—he may not have long to live.''

''I'm afraid I don't follow your reasoning,'' Frank lied, maintaining what he hoped was a neutral tone. ''Your father isn't ill, is he?''

Wetherston snorted. ''Ill? Hardly. But isn't it obvious? I would think that you, with your—your 'feelings' about how your friend Cameron could never have stolen that money and how my brother, just by virtue of his presence in the county, probably did steal it—I would think that you, of all people, would understand.''

''Go on,'' Frank said when Wetherston fell into a glowering silence.

''For God's sake, Sheriff! Do I have to spell it out for you? Are you telling me you're that naive? Are you—''

Wetherston broke off, his eyes widening in a look of sudden comprehension. "But of course," he said, a bitter smile twisting his lips and hardening his eyes. "Of course you've considered it. You probably have it all figured out, your mind all made up. But you want me to say it. That's why you're putting on this pathetic I-don't-know-what-you're-talking-about act! You want me, as a family member, to say that I have come to the same conclusions that you have. Or perhaps, like Allen, you just want to humiliate me. Either way, you want me to suggest that my brother is not only the blackmailer that we've all come to admire but a murderer as well."

Wetherston moved his shoulders in what was more of a twitch than the casual shrug he intended it to be. "Very well, if that's the way you want it, why not? For the record, then— would you care to tape my words, Sheriff? Or have someone come in to witness them and take notes? No? Very well, for the record, I, Garrick Wetherston, formally suggest to you, Sheriff Frank Decker, that my brother Allen Wetherston is not only blackmailing our father Nathaniel Wetherston but is very likely responsible for the death of Willis Ardly. Therefore I further suggest that, having proven himself capable of the simple murder of a stranger, he may very well graduate to patricide, when and if he gets our father's will revised to his satisfaction. Is that what you wanted to hear, Sheriff?"

"And Lou Cameron?"

"I don't doubt that Allen killed your friend Cameron, too. God only knows why, or what he did with the body."

Frank's stomach and chest seemed to fill with something leaden while an oddly detached corner of his mind marveled at the reaction. After all, the idea that Lou Cameron was dead was far from new. Frank had suspected it since the day after the disappearance, and when Ardly's body had been found, the suspicion had become a virtual certainty. And today, after finding Leander's name in the Carrothers paper and reading through the material at the museum, he even thought he knew why Lou and Ardly had been killed.

And yet this was the first time the words had been spoken aloud in his presence, and, somehow, that made a difference.

"You could be right, of course," Frank said quietly, "but what do you want me to do?"

"Do?" Wetherston snorted again. "What I want you to do is arrest Allen and put the son of a bitch away for life, or better, shoot him down in cold blood after you trick him into trying to escape. But I suppose those are not, in modern business parlance, viable options at this point in time, at least not for a painfully ethical public official such as yourself. Or is moral the word that I want?"

"It's good that you understand the situation."

"Oh, I understand the situation all right! Don't worry about that! Dear Allen has all the cards, that's what the situation is!" Wetherston shook his head, as much in despair as in anger. "I've worked my ass off for the past fifteen years for nothing, and my brother's probably going to kill our father any day now, and there's not a damned thing I can do about it!"

"What about the will? Have you asked your father if he's changed it?"

"To what purpose? If Allen can force him to change the will, he can force him to lie about it just as easily. And then, when Allen inherits everything, he can put on one of his wide-eyed acts and claim he's as surprised as anyone that a black sheep like himself was even mentioned in the will, let alone named principal beneficiary. 'The old man must've had some black sheep genes himself,'" Wetherston mimicked.

"Have you warned your father? Have you told him you're afraid his life is in danger?"

Wetherston shook his head. "We haven't been communicating all that well these last few days."

"Don't you think you should find a way? If you really believe your brother's planning—"

"I know I should warn him, damn it. I know!"

"But instead of warning him, you're warning me."

"I thought you should know. You're the goddamn sheriff. I thought you might have some vague idea what could be done to protect him, but obviously I was wrong!"

"I might have a reason to protect him," Frank snapped, "if I was getting the whole story."

"How much more do you want, for God's sake? I've already accused my brother of two murders! And blackmail."

"Accusations aren't proof, any more than my own gut reactions are. If Allen killed Ardly, why did he kill him? What proof do you have? If he killed Lou Cameron, why did he kill him? What proof do you have? If he's blackmailing your father with something worse than the Shriver business, what is that something? How can you be sure there even is anything worse?"

Wetherston laughed, a sharp, humorless bark. "I'm a little short on proof of murder, Sheriff, but if there's one thing in this whole screwed up mess that I'm absolutely positive about, it's that Allen is controlling our father like a puppet."

"Why? And how the hell can you be so positive it's because he's blackmailing him with this 'something worse'?"

"Because I've already tried to use 'something worse' on him myself! And it didn't faze him! He still wouldn't give Allen the boot. So Allen has to have his hands on one terrific trump card."

Frank blinked. Could Cameron and Ardly have come to Garrick rather than Nathaniel with their discovery? He had been assuming that Allen had found out about Leander's bigamy, maybe from Cameron and Ardly, maybe by listening at keyholes, and was using that as the "something worse." But if that was what Garrick had threatened Nathaniel with—

"What was your 'something worse'?" Frank asked.

For several seconds Wetherston was totally still, as if only then realizing what he had said. Then he shook his head and laughed. This time, despite the bitterness of the sound, it contained a trace of genuine amusement.

"What the hell," he said with a shrug. His whole body

seemed suddenly to relax. Pulling in a deep breath, he closed his eyes and leaned back against the door, his face angled upward toward a point on the ceiling above Frank's head. After nearly another minute of silence, he reached into his jacket pocket and extracted the ever-present bottle of chalky liquid, now almost empty, and took a swallow. Despite the air conditioning in the office, his face was beaded with sweat.

"I'm listening," Frank said.

"And I'm gay." Wetherston shook his head. "God, how I hate that word. I cannot imagine anything more infuriating or inappropriate—unless, of course, someone were to call my beloved brother 'straight.'"

Frank blinked, more from surprise than anything else. He'd been so locked into thinking in terms of the discoveries about Leander that he hadn't even considered anything else. "You're a homosexual, then?" he finally said.

"Brilliant deduction, Sheriff Sherlock," Garrick said with a forced laugh. "I thought that's what I just said. However, if it's just that you wish me to use the old-fashioned, if somewhat clinical, term, that's fine with me. It is certainly preferable to that idiotic euphemism currently in vogue. So yes, I am homosexual. But not a—what is the term? 'Practicing?' I am not a 'practicing' homosexual, in the same sense that the Pope is not—allegedly—a 'practicing' heterosexual. When one's name and face are as well known as mine, and the town is as small as Whitford, there are few opportunities for practice, let alone perfection. Which, perhaps, accounts for my total lack of gaiety in recent years."

"And your homosexuality is the 'something worse' that you threatened your father with?"

"Precisely. Although, to be totally truthful, I don't consider it all that much worse. In fact, I've always considered myself a pillar of virtue compared to my dear, 'straight' brother. Or compared to any number of the businessmen and politicians I've been forced to deal with—and set up to get laid—over the years."

"And your father? How does he feel about it?"

Wetherston laughed. "You sound like the psychiatrist he brought in a few years ago! 'How do you feel about that, Garrick?'" he mimicked. "'Your father feels your sexual preference makes you roughly equivalent to a garden slug, but how do you feel about it?'"

"How do you feel about it? Angry enough to kill him?"

For an instant, Wetherston's eyes hardened, but then he shook his head and smiled tiredly. "Occasionally, yes. But never for long. My father, that is. My brother is another matter."

"What about your wife?"

"What about her, Sheriff? Do I feel like killing her? How does she feel about my sexual persuasion? Or perhaps how and why do I have a wife?"

"Your choice."

Another laugh, tinged with real amusement. "Very well. I seem to recall that at one point you bemoaned the fact that you weren't getting 'the whole story' from me, so you shall have it." Pushing off from the door, Wetherston picked up the straight back chair, turned it around and lowered himself onto it, legs bracketing the back, arms folded and resting on the top. The jacket pocket with the nearly empty bottle of ulcer medicine in it thumped against the back of the chair as he leaned forward and rested his chin on his folded arms, his eyes pointed in the general direction of Frank's desktop.

"For a start, Gina knows the horrible truth about me. She was told of my predilections when she was purchased."

"Purchased?"

"Purchased. Just the way Shriver was purchased to be a husband to one of Allen's discards. 'Marry him, manage to bear a son, preferably his, and you'll never have to worry about money again. Or about him.' So far she hasn't managed that second goal. But, then, she isn't much more enamored of the necessary procedure than I am—which I've always assumed was one of the reasons she accepted my father's offer so readily in the first place. In any event, she has not been overly zealous in her efforts to avail herself of the Wetherston seed. She's been quite content to tour the world on an almost Allen-like expense account and stop in at the old homestead just often enough to keep up appearances and to placate Father by taking another shot at motherhood.'' His eyebrows lifted. ''Each shot has to be reported, by the way.'' He chuckled. ''At least he doesn't insist on documenting them with videotapes. Yet. But lately he's been stepping up the pressure and she's becoming more aggressive. And resourceful. She has even suggested artificial insemination, but Father, always on the suspicious side, is afraid I might slip in a ringer, so to speak, and that would never do. The genuine article or nothing. And if you're wondering why Allen's genuine but illegitimate article is being concealed rather than celebrated, you'll have to ask my father. I'm sure he has some arcane reason.''

''And you went along with your father and his 'purchase'?'' Frank asked uncomfortably when Garrick fell silent.

''I'm ashamed to say, I did. Or, more accurately, I didn't put up much of a fight. Oh, there was token resistance for a time, but that was all. I knew he'd get his way one way or another, so—''

He straightened, raising his eyes to Frank's for the first time since sitting down. ''Do you remember a boy named Mike Grey? His father, Albert, worked for the same company that employed Bob Shriver. There was a younger brother, Victor, about your age.''

''A year ahead of me, I think,'' Frank said. ''All I remember about him, though, is that the family moved away in the middle of a school year.''

''Precisely. And would you like to know why the family moved away?''

''Why don't you tell me?''

''Albert Grey was fired. He was given a comparable job two states away with a company my father owned stock in and had inordinate influence over. But there was a condition. Grey had to move his entire family there immediately and never return to Whitford. So of course he did.''

''And the reason he was fired?''

''Mike. And me. Father found out. Caught us doing our thing—things, actually—right there on the old plantation.'' A faint laugh. ''He damn near had apoplexy. But he had his way, and soon. I never saw Mike again, or heard from him. I don't even know if he's still alive.'' He shrugged. ''An object lesson in how Nathaniel Wetherston gets his way.''

''Until now?''

''Until now, Sheriff. Until Allen hit him with whatever his secret weapon is.''

Slowly, Garrick Wetherston stood up, turning the chair as he rose and setting it down facing the desk. ''So, that is the 'whole story' you wished to hear. As much of it as I am privy to, at any rate. Does it help? Does it give you something that will allow you to protect the father that, despite all that he's done to me—and to God knows how many others—I still would not care to see die quite yet, at least not by Allen's hand? Or does it just make you wonder if he's more in danger from me than from dear Allen?''

Without waiting for an answer, Wetherston wheeled about and pushed through the door. Frank stood and turned to look down through his office's lone window. After a few seconds, Wetherston emerged into the hazy, late afternoon heat. Pulling the ever-present bottle from his jacket pocket, he held it to his lips as he walked toward the gray Lincoln at the far end of the jail's parking strip. Frank couldn't tell if he grimaced or not.

A HALF HOUR LATER, Steve Waymore had replaced Phil Biggs, and Harry Truitt had come by to pick up Frank's mother, who had stopped at the office on her way out with a reminder that the microwave was ready and waiting. Frank, however, was still seated behind his desk, still trying to sort through not only the facts but his feelings about them.

Garrick Wetherston's "confession," he had to admit, had made him uncomfortable for a moment, but only a moment. Even the worst homophobe couldn't believe that Garrick's homosexuality, "practicing" or not, put him anywhere near his brother's gutter level.

Garrick's anger was another matter, however. Regardless of how justified it was, it had been festering inside him, building up pressure for over a decade. And it had been compounded for just as long by Allen's outrageous behavior and their father's monumentally expensive refusal to simply cut him off and tell him to do his worst. Like the Watergate cover-up that had turned what some had called "a second rate burglary" into a national trauma, Nathaniel's continuing cover-up had allowed Allen to grow from an irresponsible teenager into an arrogant hedonist who thought he could get away with anything, probably including murder.

And it had turned Garrick into—what? Someone so bitter that he didn't care what happened to him as long as he took his brother—and father?—down with him? Someone so angry he would do anything, including kill two strangers and his own father, in order to make sure he inherited what he thought he deserved?

Even if Garrick's suspicions about the will were right, however, Frank didn't think that Nathaniel Wetherston was in any immediate danger. Allen was already in a position to get whatever he wanted from his father, for as long as he wanted, so why should he, in effect, kill the goose from which he was squeezing an endless supply of golden eggs? Making Nathaniel change the will, though, made sense. If Garrick were to inherit everything, now or twenty years from now, Allen would be out in the cold in short order, so he had to guard against that eventuality. It did not, however, make the least bit of sense for him to hasten Nathaniel Wetherston's end.

On the other hand, if Garrick was the killer, and his pre-

sentation, well-acted though it had been, had been strictly for
Frank's benefit, all bets were off. Garrick had, perhaps dis-
ingenuously, suggested his own guilt when he'd tossed off his
seemingly casual parting remark about how all the things he'd
just told Frank might make him seem more dangerous to his
father than Allen. Could the remark have been part of his
plan? Knowing that, in any detailed investigation, much of
what he had told Frank would be discovered anyway, he could
say, when Nathaniel turned up dead, "Do you really think I'd
be stupid enough to say something like that if I'd really intended to kill him?"

But of course it was a possibility.

Just as it was a possibility that Nathaniel himself was the
killer, particularly if, as Frank was now almost certain, Lou
Cameron and Willis Ardly had discovered the same things
Sunday afternoon that Frank had discovered a few hours ago.
Nathaniel, in fact, had come immediately to mind when Frank
had seen Leander Wetherston's name in the Carrothers *Sentinel* and realized what it must mean. With Nathaniel's ob-
session for protecting the family name, he would certainly be
the one most affected by the discovery, the one most desperate
to keep it quiet. Frank had no trouble imagining Nathaniel
being caught in the act—or even helped in it—by Allen. Being either a witness or an accomplice to murder would certainly give Allen that stronger hold over his father that Garrick
was so positive existed. It was hard to imagine anything
stronger.

Allen—at least Allen acting alone rather than in concert
with or as agent for Nathaniel—struck Frank as less likely,
but he wasn't about to rule it out, particularly since Allen
would have required far less in the way of motive than either
Nathaniel or Garrick. If Lou and Ardly had come to him instead of to Nathaniel, for instance, he wouldn't have cared
about the family name or any such esoteric foolishness, but
he would have instantly recognized the power the secret
would give him over Nathaniel, vastly more than the Shriver

episode had ever given him. Allen had never before murdered anyone—at least, not to Frank's knowledge—but Frank could easily imagine him doing so if he thought he could get away with it and it would give him sole possession of such a secret.

But if Allen were the guilty party, Nathaniel would still have to have known about it. He would have to have known from the start that Lou Cameron was dead. Why else would he have invented that cock and bull story about the embezzlement?

And the same logic would apply if Garrick were responsible. Nathaniel would have to have known, or he wouldn't have made up the embezzlement story.

Sighing irritably at his inability to come to any definite conclusion, Frank stood up and glowered at the clock. It was almost time to start for Springfield to meet the Ardly boy. And, he hoped, get some answers.

But it was also late enough for Gordon Bailey to be home, he thought, as that last call from Irene flashed through his mind. What he should have done, he realized now, was drive by the Krueger lot right after Irene's call and talk to Bailey, try to set up a time for the two of them and Beth to get together and have a heart-to-heart and try to figure out the best tack to take with Irene. But, what with the Leander discoveries and the Garrick confrontation, the Irene problem had been shoved onto the back burner for the afternoon.

Picking up the phone, he dialed the Bailey home. His daughter answered with an anxious, "Mom?"

"Afraid not, Pint Size," he said. "Is something wrong?"

"Probably not, but— Look, Daddy, maybe you better talk to Gordon."

"First tell me what's going on. Where's your mother?"

"I don't know. Look, Daddy, you better talk to Gordon. Mom was really down this morning, worse than yesterday, when I told her about maybe moving in with you and about the college money and stuff. And Gordon explained about that, by the way. About the money, I mean. He said I should tell you. But Mom—'' She broke off. "Here's Gordon," she said. A second later, Bailey's voice came over the line.

"Sheriff?"

"That's right. What's going on over there?"

"I wish I knew. Have you heard from Irene today?"

"She called me at the museum this afternoon, yes. That's why I called. But where is she? Beth said—''

"We don't know," Bailey said. "The last I saw of her— Did she say anything to you about where she was going?"

"Not a word. But let's back up and get organized here. What happened? When she called me, she was practically screaming, accusing me of dragging you down to the jail and forcing you to help me steal Beth away from her."

"That part's easy enough to explain," Bailey said with a sigh. "Some friend of Irene's saw me talking to you outside the jail yesterday and told her about it. She just jumped to all the wrong conclusions. She came storming down to the lot this afternoon, probably right after she got through yelling at you, and I told her I'd gone down to see you on my own, no coercion or anything. But when I admitted what we'd been talking about—you know, about Beth moving back in with you—she blew up all over again, worse than when Beth first brought it up. Scared a couple potential customers right off the lot. Accused me of sneaking around behind her back, which I guess I was, really. And plotting against her, which I guess I was, too, the way she looks at it. Anyway, she went charging out of there, really burning rubber, and that's the last I saw of her. I tried to stop her, but she practically ran me over with her car."

"You don't know where she went?"

"No idea. I asked her, you know, 'Where the hell you think you're going?', but all she did was yell out the window, something about going home, which she didn't do. Or if she did, she either didn't stick around long or didn't bother answering the phone. I called a dozen times, but there wasn't any answer, and when Beth got home around four, the house was empty. And unlocked, which isn't like Irene, either.''

"She didn't leave a note or anything?"

"If she did, we haven't found it, and believe me, we've looked. I don't suppose you could put out one of those APB things? I know people can't be declared officially missing for a day or two, but since you're the sheriff and you used to be married to her—''

"I'll figure out something," Frank said. "You're sure she said she was going home when she left you at the lot?"

"I don't remember her exact words. I was pretty steamed, too, her barging in where I work and scaring customers away. But she definitely said she was going home. And told me where I could go, too, which also begins with an 'H'. But what difference does that make? I mean, she didn't go home, no matter what she said.''

"Maybe she did, only— Look, it's a long shot, but it's worth checking. I'll—''

"What's worth checking? Damn it, Sheriff—''

"Sorry. It's like this. Irene and I had a few blowouts ourselves when we were married. A lot, in fact. It's no secret. Sometimes, she'd jump in the car and take off, like she did with you. Half the time, she'd say she was 'going home,' only she meant to her mother's place down in Cedar River. A few times, back before Beth was born, she actually got halfway there before she cooled down and decided to turn around and come back. Maybe that's what she meant this time, too.''

"Her mother? I didn't think they were that close. She was at the wedding, but I've never even known them to talk on the phone since. And whenever I suggest driving down for a visit, Irene—''

"They weren't that close when we were married, either. Maybe that's why she never got all the way there. But that's still what she did, whether it makes any sense or not. So unless you have any better ideas—''

"No, no, I don't. I didn't mean to sound like I did. Sorry.''

"I know. It's okay. Everyone's on edge for one reason or another. Look, why don't you give her mother a call? Or, no, have Beth make the call. That way, if Irene's there and picks up the phone for some reason, she's not as likely to explode again."

"If you think it's best—"

"At this point, I don't know what the hell's best, but it's worth a try. Take a shot at it and give me a call back right away. I have to start for Springfield, but I'll stick around until I get your call."

"Will do," Bailey said. "Thanks."

Sighing, Frank glanced at his watch and decided this would be a good time to follow through on his promise to stick something in the microwave. He was taking his first bite of the frozen cheeseburger he had just thawed and was wishing he had another of the chili dogs he'd gotten at Carrothers for lunch when he heard the phone ring in the jail.

Swallowing the first bite and abandoning the rest, he punched the button that fed the call to the living quarters phone.

"Decker."

"I called." It was Bailey. "Irene was there. Had been there, I mean. I talked to her mother, and she said that she'd just got home herself, but her next door neighbor told her that Irene had come over to her house—the neighbor's house—an hour or so ago."

"The neighbor's house? What was she doing there?"

"According to the neighbor, Irene wanted to come in and wait there for her mother. Does that make any sense to you?"

"Not a whole hell of a lot. But she didn't wait?"

"No, but— Look, Sheriff, I'm starting to get scared. The neighbor said she—Irene, I mean—was acting kind of funny."

"Funny? How?"

"Didn't say. Just 'funny.' And when the neighbor didn't invite her in right that second, Irene just turned around and walked back to her car and drove off. Look, Sheriff, you don't suppose she's having a breakdown of some kind? I mean, she's been ticked off at me before, but never anything like she was today. I never thought she'd be the kind to have one, but—''

''I don't know,'' Frank said. ''I never thought so either. But something crazy's going on with her.''

''What about one of those APB's I asked about? She's not missing, but if she's acting weird and not coming home—''

''I couldn't do one officially, but I'll do something. I know she drives a five- or six-year-old red Pinto, but do you have the license number?''

''Somewhere around here, but—'' He broke off. In the background Frank could hear Beth calling out some numbers, which Bailey repeated into the phone.

''What was she wearing?''

''Damned if I know. I never notice that sort of thing. Blouse and slacks, I think. That's what she always wears.''

''Any idea the color?''

''None. Sorry.''

''Okay,'' Frank said, ''I guess that'll have to do. Like I said, I have to head for Springfield in a few minutes, but if you hear from her before I check in with you again, call. They can reach me on the radio.''

''Okay.''

''And I'll let you know if I find out anything.''

Breaking the connection, Frank consulted the sheet of phone numbers tacked to the bulletin board and located the Cedar River sheriff's department. He dialed.

''Sheriff's office,'' a gravelly sounding voice came on the line after a single ring. ''Overstreet speaking.''

''This is Frank Decker, Sheriff,'' Frank began. ''I'm—''

''After yesterday, I know who you are. Heard about your little problem up there. What can I do for you?''

''A small favor,'' Frank said, ''but it doesn't have anything to do with the murder.''

"Sorry to hear that. Found out what happened yet?"

"I've got some suspicions, but until I get something to back them up, like evidence, I'd rather not talk about them."

"I understand. Can't say I'm overjoyed, but I understand. Now what was the favor you wanted that doesn't have anything to do with your murder?"

"I'd appreciate it if you could keep an eye out for a car," Frank said, going on to give a description and license number.

"That license number's from your part of the state," Overstreet said. "Whose is it?"

"Her name's Irene Bailey. Her mother lives in Cedar River," Frank explained. "She was down there earlier this afternoon, acting a little strange, and her family up here's getting worried."

"She's not missing, then? Or wanted for desertion or anything?"

"No. It's just that—"

"Look, Decker, I can be as cooperative as the next guy, but ain't you jumpin' the gun a little? I don't run a family counseling service here, at least no more'n I have to."

"I realize that, but all I'm asking is that if one of your people sees the car, give me a call. That's all. Or her husband."

"You a friend of this Bailey? Just doin' him a favor?"

"Partly. But the woman's my ex-wife, and our daughter's getting worried, too, so—"

"Family affair, huh? Okay, I guess it'll be all right, 's long's you don't want her picked up or anything like that."

"Nothing like that. We just want to be sure she's all right."

"Okay, good enough. What's she look like? You know, so we can be sure it's her driving the car and not someone that's ripped it off."

Quickly, Frank began a description, but when he got to the curly red hair, Overstreet stopped him.

"She's not wearin' a rust-colored blouse and black slacks, is she?" he asked.

"She's wearing blouse and slacks, but I don't know the color. They could be rust and black. Have you seen her?"

"Maybe. Hang on a sec'. Hey, Bernie," Overstreet yelled, not bothering to cover the phone with his hand, "you remember that redhead that was in here an hour or two ago?"

"Sure thing," a faint, echoing voice said. "What about her?"

"Did she give a name or anything?"

"Not that I remember, why?"

"What'd she want?"

"Wanted to see a prisoner."

"Which one?"

"One we don't have and never did so far's I know. Bill or Phil something. Benson? Benton? Something like that. When I told her we didn't have anyone by that name, she just turned around and left. Acted kind of out it. Thought she might've been on something."

"You hear any of that, Decker?" Overstreet asked, lowering his voice to a normal level again.

"Most of it. Could that name she asked for have been Bender? Will Bender?"

"Hey, Bernie," Overstreet yelled, "how about 'Will Bender'?"

"Hey, yeah, I think that was it," Bernie answered in the distance.

"So, Decker," Overstreet said, going back to his telephone voice again, "looks like you were right. Now who's this Bender guy?"

"It doesn't make sense, but that's her stepfather's name. Trouble is, far's I know, he hasn't been anywhere near Cedar River for twenty years."

Overstreet was silent a moment. "See what you mean," he said. "Look, Decker, I tell you what. I'll tell the boys if they see her, they should radio in and keep an eye on her."

"I'd really appreciate it, Sheriff."

"No problem. Maybe I'll check in with her mother, too. Her name still Bender?"

"Florence Bender, yes. That'd be a help, too."

"Like I said, no problem. Least we can do, a little inter-departmental cooperation."

Frank thanked him and hung up. Inter-departmental curiosity was more like it, but he'd take whatever help he could get. Since he'd heard Bernie casually toss the names out, his worry had escalated a notch.

Irene's fits of anger were one thing. They'd been fairly frequent, even if there'd never been one as violent as the one today. But going back to her hometown, where she hadn't set foot in more than fifteen years despite a lot of false starts, was something else. As Bailey had said, a little scary.

Grimacing, Frank glanced at the clock and realized he was going to be late to meet Ardly's plane. Calling Bailey to let him know about the Bender episode would have to wait until he got back.

FIFTEEN

THE DRIVE TO Springfield took less than an hour according to the patrol car's dashboard clock. It was almost exclusively through a series of hills and valleys that Frank normally touted as some of the best scenery the Midwest had to offer, particularly when the lengthening shadows and reddish tinges of an approaching sunset gave them a new and different look every minute.

This time, however, the trip seemed to drag on forever, and Frank, his mind switching erratically back and forth between his ex-wife and whatever was going on with the Wetherstons, barely noticed anything beyond the highway and the dashboard dials and lights. Muggy air whipped in through the windows and vents, leaving a sticky film on any exposed skin.

As the last of the sunlight disappeared in the west, the off-ramp he had been watching for appeared. He followed it down to the semi-rural, ill-lighted surface street that fronted the Springfield airport. Ten minutes later, he was watching through the floor-to-ceiling windows of the waiting room as passengers descended a set of roll-away steps from a prop-driven DC-3 and walked across the fifty yards of fluorescent-lighted tarmac toward the grungy backside of the terminal building.

Frank kept his eye on a bushy-mustached, very English looking young man wearing glasses and a tweedy, three-piece suit. He was about to approach the man when a young woman hurried up and threw her arms around him. As the two walked away, hand in hand, a voice came from behind Frank.

"Sheriff Decker?"

Frank turned abruptly to find a clean-shaven, jacketless young man an inch or so over six feet looking at him hesitantly from just inside the entrance. He didn't look at all English and he didn't look much like the picture of Willis Ardly that had appeared in the *Gazette*. The accent, however, was decidedly English, even in the two words he had spoken.

"That's right," Frank admitted, feeling foolish for his mistake. "You must be Clayton Ardly."

"Right." He glanced around. "I have a case to pick up."

"Back this way and downstairs," Frank said. He had seen the baggage pickup area on his way in.

As they walked, Frank resisted the urge to skip all formalities and ask immediately about the papers. Instead, he didn't know why, he found himself asking about the flight, the weather in England versus the weather here, and a half dozen other trivialities. Finally, as they were at last in the squad car and easing into the stream of headlights the expressway had become, it was Ardly who brought up the subject they had both been avoiding.

"Have you learned anything more about my father's death? Do you know who killed him?"

"I have an idea," Frank said, "but— Look, did you find those papers we talked about?"

"I have them in the case. Are they actually important?"

"Very likely, yes. What about the ones your father took with him?"

"As best as I can tell, he didn't take them with him. He made copies and took those."

Frank breathed a sigh of relief. "What are they, then? Have you looked through them yet?"

"A bit, but I haven't read them all," Ardly said with a rueful smile. "Some of the handwriting is truly atrocious."

"But you do have them? And you know generally what they are?"

Ardly nodded in the darkness of the squad car. "As I said

on the phone, Sheriff, they're all to do with this ancestor of ours. Mostly letters from him, as a matter of fact. My great-great-grandfather, as it turns out. At least that's what Aunt Meg says.''

"Aunt Meg?''

"My father's Aunt Meg, actually. I'm most sorry I didn't think of her when you asked me who would know more about this business Dad was involved in. Aunt Meg's something of a family historian, and Dad had been conferring with her for some time, apparently. Though he never told me,'' he added hastily. "And I'm afraid, no more interested than I am in that sort of thing, her name just never crossed my mind until I found the papers themselves.''

"She does know all about this research your father was doing, then?''

"Oh, yes. In fact, the papers and the photos are hers, not Dad's. Oh, some of them used to be his, she said, but over the years she's been—well, as I said, she's sort of the historian of the family, and she's been collecting everything she can. I remember Dad rambling on about it, but I never paid much attention, so—''

"That's all right, Mr. Ardly,'' Frank interrupted the apology. "But what I'd like to know…'' He paused, swallowing to calm the butterflies that had been working up to a frenzied pitch in his stomach. "What I'd like to know is your great-great-grandfather's name. It wasn't by any chance Leander Wetherston, was it?''

From the sudden intake of breath Frank heard from his passenger, he knew he had been right.

"How the bloody hell did you know that?'' Ardly asked sharply. "It wasn't in that list you read me the other day.''

Briefly, Frank explained how he had found Leander Wetherston's name in the Carrothers paper and how, "all of a sudden, it made a sort of sense.''

"But not to me, Sheriff,'' Ardly said.

"There's more, a lot more,'' Frank said, and went on to

explain about Leander Wetherston's American descendants and the fortune they had amassed.

"But he was already married!" Ardly protested. "To my great-great-grandmother Augusta."

"Exactly," Frank said. "At the very least, Leander Wetherston was hardly the saint that his American descendants were told he was, nor was he the failure that his English family was told. For starters, he was a bigamist. And the money he used to start the bank—well, I have no idea how international law works, but there's a remote chance that you and the other British descendants may conceivably have a claim on some part of the present Wetherston wealth."

Ardly was silent for nearly a mile. "Surely you must be joking," he said finally. "Not that I wouldn't welcome a few thousand pounds falling out of the sky, but after a hundred years?"

Frank shrugged. "As I said, it's a remote chance, but your father must have had thoughts along those lines. The evening after he found out about this, he talked to a lawyer here— unofficially, at a party, but still he talked to one, and probably asked about international law."

Clayton Ardly shook his head vigorously. "No, this whole bloody affair is impossible," he said. "I haven't read nearly all of the letters he wrote to my great-great-grandmother, but in those I did read, he spoke in no uncertain terms about sending for her. It was only his death that prevented it. No, I simply cannot believe it."

"He was probably just stringing her along," Frank said. "If he hadn't been killed, he probably would have kept finding one excuse after another to delay things."

"But why? If he were deserting her, why write to her at all? Why not simply disappear?"

"At the moment, I haven't the faintest idea," Frank admitted. "Maybe I'll have a better idea when I read the letters."

BACK IN WHITFORD, while Ardly registered at the Arlington—the same hotel, at least in name, that Leander Wetherston had stayed at—Frank called Gordon Bailey, who answered before the first ring was completed.

"Bailey," he said briskly.

"Any news?" Frank asked.

"Oh, yes, Mr. Anderson," Bailey said quickly. "I'm glad you called. That deal we were talking about, it worked out fine. I'll have all the details for you tomorrow."

"Anderson? This is Sheriff—"

"That's right, Mr. Anderson, the Pinto you asked about at the lot today, there's no problem any longer."

"She came back, then?" Frank asked, finally realizing what Bailey was doing.

"Precisely, Mr. Anderson. I'll be in touch tomorrow morning. You can come by the lot and we can get the paperwork started."

"I'll do that. But if you get a chance in the meantime, give me a call. I'm at the Arlington on the Cameron business. I'll leave word at the desk they're to put you through."

"I'm sorry, Mr. Anderson, but tomorrow morning would be better for everyone concerned."

"As you wish."

Frank pressed the disconnect, phoned the jail and told Steve to call Sheriff Overstreet in Cedar River and let him know that the "non-missing person" had made it safely home. Hanging up, he turned to Ardly, who was waiting patiently by the registration desk. "Do you feel up to going through those letters tonight? I know it's five or six in the morning by your clock, but—"

"No, I'm wide awake, Sheriff, especially after that bloody good shock you gave me. If what you said is true— Well, once someone has my attention, I'm not one to dally. I'm as anxious as you to get to the bottom of this affair."

In Ardly's room, they spent the next three hours going over Leander's yellowed, fading letters, Frank growing more and more at home with the twisted scrawl. Written in the stilted style of the day, they were "newsy" letters, although the news—mostly about his rapid success in the local business community—all struck Frank as sounding more than a little egocentric, not unlike the kind that he imagined Nathaniel Wetherston would write. There was almost nothing in the letters about anyone not connected with the bank, nothing about social activities or friends. Considering the fact that his social activities consisted primarily of an extra-marital courtship followed by a bigamous marriage, however, that was hardly surprising.

There was, however, one repeated exception, but it was as much of a puzzle as the reason for the letters themselves. Again and again, Leander referred to someone named Jeremiah Ingram, whom he insisted in almost every letter was his "best friend in the colonies" and someone whom she would have to meet as soon as possible after she arrived. At first, the name was only annoyingly familiar to Frank, but after the third mention, he remembered where he had seen it before: In the 1883 editions of both the Carrothers and the Whitford papers. It had been Ingram's death that had almost crowded the visiting English off the front page in Carrothers. An obituary had also appeared in the *Gazette* a day or two later.

To Ardly, the name meant nothing at all, but Frank resolved to read through the *Gazette* obituary as soon as the newspaper office opened in the morning. It might even be worth a second trip to Carrothers to see what the more extensive coverage there could tell him. For instance, did Ingram have a son of the same name? Otherwise, since he had died weeks before Leander's arrival in Whitford—and at least a day before the tour group's stopover in Carrothers—how could Leander Wetherston even have known him, let alone become his best friend?

As for Leander's intention to bring his British wife over, there was nothing in the letters to indicate that he had been stringing her along. On the contrary, in a letter dated only two

days before his death, he actually set a date, less than a month
away. He had already taken steps to purchase the tickets, and
would send them in another letter within a week. He included
a complete itinerary, including the steamship schedule across
the Atlantic and the schedule of the train that would take her
directly to the station in Whitford. Apparently only his death
kept the tickets from being sent.

Leander must have been planning something, but there was
no indication in the letters as to what it could possibly have
been, unless it was his own destruction, which would surely
have been the result if he had carried through with his avowed
intention to bring his British wife to the American Whitford.

Yawning, Frank picked up the final letter in the packet. He
blinked. His eyelids had been getting heavier with each of
Leander's repetitious monologues, but now, suddenly, he was
wide awake. Eagerly, he began to read.

The letter, dated approximately three months after Leander's death, was signed by one Jameson Weller, who claimed
to have been an "associate" of Leander Wetherston's in his
"American business undertakings." According to the letter,
Weller had taken charge of Leander's affairs after his death.
Weller, the letter said, was in the process of liquidating Leander's holdings in the bank, which had fallen on hard times
subsequent to, perhaps precipitated by, Leander's untimely
death. Weller would, the letter concluded, forward the "re-
grettably meager" proceeds of that liquidation to Leander's
widow as soon as the liquidation proceedings were complete.

"Aunt Meg said something about that," Ardly volunteered
when Frank read the letter to him. "According to her, the
return of this money was something of a family folk tale. She
says she's always found it hard to believe that anyone in a
greedy country like America—her words; no offense meant—
could ever be as honest as this Weller person appeared to be.
She always suspected an ulterior motive. Weller could have
kept the money as easy as not, she always said, and now,
from what you've told me about the success the bank actually

enjoyed, it seems Aunt Meg was right. This Weller person must have sent the money and made up that story about the business failure so that my great-great-grandmother wouldn't come over here and learn the truth. And claim what was right-fully hers."

"Agreed," Frank said. "It was cheap insurance. However, it wasn't any 'Jameson Weller' who sent it. I doubt that any such person ever existed."

Ardly blinked. "I don't understand. The money did come, at least according to Aunt Meg."

"I'm sure it did," Frank said, nodding. "But it wasn't sent by anyone named Jameson Weller. You see, I just got through reading hundreds of pages of this same handwriting this af-ternoon—in the diaries of Leander's American widow, Dora Wetherston."

"The American widow? But why— How would she have found out about his real wife? He certainly wouldn't have told her!" Ardly shook his head, running his long fingers through his lank, sandy hair in confusion.

"Your great-great-grandmother probably wrote to Leander when she stopped hearing from him, particularly when the tickets he had promised didn't show up. And the letter went to Dora; that's simple enough. Or maybe she found the earlier letters your great-great-grandmother had written to Leander, if he was careless—or arrogant—enough to keep them. But no matter how she found out, she obviously did find out, and she made up Weller and the story about the bank 'falling on hard times.' She had one hell of a motive for wanting to keep your great-great-grandmother away, and sending that letter and a little money was a simple, cheap, and almost foolproof way to do it."

And, Frank added to himself, this "repayment" certainly explained why Dora Wetherston had carried on so much about the "anonymous charities" to which Leander had supposedly donated. Most likely, she was simply covering up for the money she sent to the British widow. And the diaries of her months of marriage—Frank now felt sure they had been written well after Leander's death, after the discovery of the British widow. Like her public statements about Leander's goodness and brilliance, the diaries were just Dora Wetherston's way of not only covering up but of saving face.

All of which Lou Cameron had doubtless figured out even more quickly than Frank had. The envelope Jennie Cameron had seen Lou carrying must have been the copies of these same letters that Willis Ardly had brought with him. And Lou's excitement— What could be more exciting than a discovery that literally turned upside down the accepted story of how the county's richest family had gotten its start? He would have been bursting to talk about it, but he would also have been eager to learn as much as he could. In fact, the reason he had returned to the museum Sunday evening was probably to reread Dora Wetherston's diaries in light of this new knowledge, to reread them and see just how much he could read between the lines.

But he—and presumably Ardly—must also have gone to see Nathaniel Wetherston. No matter how eager Lou might have been to talk about the discovery, he wouldn't have spread it around indiscriminately, wouldn't even tell Jennie, apparently, before letting the Wetherstons know what was coming. In his innocent enthusiasm, he probably assumed they would be as fascinated as he was. It probably never crossed his mind that they could seriously object to making the information public. After all, it had all happened a hundred years ago and didn't have any real effect on the present, he would have thought, unless Ardly had brought up the subject of the possible claims the British descendants might have. And even then, Lou's enthusiasm wouldn't have been dampened, not for something like this, a hundred-year-old secret that no one, apparently not even the Wetherstons themselves, had ever suspected.

But the Wetherstons—or at least one of them—had reacted

with less than enthusiasm, and, very probably because of that reaction, Willis Ardly and presumably Lou Cameron were both dead.

A LITTLE BEFORE one a.m., Frank left an almost comatose Clayton Ardly in his room at the Arlington. Ardly had been awake more than twenty-four hours, most of them spent either in the air or waiting in various terminals, so it was no surprise when the burst of adrenalin brought on by the ''Weller'' discovery wore off and his exhaustion suddenly caught up with him.

Back at the jail, Frank himself was jarred wide awake when he entered the living quarters and found his mother and Harry Truitt in the kitchen holding hands while they waited for the microwave to finish warming up their midnight snack. For an uneasy moment, he started to back out of the door, but Truitt turned and waved him in.

''Hope you don't mind me bringin' your mom back so late,'' he said with a grin, ''but that movie—Deanna Durbin, would you believe it?—was so good we stayed to see it twice. Like I always say, they don't make 'em like they used to. And then we drove around looking for an ice cream store that was still open. Had to try half the towns in two counties before we found one.'' He laughed, and Frank couldn't help but think how much younger he looked and sounded. Monday morning, in the shambles of his garden, he had been an old man, but now there was an almost boyish quality to him, despite the lines in his face and the swollen joints of his fingers.

And his mother—her eyes were downcast, almost nervous, but there was something about her face, about the smile that flickered at the corners of her mouth and around her eyes as she tried, unsuccessfully and not too hard, to pull free from Truitt's grip.

Grinning, Frank sat down to join them.

SIXTEEN

"GOOD NEWS FROM the weatherman this morning, folks. Those upper air winds have finally shifted, and that cold front's heading in our direction. Strong possibility of thunderstorms by this evening, and tomorrow—''

Frank grinned at the radio. Sure, he'd have to swelter through most of the rest of the day as even more Gulf moisture was pumped up ahead of the front, but the sauna was on its way out—at last!

Perhaps unreasonably buoyed by the prospect of cooler weather, Frank went to see George Zartman, the county prosecutor, to try to get a search warrant for Nathaniel Wetherston's house and grounds. Not surprisingly, he didn't get it.

"Come on, Frank, get serious!" Zartman said when Frank had finished his sketchy presentation. "You know I can't give you a warrant based on some harebrained theories and a few old letters! Hell, you don't even know Cameron's been killed, for sure. How are you going to justify digging up anybody's yard, let alone the Wetherstons'?" He shook his head. "No, sir. For them, you get no warrant without a hell of a lot more, like say three or four very reliable eye witnesses who saw one of them shove Cameron's car into the gravel pit."

Back at his office, Frank found himself reluctantly fending off Del Richardson's phoned request for a "Wetherston update." As long as none of the Wetherstons went public with last century's dirty laundry, he wouldn't either.

Yet.

When Richardson hung up, Frank consulted the sheet of

phone numbers on the bulletin board and dialed the state crime lab. This time he got a more cooperative technician, who told him it would be Saturday morning before Ardly's body could be released and well into the following week before the complete autopsy results would be available.

"Can't you give me *anything?*" Frank complained.

"Well, let's see," the technician said. "Three bullet wounds, you saw those, I guess."

"I did," he acknowledged impatiently.

"Consistent with his having been shot by a passenger in the car," the technician went on. "As are the bloodstains on the car seat." Two of the shots wouldn't have been fatal, but the third, seemingly by sheer luck, had managed to slip between the ribs and puncture the heart. All three bullets had been recovered from the body, and one was in good enough shape to be matched to the .22 that had been in the gun case used to weight down the car's accelerator.

"Gun's about thirty years old," the technician told him. "No way you're gonna trace that baby. Rusted all to hell inside, too—whoever pulled the trigger was lucky it didn't blow up in his face."

As for Cameron's car, they had so far found nothing helpful or unexpected, particularly no fingerprints.

"Looked like everything had been wiped clean," the technician said. "We did find some bloodstains on that spade in the trunk. Doesn't match the victim's type, so someone else was doing a little bleeding in the area."

"Type O-positive?"

"Right. How—"

"The other probable victim," Frank said, his stomach twitching at the words. "His blood was O-positive."

A call to the county coroner garnered the news that the British consulate in Chicago had been contacted and it would be the middle of next week before all the paperwork and preparations could be completed so Ardly's body could actually be put on a plane for England.

Frank was about to head out to the Arlington to talk to Ardly when Gordon Bailey called. He was at Krueger's. Frank heard the worry in his voice instantly.

"Last night when Irene got back, I thought she was okay," Bailey said. "She'd calmed down—wasn't even yelling at me anymore. And she was trying to patch things up with Beth, talking about spending more time with her, that sort of thing. But then this morning— Well, I asked her about Cedar River. She acted like she didn't know what I was talking about. And she started getting ticked off again. I know I shouldn't have, but I told her I'd talked to her mother, and that her mother said she had been there, or at least next door."

"And she denied it?"

"Without so much as a blink. Acted like she thought I was crazy. And then when I asked her where she had gone after our little shouting match at the lot yesterday, she got really uptight, said she just 'drove around,' didn't go anywhere in particular, and sure as hell not all the way to Cedar River. She got so shook, I just backed off. You don't suppose that neighbor could've been mistaken, do you?"

"I doubt it," Frank said, and went on to tell him what Overstreet had said about Irene stopping at the jail and asking to see her long-gone stepfather.

There was a whispered "Jesus!" when Frank finished, and then, after an uneasy silence, "What the hell's going on with her, Decker? You've known her longer than I have. You must have some idea."

, "I wish I did. Look, I was thinking yesterday, maybe the thing to do is for you and me and Beth to all get together and—and see what we can come up with."

"What about Irene's mother? Think maybe she'd have an idea?"

"I doubt it. Except for around the time Beth was born, we never saw that much of her. Never visited her. She'd drop by our place for a few hours every few months, mostly to see

Beth, but that was it. Might be worth calling her, though. She is the one Irene was trying to see yesterday.''

"Look," Bailey said, "I've never pushed Irene about it, but this thing with her mother—do you have any idea what it's all about? You'd think with Beth being her only grand-child—she is her only grandchild, isn't she? Irene never came right out and said it, but I always got the idea she was an only child herself.''

"She is. And no, I don't have any idea what's wrong be-tween them. I asked a few times, especially when Beth was getting old enough to wonder why we never went to see her grandmother. But Irene never really answered. Sometimes she even denied there was anything wrong at all, like it was nor-mal for a mother and daughter to live sixty miles apart and talk to each other only once or twice a year. And after while, it got to seeming normal to me, too, I guess. Or I just didn't want to rock the boat. I don't know.''

"Did you ever talk to her mother about it?''

"Never. Never saw her except when she came to see Beth.'' Frank fell silent, shocked at how much he didn't know about Irene. Damned little he did know, damned little that he had ever really tried to find out. He'd lived with her for ten years without ever knowing her well enough to find out why she didn't get along with her own mother. Ridiculous! How could two people live with a wall like that between them?

"I'll call Irene's mother today,'' he said, shying away from the memories.

"Let me know what you find out,'' Bailey said. "I'll be at the lot all day, except for the occasional test drive.''

Getting Florence Bender's number from Information, Frank dialed it but got no answer. Hanging up, he shifted mental gears and hurried to the Arlington to pass on to Ardly the information about his father's body and that it would be at least the middle of the week before it could be on its way to England.

Ardly nodded, seemingly unperturbed. "I more or less expected that,'' he said. ''My employer told me to take all the time I need, so no probs there. Right now—well, where's that museum you told me about last night? I might just want a look at this great-great-grandfather of mine after all.''

''I'll drop you off,'' Frank said, ''you and your papers, and introduce you to Laura Young.''

At the museum, Laura was eager to hear about the latest Leander developments and fascinated with the ''Weller'' letter. After barely a glance, she agreed that it almost certainly had been written by the same person who had written the diaries, presumably Dora Wetherston.

Armed with that agreement, Frank headed for the door. ''It'll be interesting to see how Nathaniel reacts to this latest little bombshell.''

''Not well, I would venture,'' Laura said with a smile, and sobered as they both remembered Willis Ardly and Lou Cameron.

As BEFORE, Frank was reluctantly admitted into the lake-side mansion by the grim-faced housekeeper. This time, Wetherston had finished his morning laps of the pool but hadn't left for his office at the bank. He greeted Frank sourly in his book-lined office-den.

''Well?'' He set aside a sheaf of typewritten papers spread on the desk before him. ''What insanity do you bring me this morning?''

''I assume you know about Willis Ardly's body being found Wednesday afternoon in Lou Cameron's car. He'd been shot with a twenty-two target pistol.''

Wetherston scowled. ''I read Richardson's lurid accounts in the *Gazette,* including your own offensive speculations. I was pleasantly surprised when you didn't take it upon yourself to rush out here and personally accuse me of murder. Is that why you're here now, to make up for that lapse?'' He sat back and speared Frank with a glare. ''Or do you merely want to know if anyone here ever owned a pistol of the sort that killed the man?''

Frank smiled. ''That wasn't my primary purpose, but now that you've brought it up, I'd be more than happy if you could give me that information.''

''All right, Sheriff. Let's just get it out of the way. I'm sure we did own such a pistol many years ago, probably more than one. Both boys, like most, went through a phase when they were in their teens. We had a target range set up in the basement, in fact. But the phase was short-lived, I'm happy to say, and the range and the guns used there have been gone for years.''

''Gone where?''

Wetherston shrugged. ''Sold, given to the gun club, lost, I couldn't say. I don't keep an inventory of every toy we've ever owned. Now, is there anything else?''

''There are no guns in the house, then?''

''Only the one I keep here in my desk.''

Frank's eyebrows arched in surprise. ''Why—''

''Just say it gives me a feeling of security that your department does not. Now if you have finished wasting my time—''

''Not quite yet, Mr. Wetherston. I thank you for the information you volunteered so nicely, but the reason I came was to talk, not ask questions. You may already have heard this, but I'm sure you'll still be interested.''

Wetherston sighed, leaning back and lacing his fingers across his tweed-vested stomach. ''Very well, Sheriff. Be quick about it.''

Frank nodded once. ''First, Willis Ardly's son, Clayton, arrived from England last night.''

''Hardly of any interest to me, despite your insane theories. Give him my condolences, if you feel it would be appropriate.''

''I'm sure he'll appreciate them. As for why his arrival may interest you, he brought some letters with him. The same letters that his father brought copies of last week. Letters written to his great-great-grandmother Augusta in England, letters written by his great-great-grandfather here in Whitford.''

''And why do you believe I should have any interest in this genealogical trivia?'' Wetherston asked with a scowl when Frank paused.

''Because,'' Frank said slowly, ''this great-great-grandfather was someone I think you're familiar with. His name was Leander Wetherston.''

For a moment Wetherston seemed not even to breathe. Then his fingers slowly unlaced themselves and his hands slid to the side to grip the leather arm rests of the chair. His Adam's apple rose momentarily. His eyes closed for a full five seconds.

''Very well, Sheriff.'' His voice had a steely edge, and his gaze was now direct. ''How much do you want, you and young Ardly?''

''I beg your pardon?''

''Don't play infantile games with me, Sheriff! How much do the two of you want? How much is it going to cost me to buy your silence?''

''You must have us confused with your son, Allen. I'm not here to blackmail you.''

''Then why are you here? Forgive me for assuming you were following in the footsteps of your friend and mentor, Louis Cameron.''

Frank scowled. ''What the hell is that supposed to mean?''

''I told you, Sheriff, don't play your childish games with me!''

''I'm not playing games, damn it! Are you trying to tell me that Lou Cameron tried to blackmail you?''

''Tried and, I'm sorry to say, succeeded!'' Wetherston shot back. ''Don't tell me you haven't realized that simple fact yet!''

''I'm afraid I haven't,'' Frank said coldly. ''Tell me about it.''

Wetherston fell silent again, his eyes narrowing as he studied Frank's still-scowling face. "You really don't believe it." Wetherston sounded astonished. "You really don't believe that your sainted friend Cameron is capable of anything so ordinary, do you?"

"Not without one hell of a lot of proof."

"How admirably loyal. But tell me, why do you think he disappeared?"

"I think he got himself killed, just like Willis Ardly."

Wetherston laughed, a short, harsh bark. "My life would be a great deal simpler if that were true, Sheriff. Unfortunately, it is not, although I would think you would welcome the information."

"I would—if I believed it!"

"Believe it, Sheriff. Profit from it if you must, but believe it."

"Convince me. You could start by telling me what did happen to him."

"He's gone on to a better life, at my expense. And at the expense of his friend Ardly's life."

"Now who's playing games? Explain!"

"As you wish," Wetherston said tiredly. "But tell me something first. Is all this going to become public?"

"I don't see how it can be avoided."

"Not even with money? I don't know how many more of you little people I can afford to pay, but, considering what happened to Mr. Ardly, I can arrange for the son to receive some of what was earmarked for the father—whatever Cameron doesn't already have. And I think I can afford one more exorbitantly salaried executive on the payroll, particularly an ex-sheriff. It might even have its advantages, public-relations-wise."

Frank shook his head angrily. "God damn it, Wetherston, I told you I'm not here for blackmail! And I would appreciate it very much if you would just tell me what the hell you think happened here last Sunday!"

Wetherston eyed Frank tiredly for several seconds. Finally, he shrugged. "Very well, if you insist, though I still find it hard to believe that I will be telling you anything you don't already know or at least suspect."

"Never mind what I do or don't suspect! Just talk!"

"In the simplest possible terms, Cameron and his friend Ardly came to me with the letters, just as you have come now. They extorted several hundred thousand dollars from me. Apparently Cameron desired Ardly's share as well as his own, the result of which desire you found in the gravel pit Wednesday."

Frank's scowl deepened. "You're saying that Lou Cameron not only blackmailed you but killed Willis Ardly?"

"Isn't it obvious?"

"That's even more insane than blackmail!"

"Believe what you want. It's true."

"Sunday night? This all happened Sunday night?"

"I can't vouch for the precise time of Ardly's death, but I would assume so."

"You rounded up 'hundreds of thousands of dollars' on a Sunday night?"

"Not all of it, of course."

"Then how—"

"I gave them whatever I could lay my hands on in cash. A down payment, if you will. No great amount, less than fifty thousand in all. And an agreement was reached. Both men would leave Whitford immediately. Ardly would return to England. Cameron would go—for the time being, at least—to San Francisco. I agreed to forward the rest of the money, in cash, to 'Lon Cramer' in care of general delivery there. He would see that half the money reached Ardly in England, he didn't say how." Wetherston smiled sourly. "But, then, I don't imagine he was too worried about that part of it, since he knew very well that Ardly would never reach England alive."

"And you sent the rest of the money?"

"Another installment, yes, though not the entire amount. Even when one owns a bank, getting one's hands on that much cash without raising all kinds of alarms isn't easy. And the money was received, if that's your next question. It was picked up Thursday morning. On learning of Ardly's death, I hired a San Francisco detective to watch the post office."

"Lou Cameron picked the money up?"

"Hardly. A young woman picked it up, presumably a new friend of his. The detective followed her."

"So you know where Cameron is?"

Wetherston shook his head. "No. The young woman managed to elude my man. However, if you would care to try the same trick yourself, you can send him your own package and hire your own detective. Or go there yourself, for all I care. If news of Ardly's body being found hasn't reached him yet, he may continue checking for further installments."

"What about the embezzlement? The note? I assume they're as phony as everything else you told me!"

"There was no embezzlement, obviously. That was just the best story I could devise in the limited amount of time I had. I typed the note myself and dropped it through the mail slot."

"And you were the one responsible for Del's anonymous tip, I suppose. Actually keeping the embezzlement story a secret must have been the last thing you wanted to do."

"Of course," Wetherston said tiredly.

"And the college money for Lou's kids? The job for his wife?"

"It seemed like a good idea at the time. Oil on troubled waters, so to speak. I thought it would smooth the situation over and cost me little."

"And Cameron—how did he get out of town? His car was at the bottom of the gravel pit, and he didn't take a bus. I had that checked."

"I'm sorry, Sheriff, but I haven't any idea. With the money he had in his pocket, including his partner's share, he shouldn't have had any trouble buying transportation and silence.''

"Very well, Mr. Wetherston, tell me all about it. Tell me everything you can remember from the time Cameron and Ardly approached you.''

"To what purpose?" Wetherston asked, irritation beginning to overcome his seeming tiredness.

"Just tell me what happened, from the start.''

Wetherston was silent a long moment, and then he sighed. "As you wish, Sheriff, as you wish.''

As Frank had suspected all along, Cameron and Ardly had gone straight to the Wetherston home Sunday afternoon after leaving the museum together. Garrick had just left, having made yet another of his increasingly frequent and vehement pleas to have Allen kicked out.

"The two of them walked into the aftermath of a pitched battle,'' Wetherston said, ''but the atmosphere didn't faze them. They were very good in their roles, particularly your friend Cameron. I never would have thought he had it in him, but he had his part down so well he seemed a totally different person. He—''

"His 'part'?''

"His part, yes. As in play-acting, conning, or whatever you care to call it. He and Ardly worked so well together, it was hard to believe they hadn't been at it all their lives. Cameron was brimming with enthusiasm, like an overgrown child, totally unlike the quiet, reserved sort I knew him to be. And it was Ardly's job to restrain him, to keep him from blurting the whole story out the moment they came in. But of course Ardly managed to keep him under control, at least until they were alone with me.''

"What makes you think Cameron was acting?" Frank asked angrily. "It sounds just like him to me.''

Wetherston shrugged stiffly, the strain of his attempt to remain casual beginning to show. "Have it your way, Sheriff, but whether it was an act or not, the results were the same.

Once the three of us were alone, here in my office, Cameron began prattling on. I thought it was some bizarre joke once I began to understand what he was talking about. But then Ardly got down to business. He reined Cameron in and explained who he was. And he showed me the copies of the letters he had brought with him. I still thought it was some elaborate joke, until he showed me the one supposedly written by my grandmother, signing herself 'Weller.' I am too familiar with her handwriting to be easily fooled. And that was when Cameron did his best work. He was most eloquent as he talked of how this 'fabulous discovery' would shed new light on everything my grandfather did, everything his widow did. Throughout his wild ramblings, however, Cameron made it perfectly clear what would happen if something wasn't done to stop him." The old man sat even straighter, his voice rising. "My grandfather would be made to look like a common criminal, a bigamist, and I would be made to look an utter fool. He was ready to destroy me, to make the Wetherston name a laughing stock!"

Wetherston broke off. Then he continued, once more under control. "I admit that, to some extent, I brought it on myself by failing to control my reactions. Except for that, I might have gotten rid of them for a paltry few thousand. I realized my mistake too late. I offered them ten thousand apiece, and they simply laughed at me. Cameron had the gall to act as if he thought I were joking! Permission, he wanted! Permission to publish the complete set of letters—in the Historical Society Quarterly, of all places!" Wetherston shook his head in wonder. "I offer him ten thousand dollars, and he makes a ludicrous suggestion like that! Imagine! Publishing those letters in that pathetic pamphlet they call a magazine." Wetherston sighed, as if with wonder. "He was toying with me, I realized then, and Ardly was enjoying it immensely."

"And then?" Frank prompted. "I assume you came to an agreement eventually."

"Eventually, yes, but not until that night. After Cameron's

humiliating suggestion, Ardly reined him in again, and they left. 'I'm sure we'll be able to work something out,' Ardly said. I've never seen anyone so smug in my life.''

''And Cameron?''

''He was still playing his part to the hilt, treating my offer as a joke.''

''Didn't it ever occur to you that he wasn't acting? That he really thought you were joking?''

''Not for one moment! I may not have known Cameron very well, but I had spoken to him a number of times, seen him at the insurance company office. And this performance of his was so out of character there simply was no other possibility.''

Frank shook his head. Wetherston had never seen this other side of Lou Cameron, and nothing Frank could say would convince him that it existed. ''All right,'' he said. ''Go on. You said you reached an agreement that night.''

''Yes. Or rather, they reached an agreement with Allen.''

Aha! Frank thought sharply. ''With Allen? How?''

A grim smile crossed Wetherston's lined face. ''He might as well tell you himself. But first let me be absolutely certain there is no way I can convince you to keep this information from becoming public knowledge. As I said, I can afford—''

''As *I* said, Mr. Wetherston, this is a murder case. Surely you don't want to open yourself up to charges of attempted bribery.''

Wetherston was silent for several seconds, his pale eyes studying Frank's features, as if trying to read what lay beneath them. ''Very well,'' he said abruptly, ''I believe you. I suspect you are a fool, but I believe you. Tell me, are you going to try to find your friend Cameron and have him extradited for murder? Or for blackmail? If everything is going to be made public, I no longer have any reason not to prefer charges against him. Or to attempt to recover the money he extorted from me.''

''And you'll testify against him if it comes to trial?''

"Of course. And it goes without saying that whatever promises I made to Cameron's wife—"

"You don't have to list every single consequence, Wetherston. Nothing is going to change my mind—for the simple reason that I don't believe any of these charges."

Wetherston shook his head and smiled faintly. "If nothing else," he said, "I will enjoy watching your face when you learn the truth, Decker. Now, if you'll come this way."

The old man stood up and, with brisk, sure steps, led the way up the broad, curving stairs to a second floor bedroom and threw open the door. Allen Wetherston lay in a king-size bed, blinking himself awake.

"Alone, I see," Wetherston said flatly. "Your friend left early."

A faint smile brought Allen's lean features to life. "Of course. During the discreet hours of darkness, as you requested. I wouldn't want anything to damage the Wetherston reputation needlessly, now would I? Besides, if I let her stay till morning, it might give her delusions of potential permanency."

"That isn't going to help you anymore. I want you out of this house by tonight."

Allen blinked, but then smiled. "Whatever you say, Father," he said, making a sweeping gesture of submission with one hand. "Is that why you have the good sheriff with you? To run me out of town by sundown, so to speak?"

"If you want it that way." Wetherston turned to Frank. "Is it too late to prefer charges of blackmail against him as well?"

"Not at all. Are you saying you'll testify against him?"

"If he is still within a thousand miles of here tomorrow morning, yes."

"I really think, Father," Allen said tightly, "that we should talk privately before you pursue this any further."

"If you're thinking those letters from my grandfather can save you, you can forget it. They are no longer a secret. The sheriff here knows about them. Willis Ardly's son is in Whitford, and he knows about them. Everyone will know about them shortly, and the sheriff assures me there is no way of stopping it.''

Allen's eyes widened. ''I see.''

''I'm sure you do,'' Wetherston snapped. ''But before you start packing, tell Sheriff Decker about Sunday night. And about his friend Cameron that he idolizes so much.''

''And what, precisely, do you want me to tell him?'' Allen pushed the covers back and sat up, revealing what looked to be silk pajamas.

''How you made a deal with him and Ardly, how the upright Mr. Cameron is no better than you when it comes to blackmail! The sheriff is still holding onto his childish illusions about his friend, it seems, no matter what I tell him.''

''And what have you told him?'' Allen asked, sliding over to sit on the edge of the bed.

''I told him how Cameron and Ardly came here with their letters and their scheme and their act, how Cameron wasn't satisfied with money but insisted on rubbing salt in the wounds with his ridiculous, hateful charade of childish enthusiasm for his 'discovery'!''

''Ah, yes, I see. His 'act,' as you like to call it. I have to admit, he did come on a little strong.''

''A little strong? He—''

''But he wasn't acting, Father, not at all. I only wish he had been. Things would have been a great deal simpler for me.''

Wetherston blinked, scowling. ''Of course he was acting! What are you trying to pull now? When a man turns down ten thousand and ends up accepting a half million—''

''You old fool! Do you have any idea how hard I had to work to get him to accept it? Without his greedy friend Ardly, your revered ancestor's indiscretions would have been all over the front page of the *Gazette* Monday afternoon.''

''You're saying that Lou Cameron did not come here to blackmail your father?'' Frank cut in.

"That was the farthest thing from his mind. That's why it took so much money."

"But—" Wetherston began, only to be cut off by Frank.

"All right, Allen, you tell me what happened. You sound as if you have a different version than the one your father just gave me."

"Gladly," Allen said, "but I doubt you'll like my version any better than his."

"Just go ahead."

Allen shrugged. "I was listening at the door of my father's office a good part of the time he was 'negotiating.' I find requests for private meetings, such as the one Ardly insisted on, quite irresistible." He smiled briefly. "Simple self-preservation. I couldn't hear everything, but I heard quite enough to make me want to hear more. So when they left, I followed. After Cameron dropped Ardly somewhere, I talked to Cameron alone. Oh, he was most happy to tell me all about his wonderful discovery. Eager, you might say. It was a gold mine, dumped right in my lap. I got the rest of the story later from my father here, though he did have a most mistaken idea of Cameron's motives. I saw no need to tell him he was mistaken, however. Not when it was to my advantage that he continue believing just as he did. So I merely offered my services as negotiator, which Father promptly accepted. I suppose he assumed that my recent experience in the field of, shall we say, negotiated silence, would make me more able to deal with Cameron than he. My only problem was how to convince Cameron that being rich but silent was better than being poor but published."

"But you finally did convince him?" Frank prompted.

"To tell the absolute truth, I'm not sure. Oh, I had no doubts at the time, but—"

"You didn't say anything about this!" Nathaniel Wetherston snapped, his face flushed with anger.

"I'm no fool, Father. If you hadn't believed what you did of Cameron, who knows what might have happened? You might have talked to him. He might even have come to understand how deeply you felt about such trivialities as the illustrious Wetherston name. He might even have agreed to suppress all that lovely information without one cent from you. And I'm sure you could, with a little pleading, have gotten Ardly to settle for forty or fifty thousand, plus an agreement to look into the international inheritance laws. But where would such civilized behavior have left me? Perhaps not totally out in the cold, but certainly in a weakened position." Allen put on a winning smile. "Don't you agree?"

"Never mind the sarcasm!" Frank broke in. "Just get on with what happened! You're not sure you succeeded with Cameron, but you say he took the money anyway. Explain."

"Of course, Sheriff. You and Father both want the truth, so the truth it shall be. I talked to Cameron for nearly an hour early in the evening, and he—"

"At the museum?"

"At the museum."

"What was he doing there?"

"Reading great-grandmother's diaries, of course. Or re-reading them, I suspect. He was having a high old time."

"All right, go on."

Allen shrugged. "There isn't a lot more. I hadn't convinced him of anything by the time I left him at the museum, and I didn't see what I could do about it. So I got Ardly away from the party long enough to talk to him, and once he realized that Cameron had confided everything to me, Ardly and I came to a quick agreement. Personally, he was happy—ecstatic, you might say—to settle for two hundred thousand. Probably would have settled for a great deal less. The problem was Cameron."

Allen paused, shaking his head wonderingly, a motion almost identical to his father's a few minutes before. "The man didn't want our money. All he wanted was to tell the world—or at least Whitford—about his discovery. And that is what I told Ardly. I had done my best. If Ardly wanted the two hundred thousand—or anything at all—it was up to him to convince Cameron. So, when Cameron showed up on our doorstep late Sunday night, I assumed Ardly had been successful.''

"That's when the deal was made?"

"Exactly. Four hundred thousand, half for each."

"You said a half million," Nathaniel broke in with new anger.

Allen shrugged. "I deserved a commission, don't you think? After all, you had left it in my hands. You didn't want to talk to them anymore, as I recall."

"However much you got your hands on," the old man snapped, "make the best of it. It's the last you're getting!"

"We'll see, Father, we'll see."

"You were saying?" Frank interrupted. "Cameron showed up here Sunday night?"

"Precisely, Sheriff. He had, he said, changed his mind, and if the offer of the two hundred thousand apiece was still open, he would take it."

"Did he say why he'd changed his mind?"

Allen shook his head. "I rather wondered at the time, particularly since he insisted on handling the money for both Ardly and himself. Once Ardly's body was found, however, it all became crystal clear."

"Not to me! If you're saying Cameron killed Ardly—?"

"Not intentionally, I'm sure. In fact, Ardly probably brought it on himself. He must have become so desperate to bring Cameron around to his pragmatic way of thinking that he got hold of a gun somewhere and tried to convince him with that. Unfortunately, Ardly was killed, not Cameron."

"You're saying they fought? And the gun went off and Ardly was killed?" Suddenly, a mixture of relief and anger flooded through Frank. This he could almost believe, and if it was true, if Lou was still alive—

"Fought, argued, whatever," Allen said. "But however it

happened, Cameron panicked. Then, when he had time to think, he realized that Father's offer was his only way out.''

"But if it was an accident, or self defense—''

''I can't speak for what went through Cameron's mind, Sheriff. I can only tell you that when I saw him, he was much the worse for wear.''

''And you didn't suspect a thing, I suppose?'' Frank asked with angry sarcasm.

Allen smiled. ''Is it a crime to have a trusting nature?''

For a moment there was silence. Frank's anger sharpened as Allen's version of events began to sort themselves out in his mind and he realized what must have really happened.

''Lou Cameron came to you for help, not money!'' Frank grated. ''He came to you to get you to back up his story that Ardly had been desperate to get the blackmail money! He was naive enough to think that you might tell the police something remotely resembling the truth. But you refused, didn't you? You saw your 'gold mine' falling right into your lap. You told him—I don't know exactly what you told him, but considering what you knew your father believed about him, I can imagine. You told Lou he'd be up for first degree murder. You told him everyone would believe that he and Ardly had gotten into an argument over who got how much money, and that you'd do everything in your power to see that he was convicted, even if it meant lying, which he certainly knew by then you were very good at. And you could certainly afford to buy however many witnesses you needed.''

Frank paused, his anger making him short of breath. ''And then,'' he continued, ''you offered him the four hundred thousand—or was it only two? Or was it even that much? And you talked him into dumping the body and the car in the water! He certainly wouldn't have done anything as stupid as that on his own, not unless he wanted the body to be found by the kids he knew damn well swam there all the time! You probably even drove him to the airport in Springfield after it was all over! Just to make sure he didn't change his mind and do something sensible, like come to me! And you must have told him where to go, too! 'Try San Francisco,' I'll bet you said. 'I've got this girl friend there who'll be glad to look after you until I can send the rest of the money.' And he believed you!''

Abruptly, Frank fell silent, breathing hard.

"An absolutely fascinating scenario, Sheriff," Allen Wetherston said with an infuriating smile, "but I don't really see what difference it could possibly make. Either way, your friend Cameron is a killer.''

SEVENTEEN

SEETHING, Frank stalked down the hall past the gallery of Wetherston family portraits and out the door, barely noticing the swampy air that descended on him like a smothering blanket.

Only during the drive back to town did his fury at the Wetherstons' sarcastic arrogance fade, allowing logic to regain the upper hand. As it did, he was forced to admit that his version of Sunday night was only marginally more plausible than Allen's. Even under those conditions, Lou would never have run out on his family. And the O-positive blood on the spade—

No, he'd been grasping at straws, desperate for Lou Cameron to be alive and, yes, almost equally desperate to strike back at that smug son of a bitch, Allen Wetherston.

Grasping at straws or not, though, he had to follow through. As long as the slightest chance that Lou Cameron was alive existed, he had do his damnedest to find him. Even if it meant getting a warrant issued for his friend's arrest.

The first order of business, however, was to call Del Richardson and follow through on his promise—threat—to the Wetherstons. It wouldn't bring Lou back, but at least it would guarantee some uncomfortable moments for Nathaniel and the expulsion of Allen.

Frank gave Richardson a brief outline of what he'd found in the 1883 Carrothers *Sentinel* and the letters Clayton Ardly had brought with him. ''If you want more details, call Ardly or Laura Young," he finished. "They're both at the museum with the letters and diaries."

As expected, the prosecutor was less than enthusiastic when Frank told him he wanted to get Lou Cameron picked up in San Francisco and extradited back to Whitford.

"For one thing," Zartman explained irritably, "you've already got Lou on the missing persons rolls. For another, unless you can honestly say you believe he killed Ardly and did all the rest, you'll be making a false statement when you file your affidavit to get the warrant."

Nevertheless, by the time Frank left the prosecutor's office he had the paperwork started. Then he spent several minutes trying to convince the San Francisco police that, first, the documents officially requesting Lou Cameron's arrest and extradition would be faxed to them ASAP, and, second, that it would be worth their while to circulate a picture, possibly even provide a dummy package for "Lon Cramer" and stake out the general delivery window for a couple of days. Except for the picture, they made no promises.

Then Frank drove out to see Jennie Cameron again. She dismissed his theory and his efforts instantly, even irritably.

"I know you mean well, Frank," she said, "but I don't believe one word. I—I hate to say it, but I...I'm sure he's dead. Once that Ardly fellow's body was found—in Lou's car—well, what else can I believe? And this foolishness you're telling me now just doesn't make sense. You know it as well as I do. Lou hated guns. He never owned one or even fired one. He couldn't kill someone, not even in self defense. And even if it happened purely by accident, he wouldn't run, not even with that Wetherston boy trying to scare him. No, he would've come to me, or he would've gone to you. He would not just run off in the middle of the night without—"

She broke off, shaking her head vehemently. "Utter nonsense."

"I know it seems like nonsense," Frank said earnestly,

"but I have to make sure. You know that. As long as there's the slightest possibility that—"

"There isn't the slightest possibility!" she flared. "Damn it, Frank, haven't you heard a single word I've been saying?"

"I didn't say I believed it, Jennie," he protested, shaken by her anger. "I don't, but I have to believe there's a chance. I know Lou was your husband, but—"

"'But' nothing! He was my husband and I did know him!"

"I know, Jennie, I know. All I'm saying is, nobody can be one hundred percent sure about anyone, not even—"

"Don't judge every marriage by your own, Frank Decker!" she snapped. "Some people are actually in love when they get married, and they get to know each other better every day they're together instead of—of just living together until they decide they've had enough!"

His face flushing, Frank started to back away, but as suddenly as Jennie's tirade had started, it ended. Her face softened. "I'm sorry," she said, reaching out and taking his hand. "I shouldn't—I know this has been hard for you, too. And that other, it's none of my business. I'm sorry."

She released his hand and pulled in a breath. "But it doesn't change anything," she went on, her voice regaining its firmness. "What I said is still true. You go ahead with whatever you feel you have to do. It doesn't matter. I know what you'll find, if you find anything at all. Because I really did know him, no matter what you or anyone else thinks."

She paused, shaking her head, a trace of the anger returning to her eyes. "You can't imagine how many of our so-called friends have taken it on themselves to tell me about that pious bastard Einar Lindstrom and how he had everyone fooled right up to the day he slashed his wrists! At least a half dozen of them have stabbed me with that particular sliver of hope, and believe me, that's the sort of 'hope' I can do without!"

"I never said—"

"I know you didn't, Frank, but don't tell me it never crossed your mind. Even if one of those crazy theories were true—which they aren't!—it would mean that Lou's entire life up until last Sunday night was a lie, and if that's the case, then the Lou I knew is dead anyway. He never existed, and it wouldn't matter if his body was found walking around somewhere! Now go, do what you feel you must.'' She turned and walked briskly down the hall, leaving him standing by the door.

Jennie's right, Frank thought as he drove back to the jail. The tiny fragment of fearful hope he had tricked himself into hanging onto was absurd. Lou was dead. He had to be.

But where the hell was the body? Had Lou's own spade been used to bury him? Where? Could the spade have been used to kill him? His blood type had been found on the blade. Frank tried to visualize some sequence of events that would account for Ardly's being shot and Lou being beaten to death with the spade, but his imagination stalled out. He couldn't even think why the spade would have been in the car in the first place. Someone must have gotten it from the Cameron house Sunday evening, while Jennie had been looking for Lou at the museum or at the party. But why? To bury Lou's body? Surely the killer—Nathaniel or Allen, or even Garrick—would have been able to get his hands on a spade without having to sneak into Lou's basement! But why bury Lou's body at all? Why not put it in the car with Ardly's? Why go to the trouble of finding two hiding places instead of just one? And why use the gravel pit, where anyone at all familiar with the area would have to know it would be found within days by the local kids, particularly during a heat wave like this one?

Unless, of course, it had been the killer's plan all along to have Ardly's body found and frame Lou for the murder?

There's an idea, Frank thought grimly. Except it would have made a lot more sense to leave Lou's body to be found and blame Ardly. Far more plausible, at least to everyone but Ardly's son.

When he reached the jail, a call from Gordon Bailey was

waiting. Frowning, Frank snatched up the receiver. "What is it, Bailey?"

"I don't know, Sheriff. More trouble, I think. Have you heard from Irene or Beth today?"

"No."

"Carrie Hyland called a couple minutes ago, all in a tizzy wondering where Beth was. She was supposed to baby-sit for Carrie again, but she hasn't shown up. Carrie called the house a half dozen times, but nobody answered, so she called me."

"Damn! Irene didn't say anything this morning, did she? About going anywhere?"

"Not a word. Last I talked to her was when I asked her about Cedar River and she kept insisting she hadn't been there. You don't suppose—" Cursing, Bailey cut himself off. "I'm going down there," he said abruptly. "I'll check in with you when I get there."

Frank didn't try to talk him out of it. Instead, he called Sheriff Overstreet in Cedar River, told him about Bailey being on his way down, and extracted a promise to again "keep an eye out" for Irene's red Pinto.

He was just hanging up when Phil told him that Garrick Wetherston was on the other line.

Sighing, he picked up the phone again. He'd had more than enough of the Wetherstons for one day. "How good of you to call, Mr. Wetherston," he said wearily. "What can I do for you today?"

"Why, Sheriff, if I didn't know better, your tone might make me think you had been infected with the Wetherston sarcasm virus." Garrick's voice was light and playful, just the opposite of what it had been Thursday.

"I don't have time for games, Wetherston."

"Ah, Sheriff! I am merely calling to thank you. And I am not indulging in sarcasm when I say that."

"What are you indulging in?"

A brief spurt of laughter, sounding not only genuine but

almost exuberant, crackled out of the receiver. "You're a hard man to thank, Sheriff Decker."

"It might be easier if you told me what you're thanking me for."

"Of course, Sheriff, of course. Two things, actually. First, there was our little heart-to-heart yesterday."

"I didn't get the feeling I was doing you any favors."

Another laugh. "At the time, I didn't think you were. But after I left your office, after I'd been driving around for an hour or so, I had myself an epiphany. Contrary to what I'd expected when I let you into my sexual closet, so to speak, I began to realize that I was feeling good."

"You'll excuse me if I have my doubts? When you left here—"

"I know, Sheriff, I know. But it took a while for the feeling to take hold, and even longer for me to recognize it. After all, I haven't had much experience with that particular feeling for God knows how many years. Could've been some novel form of indigestion, for all I knew. And even after I recognized it, it was a long time before I realized why I was feeling good."

"All right, I'll bite. Why were you feeling good?"

"I'm sure you're familiar with the old cliché about the truth setting you free, Sheriff. Well, to my total surprise, it turned out to be valid, at least in this particular case. Quite a startling revelation to someone like myself, whose family has never had more than a nodding acquaintance with the subject."

"Congratulations. Glad I could be of help. Now I have—"

"Wait, Sheriff, there's much more. That was just the start."

"Can I have the abridged version, Wetherston? I do have other things to do, especially today."

"Of course. To make it as short as possible, I spent most of the night driving around, all the way to Springfield and a half dozen other towns I don't even remember the names of, places I'd never been, roads I'd never taken before. And all the while, I kept thinking—thinking about the very things you and I chatted about. For the first time I can remember, I reviewed my own life. I looked at what it's actually been like the last twenty years—and guess what? I had another epiphany. For the last twenty years, my life has been shit!''

''Sorry to hear that,'' Frank murmured, out of the store of politeness his mother had supplied him with.

Wasted on Garrick, who went on, ''And shit it would be for the next twenty if I kept worrying about inheritances and Allen and what people would think if they knew the truth about me. And you know what?''

''What?'' Frank said automatically, although Garrick hadn't paused.

''It's not worth it, Sheriff. It's not worth it. So the hell with it! I'm no pauper; I'm a damned good administrator; I can get a job anywhere in the country. Or start my own Wetherston 'empire.' Because I sure don't need all the baggage that comes with this one. When I made that decision, I really felt good, and this time I recognized the feeling right away.''

''Bully for you,'' Frank said, looking out the window and wondering when this ''short version'' was going to end.

''And then! This morning, just when I was working up the nerve to go tell Father he could stuff his empire, your pal Richardson called to let me know you'd held a 'news conference.' He wanted my reaction. Which is the second thing I want to thank you for—dumping our dirty laundry out on Main Street.''

''You're more than welcome,'' Frank said impatiently when Wetherston paused.

''It's true, then?'' For the first time during the call, a note of uncertainty entered Wetherston's voice. ''The legendary Leander was a wife deserter and a bigamist? And Allen is being booted out?''

''I thought you didn't care anymore.''

''That's not what I said. Or if I did, I didn't mean to.''

''Then what did you mean?''

''That, under the conditions that existed yesterday, I would be better off getting out. The hassle and the deception and the ulcers weren't worth it.''

''And under conditions as they exist today?''

''If everything that Richardson said is true—is it true? You still haven't told me.''

''It was,'' Frank said tiredly, ''as of an hour or so ago.''

''Under those conditions—I don't know, not yet. I'm still thinking. If Father is willing to accept me as I am, if he'll actually turn the businesses over to me and quit second guessing me, if a few other things I haven't thought of yet, but believe me, I will, then maybe I'll stay around.''

''I'll be holding my breath for your decision. Now unless there's something else...?''

For a moment, silence, and then an oddly subdued, ''No, Sheriff, that's all.''

Without another word, Frank hung up. Garrick was no different from the rest of the clan, he thought irritably. Once his own problem is solved, not a thought in his head about anyone else, certainly not Lou Cameron or Willis Ardly.

With the next ring of the phone he forgot all about Garrick Wetherston: Jed Sparks, the postmaster, called to tell him that the package Clayton Ardly had mailed from England five days before had arrived.

Fifteen minutes later in the Historical Society museum, he and Laura Young watched as Ardly unwrapped the album and lay it, appropriately enough, on Leander Wetherston's desk in the Wetherston room.

The album was a large, bulky affair, at least two inches thick and not all that different from one in a display case in the other room. The cover, with the single, ornately lettered word, ''MEMORIES,'' almost filling it, was a good quarter of an inch thick itself, its still-resilient bulk coated with a smooth, shiny material that resembled plastic. The individual pages were heavy cardboard, attached to the spine by sturdy strips of cloth that allowed them to be turned freely.

There were very few pictures, though, considering the album's bulk. Mostly five or six inches wide, some even larger, never more than two to a page, but below every single one were names and dates, all in a delicate but legible hand. Aunt Meg's, Ardly said. Several years ago she had made a project of identifying everyone in the pictures, and apparently she had been almost totally successful.

Slowly, Frank turned the pages while all three of them studied the pictures and wondered what they were looking for.

About two-thirds of the way through, Laura suddenly clapped her hand down on the page Frank had been about to turn. "Look!" she said excitedly, lifting her hand.

A group picture almost filled the album page. Thirteen men posed on the lawn of a large house, not quite a mansion but not far from it, in two rows. Six of the men knelt in front; seven stood stiffly behind them. All were formally dressed in what passed for suits a century ago, the tiny lapels making them look as if they were one step away from Nehru jackets. The stiff, white collars, virtually up to their chins, looked terribly uncomfortable, and all had some form of cravat wrapped around the collars, many so bulky they looked more like mufflers with stickpins than ties. The six in the front row had round, derby-like hats in their hands, and one sported a cane with a massive, carved handle. All stared fixedly straight ahead, some stiffly expressionless, others with equally rigid smiles. In the background, in front of the lower tiers of brick in the house, a phantom dog made a translucent streak several feet long, an indistinct tail at one end, a fuzzy head at the other. Beneath the picture, Aunt Meg's delicate handwriting gave the date as June of eighteen-eighty-three and listed the names of all thirteen members.

The list matched the one in the Carrothers *News Sentinel*: Leander Wetherston.

"Well?" Frank asked. "What do you see that we don't?"

"It is the original tour group," Laura said.

"I can see that, but—"

"Look, there," she said, a finger touching Leander Wetherston's name. "And there." Frank's eyes followed as her finger moved to the matching figure in the picture, the second man from the left in the back row.

"Now what the hell?" he muttered, frowning as he looked from the photograph to the portrait of Leander on the museum wall.

The handsome face that looked back at him from the portrait was not the face in the group photo. Unless the portrait had been glamorized beyond recognition, it was of a totally different person. There was a resemblance, but it was slight. None of the lean handsomeness of the portrait appeared in the photo. The face was fuller, the hair thinner, without the deep waves in the portrait. The hairline itself was different, a distinct widow's peak in the portrait, receding toward premature baldness in the photo.

"Who is that, Ardly?" Frank asked, pointing at the stranger in the photo.

Ardly shrugged. "Must be great-great-grandfather Leander Wetherston."

Frank pointed at the portrait. "Then who is our Leander Wetherston?"

Ardly blinked, looking up at the portrait, then shrugged. "Looks as if Aunt Meg should've come over, not me."

"Is it possible," Laura wondered aloud, "that there were two Leander Wetherstons?"

Frank shook his head vehemently. "No way. The letters prove that. Maybe Aunt Meg made a mistake." He looked at Ardly. "Possible?"

Another shrug. "I'm not the one to ask." He leaned more closely over the photo. "Perhaps Leander is one of the others. Perhaps she jumbled the names."

But the other twelve in the group bore even less resemblance to the portrait than did the one labeled "Leander Wetherston."

"Perhaps there are other pictures of him," Laura suggested.

"Let's find out," Frank agreed.

Three pages later, the face of the man in the portrait leaped out at them. Unlike most of the others, this was not a group photo. It was a studio portrait of one man, seated cross-legged and smiling in a wooden-back, cushioned chair, his hands lying relaxed on the arms. Without a doubt, this was the Leander in the portrait—which, Frank realized now, had not been glamorized at all. The man in the photo had the same thick, lustrous hair, the same full-lipped, sensual smile and the same glint in his eyes, the same handsome features, perhaps even more striking than in the portrait.

According to Aunt Meg's delicate handwriting beneath the picture, this was a man named, not Leander Wetherston, but Archibald Mayhew.

AFTER THE THIRD ATTEMPT, made just to be absolutely sure he hadn't misdialed one or more of the long sequence of numbers the first two times, Clayton Ardly hung up the phone on Laura's desk and shrugged apologetically. Frank, who had been waiting impatiently near the extension on the other desk, suppressed a grimace as he made his way back through the maze of displays to the others.

"She must be out," Ardly explained. "Or having a lie down or watching one of her shows on the telly. Dad says— said she doesn't always bother to pick up."

"Just have to keep trying," Frank said. "Unless you know of someone else who might be able to help?"

"Aunt Meg's the only one who would know who they are," he said with a sheepish smile.

"Can't be helped. Look, while we're waiting for her to show up, let's look through what we've got again, particularly those letters of Leander's that you brought. Maybe we missed something that would—"

The phone on Laura's desk jangled. Frank, without thinking, snatched it up but caught himself before speaking. He handed it to Laura.

"Historical Society," she said and, after a moment, handed

the receiver back to Frank. "It's for you," she said with a faint smile.

"Decker."

"Frank, it's Phil," his deputy's voice crackled over the line. "Your daughter just called. She—"

"Beth? Where the hell is she?"

"Cedar River, she said, but—"

"Cedar River? How did she get there? Is her mother—"

"Frank," Phil interrupted, "if you'll just calm down, I'll tell you all there is to tell. Okay?"

"Sorry, Phil. Go ahead."

"Beth called just a couple minutes ago. She said she's in Cedar River and her mother's—and I quote—'acting weird again,' and maybe you should get down there."

"Where in Cedar River?"

"Gas station somewhere on the north side of town, didn't say which one. She just got out what I already told you, and then she said something like, 'Mom's getting back in the car. I gotta go.' And that was that."

"Damn! Whatever Irene was doing yesterday—Look, Phil, I'm going down there. Bailey's already on his way. You call Sheriff Overstreet and fill him in. If Beth manages to call again, get it to me on the radio. And call Overstreet back."

"Will do, Frank. And don't worry. The girl's okay. She didn't sound scared. It was more like she was worried about her mother."

"So am I. I'll be in touch when I get to Cedar River."

EIGHTEEN

WITH ONLY occasional use of the siren, Frank covered the sixty-plus miles of mostly winding two-lane highway to Cedar River in well under an hour. The sun glared on the windshield the entire way, the air hot and soggy as it blasted through the open windows. When, nearing Cedar River, the trees and hills gave way to flat corn and hay fields that stretched to the horizon, banks of clouds to the northwest caught his attention, but only for a moment.

Just after twelve-thirty he shoved through the door of Overstreet's office. "Hang on a sec'," Overstreet said into the phone, glancing up at Frank. He was short and wiry, somewhere in his forties, a graying terrier to Frank's St. Bernard. "Decker, right?"

"Right. Any luck?"

"Some. Got your ex-mother-in-law on the line here," he said, waggling the receiver in the air. "Managed to run down the place she works. Why don't you grab Bernie's phone next door." Overstreet gestured with the receiver toward the radio room across the hall. At Overstreet's words, the deputy in the radio room swiveled his chair around and moved out of the way, holding out the phone.

"Mrs. Bender?"

"Is that you, Frank?"

"Yes, it is. Have you heard from Irene today?"

"How could I? Even if she's in town, I doubt she knows where I work. What's this all about?"

"Look, Decker," Overstreet's voice broke in, coming at

him both through the receiver and from the office across the hall, "why don't you two just talk. Tell her the whole story. All I had time for was to tell that her daughter's in town again. Besides, all I got's this second and third hand crap, and you know how screwed up that kind of thing can get. I'll just keep out of your way and listen."

"Are you nearby, Mrs. Bender?" Frank asked.

"A block from the jail, why?"

"Could I come over and talk to you?"

"If you want, but—"

"All right. Where are you?"

She gave him the address. "It's Shelton's Footwear," she said, "but I don't have much time."

"Be there in a minute." Hanging up, Frank paused only long enough to thank Overstreet for locating the woman and to ask him to call Shelton's instantly if there was any sign of Irene or Beth.

As Frank jogged the block to the store, he was startled by a momentary breeze that felt almost cool. Glancing down the street toward the west, he could see that the clouds were getting closer and darker. Here, though, the sun glared down through air that was heavy and still after that one errant puff of wind. Another false alarm?

Irene's mother, in her late fifties, could have been Irene in another twenty-five years, her once-red hair faded. She was waiting tensely in the door of Shelton's, and hustled Frank through the store, past a customer and another clerk and into a storeroom at the rear. Shoeboxes were stacked everywhere, and a battered desk and file cabinet stood in one corner.

"I really don't have much time," she said, sounding as impatient as she did nervous. "Joanie's the only other one on today, and she hasn't had her lunch break."

"Mrs. Bender, something odd is going on with Irene. She—"

"I know. Gordon told me last night, and Sheriff Overstreet

told me a bit just now. I don't see that there's anything I can do about it.''

"I was hoping you might have some idea why she keeps coming to Cedar River. Or where we might find her.''

"I'm sorry. You know, Frank, the two of us were never very close.''

"I do know. In fact, that was my next question: Why not?''

"I beg your pardon!''

"Sorry to be so blunt, Mrs. Bender, but I'm worried about Irene—and about Beth. I'm also sorry I didn't ask the same question while Irene and I were still married. Maybe if I had—'' He cut himself off, shaking his head. "Just tell me what's going on between the two of you?'' he resumed quickly. "Does it have something to do with her stepfather?''

Her face tightened even more. "I'm sorry, but I haven't the faintest idea what you're getting at, Frank.''

"I thought Overstreet told you.''

"Told me what?''

"That when Irene came to Cedar River yesterday, she not only stopped at your neighbor's house but at the jail. She said she wanted to see a prisoner—a prisoner named Will Bender.''

After a moment Irene's mother stiffened, her lips pressing together tightly. The motion reminded Frank forcibly of Irene and her own response to situations she couldn't control. "I'm sorry, Frank,'' she said, reaching for the door, "but I don't have any more time.'' Frank grabbed her arm.

"I want an answer,'' he said flatly. "Was Will Bender ever in jail here? Or anywhere?''

Wordless, she tried to pull free.

"I want an answer,'' he repeated. "Irene's out there some-where, with my daughter—your granddaughter. Yesterday she was here, asking at the jail about her stepfather. I want to know why!''

"Ask her!'' she snapped. "Now let me go!''

"I would ask her if I could find her! But I can't, so I'm asking you."

"Is there a problem, Flo?" a male voice asked from behind Frank.

Startled, Frank turned and saw a man in his twenties, tie loosened, shirtsleeves pushed above his elbows, looking in through the door from the store.

"Mr. Shelton," she gasped, "I'm sorry, but this man insisted that—"

"I'm Frank Decker, the sheriff up in Farrell County. Mrs. Bender—"

"Does Sheriff Overstreet know you're here, Mr. Decker?"

"I left his office less than ten minutes ago. Yes, he knows I'm here."

"I see. You have no objections to my calling him to confirm that?"

"Of course not! I'm just trying to find my daughter. Her granddaughter," Frank added, looking at Irene's mother. "Overstreet can tell you all about it."

"I see," Shelton repeated slowly, his eyebrows lifting slightly as he nodded. "Very well." He glanced over his shoulder back into the store. "Take whatever time you need, Flo. I'll give Joan a hand until you're finished."

As the door closed behind Shelton, Mrs. Bender jerked her arm free of his hand and glared at him. "You're going to get me fired! Mr. Shelton doesn't like trouble, no matter whose fault it is."

"He didn't seem all that put out."

"He never does—to the public!"

"I'll explain to him about Irene. She's your daughter, so surely he can't blame you for—"

"He can blame me for whatever he wants! That's the way it is when you own the store, Frank!"

"I'm sorry, but until you answer a couple questions—"

"All right! All right! Whatever you want! Ask them and then leave me alone!"

Startled by her vehemence, Frank stepped back a pace and looked down at her, seeing again in her anger the resemblance to Irene. "Do you have any idea at all why she might have come here? Or where she might be?"

"I already told you I don't!"

"What about her stopping at the jail yesterday and asking about Will Bender? Was he ever in jail? Irene never mentioned—"

"She wouldn't!" Mrs. Bender snapped. "It was all her fault, so it's no wonder she never talked about it!"

"What was all her fault, Mrs. Bender?"

Her lips pressed together, the image of Irene's tight-lipped anger. Finally, with a harried glance toward the door Shelton had closed, she let out her breath in an explosive sigh.

"She put him in jail," she said bitterly. "She made up stories about him and got him put in jail! That was the final straw. When he got out—after I forced her to go down to the jail and admit to the sheriff that she had lied—he left. Will left me. She drove him away, just like she drove away every man after him."

"What sort of stories?" Frank asked.

"Complete lies! I can't imagine where she even heard of such things."

Frank's eyes widened as he recalled his last meeting—confrontation—with Irene, his own accusations based on Beth's worries. "Abuse, you mean? Irene accused her stepfather of sexually abusing her?"

"Lies!" she repeated, turning away from Frank, shaking her head angrily. "All lies. She admitted it, too late to do Will any good. The damage was done. He just couldn't take any more."

Frank almost shivered at her words, the angry, defensive tone so similar to Irene's. He hated to think his own accusations—unfounded, as it had turned out—had triggered whatever was happening to Irene. But it had, it must have, stirring up old memories—

"Are you positive they were lies?" he forced himself to ask.

"Of course they were lies!" Mrs. Bender hissed. Without the gray in her hair, he could have thought Irene stood there with her back to him. "Will was not that kind of man. He couldn't have been. And he wasn't the only one. She drove away every man I ever had anything to do with! By the time she married you and moved out, it was too late for me. Why do you think I'm here, slaving in this—"

She cut herself off and threw a panicky glance at the door, as if afraid Shelton had his ear pressed against the other side.

"Is there anything else, Sheriff?" she asked stiffly, her back still toward him.

"Where is Will Bender now?"

"I have no idea. After being publicly humiliated that way, he certainly couldn't stay in Cedar River. She admitted she lied, so they had to let him go, but once the accusations were made—half the town was like you—'Where there's smoke, there's fire!'"

"You've never heard from him?"

She shook her head. "Can you blame him?"

"But you're positive he isn't around Cedar River somewhere? Does he have relatives in the area? Anyone who would know where he is?"

"So you can harass him again? After all these years? No, he had no people here, lucky for him. Shame enough to be accused in front of friends and strangers."

Frank was silent a moment, thinking. "The neighbor who talked to Irene yesterday—what's her name?"

"You are not talking to Thelma!" She jerked around to face him. "Not about this. No! I will not allow it."

"All right." He raised his hands, palms outward, in a placating gesture. "I won't. Just calm down. I'm not accusing anyone of anything."

"Are you finished?"

"If that's all you— No, one more thing. Where did you

live when this happened? Irene sometimes talked about a house by the river.''

She laughed, a short, harsh sound. ''I'm sure she did. That's where we had to live after her antics forced Will to leave. The only place I could afford. It was torn down years ago, that whole block. Should've been torn down before we moved in.''

''Where was it?''

''612 River. Third hovel from the corner.''

''And the house where you lived before that? With Will Bender? I promise not to talk to any of the neighbors,'' he added when she started to shake her head, ''except to ask if they've seen Irene and Beth in the area today. All right?''

Reluctantly, she gave him an address on Twenty-fifth.

As Frank opened the door and walked through the store, Shelton looked up from the cash register where he was giving change to a matronly looking woman wearing a flowered print dress and sneakers. ''Thank you very much, Mrs. Creighton,'' he said, patting the change into her hand and moving quickly toward Frank.

''Sheriff Decker,'' he said, catching up to Frank at the front door, ''is everything all right? I called Sheriff Overstreet, and he explained the situation. If there's anything I can do to help…?''

Frank glanced sideways to where Mrs. Bender was emerging uneasily from the back room. ''Thanks, Mr. Shelton. Nothing right now. But if we find Irene—Mrs. Bender's daughter—it might help if you could give her some time off to talk to her. If she wants to, that is. It's all a little confused right now.''

''Of course. I understand. Flo is free to take whatever time she needs. With pay, of course.''

''That's good to know. I'll be in touch, one way or another.''

Outside, the sun had vanished behind a blanket of whitish-gray clouds. The air, still thick and damp, was now moving in erratic gusts. To the west and north, a wall of heavier, almost pitch black clouds reached halfway from the horizon. Lightning flickered in their depths as Frank slid into the squad car and pulled away from the curb. The front must have already reached Whitford, he thought as he flipped on the short wave, already tuned to the National Weather Service frequency.

In the usual monotone, the announcer outlined the areas under watches and warnings. Both Cedar River and Whitford were, so far, under only a severe thunderstorm watch, but more than half the state was under a tornado watch. No funnels had been sighted, but the watch would last another five hours.

As sheriff, he should be in Whitford. Should never have left in the first place.

"Decker, you back in your buggy yet?" Overstreet's voice crackled from the two-way.

"Just got here, Overstreet. What is it?"

"Your ex's new guy is here. He says—"

"Decker? This is Gordon Bailey," another voice broke in. "I've been talking to the neighbors, but nobody's seen Irene today. Overstreet said you'd been talking to Mrs. Bender herself."

"Just left her, yes. And I've got a couple other places to check, places where she and Irene lived years ago. Did she ever tell you anything about them? Or point them out to you?"

"Not a word. I knew her mother lived here, but that's all. What about you?"

"Never said a thing, except that she once lived in a house by the river. Look, you stay where you are, and I'll let you know if I find anything at either place."

"Any idea yet what she's doing down here?"

"Not yet. Sit tight and I'll let you know."

The Twenty-Fifth Street address was easy enough to find, but there was no sign of Irene or her car. Without asking about her at any of the neighbors' houses, Frank stayed in the squad car and drove east. It took two stops to ask directions before he found the river and the street named for it.

One side of the six hundred block, the side away from the river, was lined with small rundown houses, one a converted house trailer. A dingy looking tavern occupied one corner. A church, apparently abandoned, cowered at the other end of the block. On the other side, toward the river, there were no buildings and no fences. The first fifty feet beyond the cracked and uneven sidewalk was bare except for grass and weeds and broken glass and a few unplanned, half grown trees. Beyond that, the ground dropped out of sight toward the river. Several trees grew on the slope and by the river's edge, only the tops visible from the sidewalk. The far bank, weighted down by the grimy backsides of warehouses and factories, was clearly visible down to the polluted waterline.

Irene's red Pinto was in the middle of the block on the side of the street toward the river, sandwiched between a brown van and an ancient, rusted-out Dodge. Frank pulled up behind the Dodge.

He walked uneasily toward the Pinto, his mind trying to reconcile what he saw with the "riverfront home" that Irene had made sound like something out of a Norman Rockwell painting. The two images didn't match any better than Irene's sparsely described but seemingly affectionate memories of her years with her mother matched the actual relationship between the two women.

The door to the tavern across the street burst open.

"Daddy!"

Beth came flying across the sidewalk and out into the street. She was across before he could shout for her to be careful. They came together on the sidewalk a few yards from the Pinto.

"I wanted to call you but they wouldn't let me use the phone, so—"

"Where's your mother, Pint Size?"

"Over there," she said, pointing toward the river. "She's just standing there, on some kind of wall or something. It's like she doesn't even know I'm here!"

Frank hugged her briefly. "It's okay. Gordon's in town, too. We'll make sure nothing happens to her."

"But what's she doing here, Daddy? What's happened to her? She's never dressed like this before, and the way she was trying to see Grandma yesterday—"

Frank shook his head as he led her back toward the squad car. "I don't know, Pint Size, but she'll be all right. You wait up here by the car, okay? I'll go talk to her."

Ordinarily Beth would have resisted his request energetically, but now she simply nodded and made no move to follow him.

His stomach twitching, Frank walked in the direction Beth had pointed, following an almost-path through the weeds. Broken glass and bottles crunched more thickly under his feet as, slowly, the trees on the near side of the bank rose up into view. From the top of the bank he looked down the steep, jaggedly uneven slope. At the bottom, a dozen feet up from the scummy surface of the river, were the remnants of a concrete retaining wall.

Irene was standing on the crumbling wall, her back to him, looking startlingly like she had when they had first met—right down to the tight sweater and short skirt.

For a long moment, he stood silently, the only sounds the muffled clanks and rumbles from the grimy factories across the river.

Slowly, cautiously, he moved down the slope, wondering how Irene, in unaccustomed high heels, had made it without falling. He stopped a dozen yards away, bracing himself against a crooked tree trunk.

"Irene," he called softly. For a moment he didn't think she had heard him.

Her shoulders straightened slowly. A moment later her hands went to the waist of her skirt. As she turned, her fingers slid around the waistband. As if by magic, the skirt became two or three inches shorter.

He'd first seen her do that trick the day she started work on the assembly line at Leverentz, where he'd already been a tech for almost a year. She was one of the few who wore skirts instead of slacks. He remembered how the length had changed from hour to hour but had always seemed to be the shortest when he was called over to repair the equipment on adjacent lines.

She was smiling when she turned to face him, the same seductive but uncertain smile he had seen all those years ago whenever he had looked up from his work to steal a glance at her.

A smile he hadn't seen for fifteen years.

For an instant, he found himself thinking, as he had then, how beautiful, how incredibly sexy she was.

In another instant, the smile was gone, and his thoughts vanished with it, replaced by the icy realization that that was all they had ever had between them. He hadn't known—or ever wanted to know—who or what she really was. Any more than she had known—or wanted to know—who or what he really was. And once they were married, instead of getting to know each better over the years, that damned wall had grown up between them. Long before their divorce, the wall had become, by mutual consent, complete and impassable, impenetrable even to their sporadic and perfunctory sex.

Sometime in the last few seconds, he realized, her eyes had gone blank. Now they were taking on a puzzled look. He had to fight the urge to rush forward, to grab her, to keep her from losing her footing. But any sudden movement might only startle her into doing precisely that.

"Irene," he said, his voice barely carrying over the industrial noises from across the river, "why don't you get down off that wall and come over here? Beth's worried about you."

"Beth?" The puzzlement on her face deepened. Her body

swayed dangerously. He took a slow breath of pure terror as his stomach knotted and twisted.

But then she was steady again, her eyes darting about warily. Hastily, one ankle almost turning as a high heel wobbled, she stepped down from the crumbling wall. Frank ran to her and grasped her hand.

"Come on," he said. "Beth's up at the car. She's worried about you."

She allowed him to help her up the steep slope, offering no resistance. "How the hell did I get here?" she said, half under her breath. She sounded more frightened than angry.

"You drove, just like you did yesterday."

He felt her tense and pull back for a moment, but then she was following along again. "I really was here yesterday? You weren't lying, you and Gordon?"

"We weren't."

"What was I doing?"

"Trying to see your mother, apparently. And asking at the jail about your stepfather. Today you were just standing there on the retaining wall."

For a moment, it seemed that comprehension flooded her face, but then it was gone, replaced by a frown, as if she had remembered something only to lose it an instant later.

"Jesus," she murmured. Again she sounded frightened, and he squeezed her hand in what he hoped was a comforting way.

"Don't worry," he said. "It'll be okay."

"That's easy for you to say!" she snapped, suddenly angry, but just as suddenly the anger passed and he felt her hand go limp in his.

They reached the top of the bank, level ground. Beth, watching from the side of the squad car a good fifty yards away, ran pell-mell toward them the instant she spotted them.

"Gordon's on his way over," she yelled. "That Overstreet guy called on your radio, and I figured out how to answer it,

so they know where we are and they're both coming right
over.''

Lurching to a stop, Beth gazed worriedly at her mother.
Finally, Irene looked up at her and their eyes met. Irene
smiled uncertainly and reached out to take her daughter's
waiting hand. Suddenly they were hugging.

No ONE, least of all Frank, knew how things were going to
be for Irene, but he was less worried after talking with Bailey
again. Frank saw the concern in the man's face as he listened
to Frank's hasty recounting of what Irene's mother had said.
Despite the slick, glad-handing image Bailey hid behind on
Krueger's lot, he seemed both bright and caring—more caring, Frank realized uncomfortably, than he himself had ever
been. Bailey was also a hell of a lot better at tearing down
walls between himself and other people than Frank. He'd de-
molished the one that had been building between himself and
Frank in that one visit to the jail, simply by telling the truth.
And now that Gordon and Beth were on the same side and
had at least some hints about what had triggered Irene's
lapses, her retreats into the past, other walls would start to
come down. Frank was sure of at least that much. Even before
leaving Cedar River, Bailey had convinced Irene's mother,
despite her continued nervousness, to agree to a visit and a
''serious discussion'' either this weekend or the next. If anyone could get the truth out of her about Irene's stepfather, it
was him, and even if it turned out, as Frank suspected it
would, that Irene had been abused and then forced to lie about
it— Well, with the outgoing and supportive Bailey, she had
a chance, certainly a better chance than she had ever had with
Frank.

On the drive back to Whitford, Frank set a modest pace in
the squad car while Irene followed with Beth in the Pinto and
Bailey brought up the rear in his Krueger loaner of the month.
The weather, to Frank's surprise, grew less threatening. According to the weather bulletins the squall line, after drenching

an area twenty or thirty miles to the west, had "fallen apart" even more rapidly than expected. The sun even appeared briefly in the midst of a patch of brilliant blue as Frank left the three of them at the Bailey home and headed back to the Civic Center. All weather watches were still in effect, the radio repeated, and the front itself had picked up speed and was due before sundown.

At the museum, Ardly was still working his way through Dora Wetherston's diaries. "What did Aunt Meg have to say?" Frank asked.

Startled, Ardly looked up and shook his head. "Nothing yet. I've been trying every half hour, but she hasn't answered yet." He glanced at his watch. "It's almost nine-thirty over there. I suppose I should start trying more often, so she doesn't slip in and go to bed between calls."

Ardly went over to Laura's desk and dialed as Frank hurried to the extension on the other desk. After almost a minute, Ardly suddenly grinned and waved to Frank to pick up the phone.

"Aunt Meg? This is Clayton," Ardly said loudly. "Sorry to ring you up this late, but this is important."

"What? Clayton?" a woman's robust but confused voice was asking as Frank got the receiver to his ear. "Did something happen to him, too?"

"No, no, Aunt Meg, this is Clayton speaking. I'm quite all right. I just have something to ask you."

"Ask? Ask what? Clayton? Did you say you're Clayton?"

"That's right, Aunt Meg. I'm calling from America."

"From America?" Suddenly the voice softened. "You're calling from America? The cost— Well for heaven's sake! What about? You mustn't dawdle!"

"You remember that old photo album, the one Dad borrowed from you a few weeks back?"

"Of course I remember! You're not calling all the way from America to ask me that, surely?"

"No, Aunt Meg, I mean, do you remember when you put all the names and dates in it?"

"I'm not likely to forget. I talked to more relatives than I ever want to again, I'll tell you."

"Are you—I don't mean to sound disrespectful, Aunt Meg, but are you positive you put all the names in the proper places?"

"If you've found any mistakes, my boy, they aren't mine!"

"In the picture of the group that Leander came here with, could there be any errors?"

An indrawn breath, not quite a sigh. "Anything is possible, I suppose, but it's not likely, not in that one. That same picture—or one taken at the same time, to be more precise—is in the files of the local Preservation Society. The names are all noted on the back of the photo in their files, so if there are any errors, they're the fault of someone else."

"Then the man second from the left in the back row actually is Leander Wetherston?"

"If that is what I wrote, yes! Now what's this about, Clayton?"

"There's another picture, a portrait, of someone you labeled Archibald Mayhew."

"What of it?"

"Who was he? I hadn't ever heard of him."

"I'm not the least surprised, no more interest than you've ever shown in such matters. I doubt that you even knew these photos existed before your poor father asked you for them. Many's the time we talked, and he lamented your total lack of interest in anything beyond what you found on the telly. He—"

"Please, Aunt Meg, who was Archibald Mayhew? Do you know anything at all about him?"

"Of course I do. He was, to put as charitable a face on it as I can, the black sheep of the family. But why on earth do you want to know about him? I thought your father was attempting to learn more about what became of Leander—"

"He was, but— It's a long story, Aunt Meg, longer than I can afford to tell you at these rates. I'll tell you all about it when I get back. But right now, just tell me what you can about this Mayhew person."

"Very well, but it's not nice, not nice at all. He was a right nasty creature, though he did have a way of getting round people, they say."

"Did he go to America, too?"

"Not willingly. You might say he was exiled."

"For what? And who was he? You still haven't told me that."

"Leander's second cousin, my dear, and no love lost between them! Mayhew was—well, a 'complete wastrel' is what Leander called him."

"Leander?" Clayton repeated, sounding puzzled.

"Those letters I lent your father aren't the only ones that still exist, you know. I've a good half dozen other boxes, some from earlier times, some from later. Some of our ancestors were quite the packrats, I'm happy to say."

"You said Mayhew was 'exiled' to America?"

"Perhaps that isn't the proper term. Other members of the family—including, in all likelihood, Leander—combined their resources and put up the money to send him away in order to avoid the humiliation of having him arrested and tried."

"Arrested? For what?"

Aunt Meg was silent a moment before going on in a lower, more confidential tone. "Nothing one wants in one's family, Clayton, dear. He was a thief and a forger, a brawler and a drunk, but worst—he assaulted Leander's wife."

"Augusta? My great-great-grandmother?"

"Why, yes. How did you know her name?"

"I just got through reading those letters you gave Dad, the ones Leander wrote to her from America. But what happened to Mayhew?"

"In eighteen-eighty-two, after assaulting Augusta—he claimed she 'led him on,'—sheer nonsense, I am quite sure—

he was presented with a one-way ticket to America. And that is the last anyone in the family ever heard or saw of him. No loss, my dear.''

''He never came back?''

''He wouldn't have dared. Had he so much as set foot in England, he would have faced arrest, no matter the humiliation to the family.''

''Could he have known about Leander's tour?'' Frank broke in.

''Clayton? Who—''

''This is the local sheriff, Aunt Meg, Sheriff Decker,'' Clayton said hastily. ''He's trying to find out what happened to Dad. He's been on the line, too, and—''

''You could have told me!'' she said resentfully. ''What I've been telling you about the family—''

''It's all right, Aunt Meg, please. I'll explain it all when I come home, but right now, do answer him, please. It could be very important.''

There was a brief silence, and then, ''If you're quite sure, Clayton.''

''I'm quite sure.''

''Could Mayhew have known about the tour?'' Frank repeated.

''He could have, I imagine,'' Aunt Meg said, still a bit reluctantly. ''He was rumored to maintain a correspondence with several of his—his former lady friends.''

Frank could almost see the old woman's nose wrinkling as she spoke the words. Thanking her, he hung up.

Now that makes sense, he thought with grim excitement as Ardly said his good-byes. As Aunt Meg had talked about who and what Mayhew had been and done, particularly about his supposed assault on Ardly's great-great grandmother and his criminal activities, the events of a hundred years ago had come clear in his mind. But before he could even begin to explain his ideas to Laura or Ardly, the phone rang and Laura picked it up.

"For you, Frank," she said after a moment. He picked up the extension.

"Decker."

"Frank, it's Phil. You better get the hell over here. Martha Winters is here. You know, Wetherston's housekeeper out at—"

"I know, Phil. What does she want?"

"She says Garrick just showed up at the Wetherston place, and he ran her out. With a gun."

NINETEEN

FRANK RACED FROM the museum.

At the jail, his mother took a moment from comforting Martha Winters to assure him that Phil Biggs was indeed on his way to the Wetherston estate. The housekeeper, seated in Frank's chair, still reminded him of Nurse Ratched, but now it was after the patients had staged their revolt. Despite his mother's attentions, the woman seemed less devastated than offended.

"What happened, Martha?" he asked.

"I've told your deputy."

Frank bit back a curse. "Tell me."

"Garrick Wetherston had a gun," the housekeeper said. "He sent me away."

"Yes, but what else? What did he say?"

"I fail to see—"

"Just humor me, Martha. Please, as much detail as you can."

After a huge sigh and a brief, exasperated stare, she began. Garrick had come back to the house "maybe not quite grinning from ear to ear," but happier looking than she had ever seen him. "He even waved hello," the housekeeper added, with her eyebrows raised. "Before he went in to see his father."

But Garrick's good mood hadn't lasted long. Not two minutes later he burst out of the den and ran up the stairs.

"Then what?" Frank prompted.

"He came back down looking ready to spit nails. And then

Allen came down," she went on, "practically on Garrick's heels. He looked like the cat that ate the canary. Stood there at the foot of the stairs, laughing." Martha slowly shook her head. "I thought Garrick would explode!"

"That's when he pulled the gun?"

She shook her head. "He started back to the den, but he turned around and went out the front door instead. When he came back in, that's when he had the gun."

Frank nodded. Garrick sometimes carried a lot of cash. Long ago, Nathaniel had wangled him a permit to carry a .38 police special. So far as Frank knew, Garrick had never used it. Frank would not even have known the gun existed if he hadn't noticed the permit application in the files he had inherited from Butterfield.

"What was he doing with it?" he asked now. "Threatening Allen?"

"He wasn't pointing the gun at him, if that's what you mean. He just had it in his hand, but the way he was looking—" She shuddered. "When he saw me, he told me to go home, I wouldn't be needed anymore. Believe me, I didn't even close the door on my way out."

"What about earlier today? Did you hear anything between Allen and his father? Any arguments or disagreements? Particularly after I left this morning?"

Martha shrugged. "I couldn't say, but the two of them were in the den for nearly an hour."

"Talking about...?"

"I do not listen at keyholes, Sheriff."

"I'm sure you don't. But what about afterward? What did they do?"

"Let's see. Allen was in his room most of the day, except when he came down to tell me to call Hillman's."

"The auto shop? What for?"

"To tell someone to come pick up his Mercedes. He wanted it serviced, and he wanted it back this afternoon."

"Was he upset? Angry?"

"He was his usual self," she said, sour-faced.

"And Nathaniel? Angry? Upset?"

"Very much so. And with good reason, I'm sure. Ever since that boy arrived—"

"Did Nathaniel do anything?" Frank cut in. "Go anywhere?"

"He went out, yes. He said he was going to speak to his lawyers. And perhaps visit his grandmother's grave."

"Dora Wetherston's grave? Did he say why?"

Her lips tightened. "I am his housekeeper, not his wife."

Frank grimaced and turned away. Did it matter precisely how Allen and Nathaniel had spent the day? No. What mattered was that Allen was still there. Somehow, he had the upper hand—again. Maybe he'd played the Mayhew card, if he had it.

More likely, he had something up his sleeve Frank hadn't discovered yet. But whatever Allen's ace in the hole was, he had played it by the time Garrick made what he had expected to be his triumphant entry. And when Garrick tried to announce the conditions under which he would consent to stay on, Nathaniel had told him Allen still wasn't being cut off. Might even be put in charge.

Then Garrick had raced upstairs to confront Allen, and naturally Allen had rubbed Garrick's nose in it.

After twenty years of anger and frustration, climaxed by the emotions of the last twelve hours, it was guaranteed to push his brother over the edge. Last night Garrick had decided "to hell with the Wetherston empire." Not that big a step to "to hell with everything." To a Wetherston, the distinction was probably a small one.

The department radio crackled to life. "All quiet out here, Frank," Phil Biggs reported.

"Is Garrick's car—that big gray Lincoln—still there?"

"In front of the garage, Frank."

"Okay, Phil. Stay in the squad and watch. I'm going to try

phoning the house. If that doesn't get me anything, I'll head out your way.''

Someone at Wetherston's end picked the phone up after a dozen rings, said nothing, and hung up almost immediately. When he tried a second time, he got a busy signal. The phone was off the hook.

Turning from the phone, he saw his mother looking at him, her face smooth with anxiety. ''Call Steve,'' he said. ''Ask him to come in early. And keep trying the Wetherston place, just in case.''

She nodded but made no move toward the phone.

''It'll be all right, Mom. Garrick's not going to shoot anyone.'' I hope, he added to himself as headed out the door.

THE SKY WAS DARK gray and the wind gusty as Frank descended the Wetherston drive. Lightning flickered deep in the clouds to the west. The storm had raised static on the squad's radio, and now he heard thunder, a dull drum roll in the distance. This one wouldn't break up the way the last one had, the weather bulletins assured him. The line of oaks beside the drive rippled nervously.

Garrick's gray Lincoln was skewed in front of the huge garage, blocking two of its four doors. Next to it was the other squad car, Phil Biggs behind the wheel. The deputy alternately glanced at the front of the house and at Frank as he rolled to a stop a dozen feet behind Phil's squad. Phil started to get out, but Frank waved the deputy back in and climbed out himself. The wind, still damp, had turned chilly, each gust from a different direction. Past a narrow break in the trees, he saw whitecaps crawling across the lake as he came up to Phil's window.

''What's up?'' he asked.

''Not a damn thing, Frank, not one sound. You don't suppose he's killed them, do you?''

Frank shook his head. ''I doubt Garrick's killed anyone, Phil.''

"So, what now?"

Frank felt his stomach twitch. A chill unrelated to the wind skittered through his body as he faced the massive house. The front door stood wide open, as if in invitation.

"Now I guess I earn my money for a change," he said, with a nervous grin.

"You got a gun?"

Frank shook his head.

"You want mine?" Phil twisted to unsnap his holster.

"Thanks, no," Frank said. "I'm not going to shoot anyone, and one of those things in my hand might set Garrick off."

"But if he killed Lou and that Ardly guy—"

"He didn't."

Phil frowned uncertainly. "What if you're wrong?"

"Then I'm wrong. And maybe you get to run in a special election to replace me."

Phil swallowed and settled back into the seat. "You could just leave them alone until they—until they do whatever they're going to do to each other," he said quietly, staring at the house.

"Tempting, but no."

Phil shrugged, more of a twitch. "You're the boss."

"Out here, anyway." Frank stood watching the house, alternately wishing he could be more like Butterfield and being glad, at least for Garrick's sake—and maybe his own—that he wasn't. After a long half minute, he pushed away from the squad and slowly followed the flagstone walk to the front door. He felt his heart pounding, his stomach knotting painfully.

The first drops of wind-driven rain pelted his back as he stopped in the open door and peered down the shadowed hall. Not one light had been turned on, despite the dark sky.

"Garrick!" he called. "Garrick Wetherston. This is Frank Decker. I'm not armed. I'm coming in."

No response. Probably they were in the den at the far end of the hall and hadn't heard him. Or upstairs in Allen's room.

Frank stepped inside, resisting the automatic impulse to shut the door against the rain. Better some water damage to the plush carpet than to cut off a potential path of retreat. Cold, dry air still pumped out of the air conditioning register nearest the door, but it was overwhelmed by the wind and rain. One of the portraits lifted and banged against the wall, the subject staring at Frank as if he were somehow to blame.

He found a light switch and flipped it. Three overhead lights spaced along the hall came on. The door to Nathaniel's den was shut.

Frank walked slowly past the broad, sweeping staircase to the second floor, past the ceiling-high sliding doors to the formal dining room. He stopped just short of the door to the den and listened. No voices.

"Garrick," he repeated loudly, "this is Frank Decker. If you're in there—"

"Sheriff! Thank God—" Allen's terrified voice began but was cut off by Nathaniel's, filled with tightly controlled anger.

"Shut up, Allen! You've done more than enough today! Sheriff, perhaps you can talk some sense into Garrick."

"I might have better luck if the two of you stayed out of it!" Frank snapped, with so much anger he surprised himself. Then, more softly: "Garrick, can you hear me? I'm not armed. We have to talk."

Several seconds of silence.

Finally, Garrick's voice came through the door. It was high-pitched and tense but as tightly controlled as his father's had been. "We have talked, if you recall, Sheriff. Those thanks I offered you earlier were, it seems, premature."

"I've learned a lot since then, Garrick."

He heard a harsh sound, maybe a snort, maybe a laugh. "So have I, Sheriff."

"Look, Garrick, you haven't killed anyone yet. I don't think you want to start now."

The sound again. "Wrong, Sheriff. I most certainly do want

to start now. I just haven't worked up the guts to pull the trigger. Yet.''

Frank's heart thumped so hard the badge over his shirt pocket bounced. This wasn't what he'd signed on for. An occasional rowdy drunk throwing a punch or two, that was about the worst he'd expected.

''Maybe you don't really want to pull it, Garrick.'' Frank paused, sucking in his breath. A roll of thunder in the middle distance struck him as a curtain raiser.

''I'm coming in,'' he said, surprised his voice didn't break. ''Don't do anything dumb.'' He reached for the knob, half expecting a warning to stay out, half expecting the door to be locked. Not a sound from inside. The huge brass knob turned easily in his hand.

As the door swung back, Frank held his hands out, palms up. The chilled, dry air of the den enveloped him as he stepped inside.

Halfway along the book-lined wall on the right stood Garrick Wetherston, a gun huge in his hand. Without tie or jacket, he looked thinner than ever. Sweat—in this cold room!— beaded his forehead and darkened the side of his shirt from armpit to belt.

The gun. Light shimmered on the blued barrel. A gun very much like the .38 that lay in a locked drawer of Frank's desk. Deadly. Stopping power, they called it. Not like the twenty-two that had killed Ardly only after three point-blank shots.

Garrick was aiming the gun diagonally across the room at Allen, who leaned stiffly against the paneled wall between Nathaniel's massive desk and the French doors that opened on the glass-enclosed swimming pool. Nathaniel sat in the plush swivel chair behind the desk, his hands thrust deep in the pockets of the heavy tweed jacket he still wore over his vest. The chair fidgeted continually, like a rocking chair with a range of two or three degrees, although the old man appeared motionless. His gaze darted toward Frank, then returned to Garrick.

"Shut the door," Garrick said.

Frank pushed it shut without taking his eyes off Garrick. He took a step forward.

"Stay back, Sheriff."

Frank stopped. "You won't shoot me, Garrick."

"I don't think so, no. But as I said, I've been trying to work up the nerve to shoot my dear brother for some time. If you try to take my gun away, that might be just the impetus I need." A smile twitched at his bloodless lips. "Yes. That might do it. Why don't you try?"

Not a chance, Frank thought, as thunder commented in a long, low, growl. "If you kill your brother, you'll never get your inheritance," he pointed out. "Or have you decided you really don't care?"

A scowl crossed Garrick's face, coupled with an abortive motion of his left hand toward his stomach. Then the smile returned, edged with pain, but one of genuine amusement. "I hadn't thought about that, but do you know, I suppose I must have."

"You'll lose more than your inheritance, Garrick."

"Too true, Sheriff. But you recall the little discovery I told you about this morning, don't you? The discovery that I still had the capacity to 'feel good,' even after all these years? Well, once I do this, I'm pretty sure I'm going to feel good— or at least better than I'll feel if I don't do it. My problem is getting over the hump, so to speak. Jumping out of the plane and yanking the ripcord. Actually pulling the trigger." The knuckles of the hand gripping the gun were white. "Are you sure you don't want to try to take it away from me? Give me that little shove out of the plane? I promise I won't shoot you if I can possibly avoid it. Just my dear brother. Think how much better and cleaner the world will be without him."

"I'd sooner talk a little more."

"As you wish." The pain of his ulcer was crowding out the smile. "I assume you've guessed that the information you gave the editor of our esteemed local tabloid this morning is badly in need of an update.''

''About your brother being on the way out?''

''Precisely. I don't suppose you have any idea what he did to save his worthless hide this time? That is something I would very much enjoy hearing you talk about. I haven't been able to get word one out of either of these gentlemen.''

''I have a couple of ideas.''

''Let's have them, then. If one actually proves to be right— and if I can find a way of overcoming it—I might even be persuaded to let him live.''

Beyond the French doors, as unreal as if on a movie screen, whitecaps scoured the lake. The wind-driven drops of rain pelted against the glass of the enclosed swimming pool.

Swallowing, Frank discovered that his mouth, his whole throat, were desert dry. His eyes fastening on Allen and the old man, he said, ''I assume you know about Mayhew. One or both of you must have learned about him from Lou Cameron and Willis Ardly last Sunday.''

Nathaniel inclined his head fractionally, once. ''I know about Mayhew,'' he said, his voice as stiff as his body. Allen nodded nervously.

''Mayhew?'' Garrick broke in. ''Who or what the hell is a Mayhew?''

Frank explained what he and Laura and Ardly had found in the album and what they had learned from Ardly's Aunt Meg. ''Mayhew must have learned about the tour from one of his girl friends,'' he finished. ''He caught up with it in Carrothers, killed Leander, and took over his identity.''

A bark of laughter erupted from Garrick. ''All this effort to save the Wetherston name! And it doesn't even belong to us!'' Thunder joined his laughter, making something in the room rattle. ''Leander the farsighted founder of the Wetherston empire was really Archie the rapist, swindler and murderer!'' Garrick's eyes glittered. ''Is that why you're keeping my beloved brother on the payroll, dear Father? Because if it is—''

He broke off and glanced at Frank. ''Archie Mayhew will be the subject of your next news conference, won't he, Sheriff?''

Frank nodded, glancing toward the French doors as a half dozen near-simultaneous lightning flashes lit the pool enclosure. Rain now blasted against the glass in wind-driven sheets. The trees above the pool whipped wildly, and the lake was almost a froth.

''It will,'' Frank said.

''Does that make a difference, Father?'' Garrick asked.

The old man shook his head.

''This has gone far enough, Sheriff,'' Allen broke in, his voice a demanding whine. ''Can't you—''

''Shut up, brother dear!'' Garrick ordered, almost screaming. Allen shut his mouth with an audible click.

''Sheriff,'' Garrick went on more quietly, ''you said you had a couple of ideas. Mayhew, though fascinating, seems not to have been the one I was looking for. I assume you have more.''

Frank was silent a moment. He hadn't thought beyond Mayhew, not in any detail. His earlier idea—that Allen's hold on his father was that he'd helped Nathaniel kill the two men and dispose of their bodies, or perhaps even had done it all himself under Nathaniel's orders—couldn't be true, or Nathaniel wouldn't have earlier been on the verge of kicking Allen out because of Frank's threats to expose the first of Leander's—Archie's—long-closeted skeletons.

No, the hold had to be something Allen had kept to himself until today, until he was forced to use it. Something that would give him control, but which he hadn't wanted to use. Something—

Suddenly, Frank knew what it was. Just as suddenly, everything Allen and Nathaniel had said and done since Sunday made sense. "It's Shriver all over again," he said in grim wonder, "in spades."

"Shriver?" Garrick echoed. "But—" His eyes widening in sudden comprehension. Jaw clenched, he stared at his brother. "You did kill them!" he grated. "Both of them! And you—" His glare switched to Nathaniel. "This morning he told you! But instead of turning him in, you're protecting him and—and the 'name' that isn't even ours!"

For a moment Frank thought Garrick would pull the trigger. He could almost hear him seething. Not because of the killings. Not even because Nathaniel was covering up. No, the "injustice" of it all, the infuriating injustice of it all. Allen winning—again. Garrick frozen out—again. Lou Cameron and Willis Ardly had become mere stage props in the Wetherston drama. All that mattered to Garrick was that Allen was getting away with murder—literally this time—and there wasn't one damn thing that Garrick could do about it, short of turning to murder himself.

Garrick straightened. "I don't suppose there's a chance in hell you can prove it." He sounded weary. "Is there, Sheriff?"

"With your father's testimony, I probably could."

Garrick snorted derisively.

"Or if we could find Lou Cameron's body," Frank went on. "And whatever evidence is with it. At the very least, we could prove that Lou was dead when these 'negotiations' between him and your brother were supposedly taking place."

"But you can't find the body." The gun, which had started to droop, jerked up as lightning flashed. Less than a second later, thunder rattled the French doors.

Frank shook his head. "If I can get a search warrant—"

"For where?" Garrick demanded. "The house and grounds? The lake? Every damn gravel pit in the state?" He glared at his brother. "Like great-grandfather, like great-grandson! Getting away with murder must be in the genes! They never found Leander's body either!"

"Nobody knew Leander was dead," Frank said, "not until Lou—"

Frank stopped. The countless bits of seemingly irrelevant and contradictory information he had been dumping into his own shadowy mental warehouse for days suddenly formed a pattern, like iron filings attracted to a magnet. Clustered around the framework formed by murder now, by murder a century ago, they formed a pattern.

A pattern that explained, first, those things the simple fact of Allen's guilt had not explained.

Almost like magic, he saw the rest of what had to have happened a hundred years ago. Why Mayhew had continued to write to Leander's widow, why he had repeatedly referred to the already-dead Arthur Ingram as his best friend. Why Lou—Lou, not the killer—had stopped by his house Sunday evening and picked up the spade.

And he knew where Lou Cameron's body was. Why it had been disposed of separately from Ardly's.

It hadn't been part of a scheme to blame Ardly's death on Lou. Like everything else Allen Wetherston had ever done, it had merely been convenient.

"Lou Cameron and Leander Wetherston are in the same grave, aren't they, Allen?" Frank said quietly.

"You're insane, Sheriff!" Allen snapped, but not quite quickly enough. A kind of terror, the look of a trapped animal, had filled the younger Wetherston's eyes for a moment before he could regain control.

"They're both in Ingram's grave," Frank went on, seeing again a telltale flicker in Allen's eyes. He turned to Garrick. "You can give me the gun, Garrick. I know how to find Lou's body. I know how to prove enough of what happened to put your brother away."

Garrick scowled, the gun not wavering. "What kind of trick are you trying to pull, Sheriff?"

"No trick, Garrick. It just now hit me what happened."

"Then tell me what happened. Who the hell is this Ingram and why is Leander or anyone else buried with him?"

"He was someone who died in Carrothers just a day or two before the 1883 tour came through Whitford," Frank said. "I saw his obituary in the Whitford paper, and a lot more about him in the Carrothers *Sentinel*. He had been quite a prominent citizen up in Carrothers. Leander—Mayhew—mentioned him over and over in those letters to Leander's wife Augusta, Ardly's great-grandmother. He said at least a dozen times how this Arthur Ingram was his best friend here in Whitford and how she simply must meet him as soon as she arrived. But before Mayhew—"

Frank broke off, trying to organize his ideas into some form in which they would make sense to Garrick.

"You have to remember what Ardly's aunt told us about why Mayhew was kicked out of the family and sent to America," Frank said. "The last straw was when he assaulted Leander's wife—but he insisted she had 'led him on.' Maybe, in his eyes, she had, or maybe they had been having an affair and she wanted to break it off. Or maybe she had simply resisted all his advances, and he couldn't stand it.

"But whatever happened, Mayhew got kicked out of the family, exiled to America, and he blamed her for it. He hated her. And then, after he'd been in America a year or so, he heard about Leander's trip. Ardly's aunt said she thought Mayhew kept in touch with some of his one-time girl friends, of whom he apparently had several. He caught up with the tour group in Carrothers, the day before it came to Whitford. He killed Leander and, I suppose, figured that Ingram's freshly dug grave was a handy place to get rid of the body. A few weeks later, he showed up in Whitford, using whatever identification and money the real Leander had had with him. In Whitford—but you know Leander's story, how he got all the local investors together to start a bank, how he put in hefty chunks of his own money—which he'd undoubtedly gotten by means of more forged letters or telegrams.

"And all the while, right up until his death, he kept writing to Leander's widow. He was planning for her to come over, just like he said. But he wasn't going to be here when she arrived. He couldn't be, or his whole scheme would've fallen apart. No, he was going to take all the money he could get his hands on—probably even sell the house he'd built—and vanish while she was on her way over. And he was going to arrange for her to find the real Leander's body!"

Frank shook his head in numb wonder. "He must have really hated her for whatever he thought she had done to him in England. This would be the perfect revenge. She'd be stranded, penniless, thousands of miles from home, staring at the rotting corpse of the husband she'd thought was waiting for her, alive and prosperous. But Mayhew died before he could set things moving. And Lou realized all these same things. He must have, once he started talking to Ardly!"

Frank turned again toward Allen. "And he told you all about it, didn't he? Sunday evening, when the two of you were at the museum, alone. He told you everything he'd figured out from the letters and the diaries, but he also told you about the proof he'd just realized might still exist—the proof that Mayhew had existed and that he really had killed Leander. He told you he was pretty sure where to find Leander. He told you that if Leander was anywhere, he was in Ingram's grave. And knowing Lou and his wild enthusiasms, it wouldn't take much to talk him into going out, right then and there, to check, to look up the old records in the museum and find out where the graveyard was and drive out to take a look. That's why he came by and got the spade from his basement, to dig up Ingram's—and Leander's—grave!"

Frank found himself almost laughing at the thought of that midnight excursion. Lou would have been beside himself with excitement from the moment he and Ardly had met. First, a hundred-year-old mystery that no one had suspected even existed, a mystery whose elements would, all by themselves, turn the town upside down. And then a solution even more bizarre than the mystery itself, and finally a dark-of-night trip with Allen Wetherston to—

The excitement vanished. For a moment, Frank had been sharing it with Lou, but the harsh reality of how that midnight excursion had ended blotted the pleasure out. Lou had probably dug his own grave. Frank couldn't imagine Allen Wetherston soiling his hands with hard work.

Sobering, he turned to Garrick. "Good enough?" he asked grimly. "Will you let me have that gun now?"

Garrick stood motionless, his eyes going from his brother to Frank and back again. The only sounds were the rain sweeping against the glass around the swimming pool and the continuous rumble of thunder. Finally, reluctantly, the finger that curved around the trigger relaxed. Then the hand and arm softened, as if a steel framework inside them were melting.

"I guess you were right after all, Sheriff. I really didn't want to pull the trigger, God knows why. Dear Allen must've gotten all the killing genes this generation." Garrick's hand drooped to his side. As it did, Allen's half-hearted facade of confidence crumbled completely, his eyes filling with the same trapped look of terror that Frank had glimpsed there before.

Frank started to step forward, intending to take the gun from Garrick's now limp hand.

Outside, there was a blinding flash. One of the trees at the lake shore exploded, with a sound like the sizzling scream of torn fabric amplified to deafening proportions. A half-dozen glass panels shattered on the apron of the pool.

The lights in the den went out, leaving Frank, who had been facing the French doors and the lightning flash, blinded. Even so, his lunge brought him to Garrick almost in time.

But not quite. As he grasped at Garrick's now empty hand, his vision began to clear. Even in the dim light from the French doors, even past the lingering green afterimage of the lightning bolt, he could see enough:

Allen had the gun.

TWENTY

STUMBLING BACKWARD, trying to get a better grip, Allen almost dropped the gun.

Before Frank could react, Allen was out of reach, his back against the wall beside the French doors. Then he got his finger through the trigger guard. The muzzle jerked upward to point at Frank.

A moment later, the lights flickered and came back on. Allen laughed sharply.

"Well, Father," he said, darting a sideways glance at Nathaniel, "it's nice to see that God's on our side, too. That spectacular little distraction He sent just now was a nice touch, don't you think?"

He was smiling now, almost smirking. "However, Sheriff," he went on, gesturing with the gun, "God helps them as helps themselves, I think the saying is, so I'd appreciate it if you and my brother would stand just a little bit closer together. Just in case either of you is thinking of doing something foolish."

Frank stood unmoving. Garrick slumped a step closer.

Allen, nodding approval, stepped away from the wall, all confidence now. Glancing over his shoulder at his father, he perched on the outer corner of Nathaniel's desk.

"You can't—" Frank began. Allen cut him off with a bark of laughter.

"But I can. Everyone has been so cooperative, I really believe I can. But just to make sure— Tell me, Sheriff, how is it you happened to show up so conveniently? From the way you were talking to my sanctimonious brother through the door, you obviously knew what the situation was, which means—what? Martha? Martha called you?''

"She came to the jail," Frank acknowledged.

"Ah, even better! Absolutely marvelous!" He waggled the gun. "Not only does this useful weapon belong to my brother as recorded by our estimable Sheriff's office, but, thanks to Martha, everyone knows Garrick was the one last seen brandishing it. And for all they know, he's still the one!''

He paused, the smirk becoming broader. "Yes, I see just how to do this! For a start, I shoot you, Sheriff, and then, from much closer range, I shoot my brother. And then, with the gun in his hand, I fire it again, probably into his body. That will put powder marks on both our hands, and it will look as if he shot you, and then, in an absolute panic, I jumped him and the gun went off. Alas, he was killed in the struggle.''

Allen looked almost gleeful. "Well, Sheriff? Will it play?"

Frank only shook his head. He felt numb, except for the spot on his chest at which the gun now very steadily pointed. That spot tingled in grim anticipation. "What about your father?" he asked. "Will you kill him, too?"

Allen's brows arched upward as he shot another glance over his shoulder at Nathaniel. "Now why would I want to do that? We're in this together, he and I. We're a team. I thought you realized that.''

"That was before you decided to kill family members."

"Ah, but you heard my brother, my wild-eyed faggot of a brother. He wanted to kill me. This will be, strictly speaking, self defense. After what we've been through this past week, my father can certainly see that. Can't you, Father?''

Allen glanced in the old man's direction, but there was no response, no motion. Even the slight rocking of the swivel chair had stopped.

Allen shrugged. "I'm sure he'll eventually see the wisdom in this course of action. Salvage what can still be salvaged. Isn't that right, Father?" he asked more loudly, more deliberately. "Without Cameron's body, nobody can prove a thing. And now that my brother has gone berserk, we can find a way to blame the whole affair on him, if necessary. That is, if, by some miracle, Cameron's body is found. As I recall, my hermit-like brother had absolutely no alibi for Sunday evening."

"Is this how it was with the others?" Nathaniel asked abruptly. His voice was strong, but hollow sounding.

Allen frowned. "Still with us, then, Father? I was beginning to wonder if you had gone catatonic."

"Is it?" the old man repeated.

"If I knew what the hell you were asking, I might be able to answer."

The old man turned his head slightly, his expressionless eyes fastened on Allen. "I don't know precisely what I'm asking. Just tell me about it. Tell me about Ardly and Cameron."

Allen's frown deepened. "I already did, as much as you let me. You said you didn't want to know any more. 'Keep the sordid details to yourself,' I think were your exact words."

"I've changed my mind."

"Or lost it!" Allen snapped.

The old man was stiffly erect in the chair now, his hands resting on the edge of the desk. "If you expect me to back you up, tell me about the others. Now!"

"There's nothing to tell! I killed them! What more do you want?"

"Did it bother you? Did you enjoy it?"

"For God's sake, Father! All right! All right! No, I didn't enjoy it. I don't enjoy killing people. It was—it was—"

"Convenient?" Nathaniel prompted.

"Yes, convenient! For both of us, don't forget! I saw a chance to get rid of them, and I took it! And Cameron, with his absurd enthusiasm, made it easier than I ever could've hoped for. He not only dug his own grave, he climbed into it. As for the other one, he was so eager to get the money I'd promised him, he didn't question anything I said or did.''

''You shot them both?''

''Damn it, Father—''

''You shot them both?'' Nathaniel repeated flatly.

''No! I bashed in Cameron's head with the spade while he stood in the grave he'd just dug for himself! Ardly's the only one I shot! With that damned target pistol!''

''You've had it all this time? In case you ever wanted someone dead? Is that why you took it?''

''Hell, I don't even remember taking it!'' Allen snarled. Lightning flickered over his face. ''I found it in some of the junk I took with me when I first went—when you first shipped me off to California. What with the crime rates lately, I started carrying it around in the car.''

''But you didn't enjoy the actual killings? They certainly couldn't have been very difficult. And you seem to be looking forward to killing the sheriff and your brother.''

''Father, for God's sake, what's the point?''

''I merely want to learn more about you, about my 'partner', as you put it.'' Nathaniel's eyelids drooped slightly, as if he were calculating. ''Now tell me, did you enjoy it?''

''No! Need I remind you again that it was for a good cause?'' Allen paused, grimacing. The kind of face you make when you find something distasteful in your soup, Frank thought.

''Killing Ardly was downright unpleasant, if you must know,'' Allen said. ''I had to shoot him three times. 'Who would have thought the old man had so much blood in him?' And then all the work of disposing of the body—''

He broke off, glaring at his father. ''Is that enough? Or do you want every grisly detail up until the time you started helping?''

There was a long silence. Finally, the old man's gaze dropped, and he slumped. ''I shouldn't have been surprised,

I suppose," Nathaniel said softly, "not by the descendant of Archie Mayhew."

Allen laughed harshly. "And don't forget great-grandmother Dora's contribution to the gene pool!"

"What?" Nathaniel looked up sharply.

Allen laughed again. "Don't tell me you haven't figured that out yet!"

"Figured what out?"

"That she killed great-grandfather Leander, of course! Or no, make that great-grandfather Archie."

Nathaniel drew himself up. "That's insane! What makes you think—"

"For God's sake, Father, wake up! I've known—suspected, anyway—since you first told me that pathetic story about how you took her out for 'her last boat ride' the week before she died."

His father stared icily. "What are you talking about?"

Allen shook his head in mock pity. "You can't possibly be that naive. Are you trying to tell me the idea that old Dora knocked great-grandfather off never even crossed your mind?"

"Of course it didn't!"

Allen laughed again. "I'll leave it to the Sheriff, an objective observer if there ever was one. I don't suppose you've ever heard the story of Dora's last boat ride, have you, Sheriff?"

Frank managed to shake his head.

"Very well, it goes like this. In those last months, according to Father here, Granny Dora wasn't all that lucid. Her mind kept wandering, and every so often she would think that he was Leander—or Archie, I mean." He shook his head. "It's going to take a while to get used to that name, you know. 'Archie.' But as I was saying, when Father was younger, he looked a lot like that old rascal Archie. Not that you'd believe it now, of course. Anyway, one day she insisted Father take her out on the lake in a little boat. Well, he talked it over with the doctor, and the doctor said it couldn't hurt, she didn't have long anyway, make her last days happy, so they went. And when he was looking at something in the water along the side of the boat, she suddenly thought she was back there on her last ride with Archie and she thought she saw him start to fall in and she tried to grab him and keep him from falling, but she lost her balance and fell right on top of him. They both almost went in. Now doesn't that sound a bit suspicious to you, Sheriff?''

"She wasn't trying to save him?" Frank asked. "She was trying to push him in?" Probably true, he thought, momentarily distracted from his own imminent death. After all, Archie's dying at just the right time had been a remarkable coincidence.

"She must have come across one of the letters to the English wife *before* Archie died, not after," Frank mused. "Maybe she even found out he was planning to steal everything in sight, even sell the house, and desert her. That would certainly give her motive enough. And killing him gave her an even stronger reason to heap praise on him posthumously. She was just trying to convince everyone he'd been the perfect husband. After all, who would ever suspect her of killing someone she idolized?"

"Exactly. See, Father? You see how obvious it is? She damn near killed you, thinking she was pushing old Archie in, just like she'd done sixty years before." He chuckled. "As the good sheriff just said, she certainly had plenty of reason." He paused, smiling. "Almost as much reason as I have right now."

"Wait!" Nathaniel said. "You can't—"

"But I can! We've already been through all that. So unless you intend to turn me in…"

The old man blinked. Then he shook his head slightly. "No," he said softly, "I won't turn you in."

"Then we can get down to business." Allen's eyes focussed on Frank, and Frank found himself wondering if, somehow, he could lunge at Allen and get the gun. If he were hit, if it weren't in a vital spot, he was big enough that maybe, just maybe the adrenalin pumping into his bloodstream would keep him going long enough to get the gun.

It wasn't, he thought grimly, as if he had a choice. Doing nothing was as good as suicide.

The tingling, aching spot on his chest expanded to cover his entire body. "You still don't have a chance, Allen." He wasn't surprised to hear his voice crack, nor to feel his legs tremble as he moved a short sideways step to the right, away from Garrick.

"Stay where you are!" Allen snapped.

"What are you going to do, shoot me?" Frank wasn't sure where the words came from. His voice seemed to be on automatic pilot. If he could just get his body to work that way, too, the way it had worked years ago when he had stood on the edge of the gravel pit and worked up the nerve to take a running jump into the icy water forty feet below.

Garrick, perhaps sensing what Frank was doing, took a sideways step in the other direction, toward the desk. The gun twitched toward Garrick.

Frank lunged.

He hadn't covered more than a fraction of the distance when he heard a shot.

Then he was crashing into Allen, slapping blindly at the gun. As his palm struck the barrel, the .38 went off, the sound slamming at his eardrums, the flame biting at his hand.

Allen tumbled backward. Frank, unable to keep his balance, thudded on top of him, his face almost ramming into Allen's.

He felt warm blood on his chest.

He had felt no impact from the bullet, but the blood—

For a moment, he seemed paralyzed, unable to make his arms work to throw himself off the other man, but at last, with a lurch, he rolled onto the floor and scrambled to his feet.

He looked down.

The blood was not his. It was Allen Wetherston's.

"I should have done that years ago," a thin but rock-steady voice filtered through the ringing in Frank's ears.

His eyes snapped toward the voice.

Nathaniel Wetherston, still seated behind the desk, was once again stiffly erect in the chair. A gun—the gun from the desk, the gun he had told Frank six hours earlier gave him a "feeling of security"—was in his hand. Grimacing, he brought the muzzle around and jammed it against his own temple.

"And this," Wetherston said, his voice little more than a whisper.

The echoes of the shot were drowned in a clap of thunder.

TWENTY-ONE

THE STORM HAD PASSED without Frank's even noticing. A late afternoon sun slanted under the line of oaks and glistened off the wet grass as he and Phil Biggs watched the Hensley Funeral Home ambulance pull out of the drive with its double cargo, followed by the car with Del Richardson and his photographer. The air was pleasantly cool and surprisingly dry.

"Need me for anything more, Frank?" Phil asked. "How's your hand?"

"Aches a little, that's all," Frank said, flexing his fingers. "And I promise to let Doc Starret make absolutely sure nothing's broken."

"Today, Frank, not the day after tomorrow or next week."

"I'll do it, Phil, I'll do it."

"Make sure you do. I know how easy it is to let something like that go. But all those little bones in the hand— The time I bunged mine up in that softball game, I didn't find out—"

"For five days, when it got so sore you finally went in, and it took twice as long to heal as it should have," Frank finished for him. "I'll see the doctor this evening, I promise. Now get the hell back to the office and punch out before overtime sets in."

Phil started slowly along the flagstone walk toward his squad, still in front of the garage with Garrick Wetherston's huge gray Lincoln and the other squad. After a half dozen steps, the deputy stopped and turned. "Now that we know for sure about Lou, you want me to go see Jennie and the kids?"

Frank shook his head. "I'll do it. I have to. Now go!"

Still moving slowly, Phil climbed into the squad and drove away.

"It's nice when people worry about you," Garrick Wetherston's voice came from the hall behind him. Frank couldn't detect even a trace of the usual Wetherston sarcasm. Instead, the man sounded as if he meant precisely what he was saying.

"It is," Frank agreed, turning. "Are you going to be all right? You might be able to use Doc Starret, too."

"No, I'm all right. Now." In the past hour, Garrick had vomited twice, first a few seconds after the shooting, when he'd seen the mess that even a small caliber bullet makes of a head, again a few minutes later when he had located a fresh bottle of his chalky ulcer medicine and had tried to down too large a gulp. "Besides, we aristocrats have our own personal physicians, didn't you know?" he added with a weak smile. "Edwards should be along any minute."

Frank only nodded, still wondering if he had done the right thing by not arresting Garrick for his part in that madness back in the study. There were probably a half dozen crimes he could be charged with, but somehow—

"I'm sorry." Garrick's voice was unsteady again. "For the whole damned Mayhew family, all four generations of us, I'm sorry."

"I'm not the one that deserves an apology. Try Leander's real descendants." And Lou. Lou above all others.

"I know, and I will." Another even weaker smile. "I'm not much more accustomed to apologizing or making amends than anyone else in this family ever was, so I thought I'd practice on you."

"And now that you've had your dry run?"

Garrick made a faint, shivering shrug. "I'll talk to Ardly. We'll work something out. There's enough in the till to go around, especially now that we don't have to worry about Allen's allowance anymore. If you see Ardly, tell him."

"Tell him what? That you want to see him to discuss terms?"

"Something like that, I imagine. And I suppose I should do something about the Shriver boy."

"It wouldn't hurt. He could use a friend about now."

"Couldn't we all..." Wetherston pulled in a deep breath, fumbling in his jacket pocket with one hand. "Is it all right for me to have someone clean up in there?" His voice was stronger as he pulled the bottle from his pocket and gestured toward the den with it. "You are through, aren't you? No one will accuse me of destroying evidence?"

"We're through. You can have someone clean up."

Nodding his thanks, Wetherston unscrewed the cap and downed a swallow of the chalky liquid. Frank watched silently, his thoughts shifting bleakly to the task ahead: Talking to Jennie Cameron.

First he'd have to clean up and put on a fresh uniform. Learning the truth about Lou would be hard enough without the messenger being covered with blood, even if that blood did belong to Lou's killer. Particularly if it belonged to the killer.

But at least Jennie—like himself—would now have her faith in Lou vindicated. She would know for certain that their life together hadn't been the lie the Wetherstons had tried to convince her of. She would have her memories unsullied.

And she would know that during his last moments, as he found the long-buried body and realized that the puzzle was solved—she would know that in the instant before he was struck down, he had been as happy and excited as at any time in his life. A small comfort, and cold, but it would be something.

Sucking in a deep breath, feeling the blood-soaked shirt shifting uncomfortably on his chest, seeing Jennie Cameron's stoic face floating in the air before him, he turned his back on the last of the Wetherstons and walked to the squad car.

SECOND ADVENT

TONY PERONA

A NICK BERTETTO MYSTERY

When the beloved patriarch of his hometown dies of a shocking suicide, investigative reporter Nick Bertetto is called in to investigate what Martha, the victim's granddaughter, insists is not suicide, but murder.

It's clear that Martha has the most to gain from a murder investigation—suicide would void her grandfather's bequest of his fortune to her religious organization—Children of the Second Advent. And as Nick digs deeper, a dark picture emerges of fanaticism, con artists, "miracles," and a killer dead set on making sure there will be no second coming…or second chances.

"My kind of writing, my kind of characters."
—Ed Gorman, author of the Sam McCain mysteries

"A winning first novel."
—*Mystery Scene*

Available December 2004 at your favorite retail outlet.

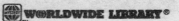
WORLDWIDE LIBRARY®

WTP514